PIPER J. DRAKE

HIDDEN
IMPACT

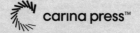

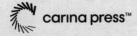

carına press™

ISBN-13: 978-1-335-93229-7

Recycling programs
for this product may
not exist in your area.

Hidden Impact

www.CarinaPress.com

Printed in U.S.A.

To Joy, for answering random texts
in the middle of the night and reading snippets
of hanky-panky scenes on request. You were the
first to read this when it was just three proposed
chapters, and I hope you enjoy the whole book.

HIDDEN
IMPACT

Chapter One

"I need your services. Whatever they cost, I'll figure out how to pay...somehow."

Gabriel Diaz scowled and didn't bother looking at the latest person to approach him, instead keeping his attention on the crowded room. He figured the slight woman was minimal threat to anything but his temper. "Look, lady, I don't know what you think you're trying to get, but I guarantee you I'm not into whatever you have in mind."

Jesus, this celebrity bodyguard gig was getting old. Fast. He'd had so many propositions tonight from plastic women as shallow as they were vain, he couldn't stand another whiff of expensive perfume. And he only had himself to blame.

He'd been the one to insist their team take on the easy jobs in the downtime between their real engagements. It kept a steadier flow of income for their private military contracting business, and the executive-level connections had an even more significant value than simple dollar signs. That being said, he'd overestimated his tolerance for the glitzy after-parties this particular client liked to throw. And apparently everyone from the socialites to the groupies hot enough to be allowed into the party were partaking of the food, booze and eye candy. Personal security included.

Course, they didn't use the business terms. No. They all whispered a different word behind their hands. *Mercenaries*.

Whatever. He could give a flying…

"N-no. I mean…w-what I…"

He gritted his teeth. Why couldn't she take a hint and bug out? He was going to be forced to send her away crying or some shit. "What you need to do is take yourself off to find another man."

There was a sharp intake of breath. Good. Maybe she'd finally go and warn off other hopefuls, too.

"What you need to do is hear me out." Steel edged her voice now, and maybe a bit of desperation.

It was the former, not the latter, that made him take a real look at her.

Her eyes caught him first. Deep emerald green. Shocking, actually, set in a delicate Asian face framed by a cascade of hair so black the lighting caught blue highlights. Her features were naturally beautiful, accented with a minimal amount of makeup. Very different from the majority of the people in attendance, regardless of gender.

Color leached from her face as she must have realized she had his full attention. But she didn't back away or break eye contact. Good for her. Lesser men had balked when Gabe had stared them down.

"My little sister is missing." The edge was gone from her words but the desperation was still there.

Anger washed away. Damn. "I'm sorry, miss. But the police are the people to contact."

Political targets, reporters and prisoners of war were the kidnap victims private military might be contracted to locate and retrieve. The kind of people held for ransom in places so far off the radar, even sunlight might not find them. And those weren't his team's specialty.

The woman in front of him was a normal civilian. Willowy, slender. The thought of a little sister conjured up images of some tiny waiflike kid. He and his partners were heavy hitters, not the kind of people you sent in to do anything but cause strategic destruction. They went into hot spots overseas and did the things politicians didn't admit to knowing about at these glitzy events, things a US uniform wouldn't be doing. Delicate, gentle—the sort of handling a traumatized girl retrieved from a kidnapping situation would need—was not their forte.

The older sister shook her head. "I've spoken to the police and the US Embassy. No one will do anything, not yet. And by the time they believe something's actually wrong, I might never find her."

Missing persons cases were tough. She was right about the time crunch. There was only a short window before the abducted was more than likely dead. Considering what could have already happened, death might not be the worst thing either.

Definitely not going to add to what this woman was already imagining. Hopefully she didn't know what *could* happen.

"You'd do better hiring a private investigator." He drew his eyebrows together, tried not to let the urge to squirm under her very direct stare show. Damn. Give him vapid groupies and a clueless entourage and he had no problem staring them down. This woman, it was like she could see straight through him and know how much he didn't want to cause a scene at this very moment. There was nothing good he could do for her.

"A private investigator doesn't have the international resources I think your company has. And I asked—you're the best. Henderson only hires the A players for his events and he likes to brag about the mercenaries he has on his payroll. He wouldn't risk bragging about you if you weren't the real thing. If you're not the right person to talk to, maybe you have someone else in your organization? Someone I can present more details to so they'll understand?" If she'd whined at him, it'd be easier to tell her to get lost. Even tears.

Great, man. You'd rather make her cry than help her.

Damn straight.

But she was being reasonable and calm, businesslike without giving up any of the urgency she'd had from the moment she'd approached him. The lady definitely had experience negotiating. And their organization didn't. The sort of strategy and the tactical strikes they made were a lot more final than any verbal agreement. People didn't hire private military contractors like the Centurions for delicate jobs like this, not when the package was likely to be so fragile.

The Centurion Corporation took contracts internationally for more…potentially volatile situations. Their jobs had more to do with combat force augmentation, local populace liaison, community patrolling and "black bag" jobs that wouldn't be explained or reported to the US citizens. There were other private organizations with divisions to handle situations like this woman's missing sister. But he didn't know of any with a likely price tag any normal individual would be able to afford.

"I'm gonna be honest, because you seem like a nice person and you're still giving me no other choice." He leaned forward, looming over her so his whispered words could be understood despite the blaring music around them but no one else would hear. "Save your money. Don't give it to anyone who promises to get your sister back alive. Doesn't matter how long they listen or what they promise you. If she's out of the country, it's going to take anyone way too long to get her back in one piece. Put it towards her memorial."

Harsh. No one wanted to tell a person their loved one was probably already dead, and almost certainly would be before anyone could find them. But feeding her false hope wouldn't do her any favors. And he really wanted her to walk away.

She'd stood absolutely still as he'd spoken. Hadn't given any ground or shrunk away from him. As he straightened, he cast his gaze around the room in a safety check before looking back down at her.

Her face was frozen, but it was her eyes again. Sheer and utter devastation, shattered hope and some emotion bordering on hate welled up with her tears. Then dark lashes came down, releasing him from the shock of it, and when she opened her eyes again there was nothing but cold calm. "I won't thank you for your advice, but I do for your honesty. *Xiè xie.*"

Thank you. In Chinese. Mandarin, he thought.

He didn't know Mandarin or Cantonese but he knew the words for *please* and *thank you* in a lot of languages. There were a lot of situations where someone was saying those words to him or his people. He made it a practice to try to reciprocate when appropriate when out in other parts of the world. Sometimes with genuine sincerity, sometimes with sarcasm as they tried to kill each other.

He'd stop thinking along those lines for the time being.

She turned and walked away, head up and shoulders straight. Her hips rolled slightly as she strode with purpose in three-inch high heels—as if she had someplace to be and he hadn't broken her hope to pieces. And wow but the silhouette of her very tight behind in the little pencil skirt she wore did awful things to his libido. If he wasn't already going to hell in a handbasket, he definitely would be now.

"Trouble?" Marc's voice murmured in his earbud.

Only if he ever saw her again. He lifted his wrist and spoke into the tiny microphone attached to his shirt cuff. "No."

"Looked pretty tense from where I'm standing." Of course Marc'd seen the exchange. They were positioned around the perimeter of the event. Each of them could survey the crowd and had direct line of sight on at least two of the others on their team.

"Keep eyes on her in case she does something crazy." His first priority was the safety of his client, and wouldn't it just suck if the woman went ballistic because he'd turned her down?

"Roger that."

Qīng wā cào de liú máng.

That was a complete and total fail. Yet again, Maylin blinked back tears and struggled to maintain her composure. The party was over now and she'd only need to finish overseeing her team's cleanup of the catering equipment. Then she could bury herself in a tray of egg tarts and try to figure out what her possible alternatives were at this point.

If there were any.

With every day, every hour, her chances of finding

An-mei were dwindling. It wasn't as if her family would be of any constructive help either, even if they did somehow realize the reality of An-mei's disappearance.

Watching her staff carefully wrap up any leftover food and clear away the chafing dishes, she seized the thought of family to take her mind down safer paths for the time being.

Thank goodness her stepmother hadn't been there to witness either Maylin making a fool of herself or the cursing to follow. Though with a body like that man had, she rather doubted the big bodyguard ever had to settle for frog-humping, curse or no. When she'd first approached him, she'd not realized just how big he was in the midst of all the milling partygoers. She'd thought he'd been standing on a step or part of a raised stage. Nope. Both his feet had been firmly planted on the same floor as hers and he'd stood head and shoulders over the crowd. It'd taken her by surprise, made her stutter like an idiot.

First impression was key.

A lesson from her mother, her real one. And one she should have kept in mind rather than blowing her last chance to find someone to listen, to help her find An-mei.

"Cleanup is complete, Miss Cheng." The young man didn't come within arm's reach. Not that she'd ever strike out, but her entire catering staff was familiar with how clumsy she could get when distracted. Few ways to be more distracted than humiliating oneself at a high-profile event thrown by one of her best clients. Luckily, no one seemed to have noticed her discomfiture but her own staff, and they were like family. The kind of family a person chose instead of having been born into. When it came to relations by blood, only An-mei had been the family of her heart. Maylin would do anything for her little sister. Anything to get her back.

"Thanks, Charlie. Let's get out of here and head home, then." She nodded to one of the venue's regular security guards and stepped out into the cool night hoping to clear her head.

It must've only stopped raining a short while ago. Not a surprise for Seattle. The sidewalk pavement shone silver in the light of the streetlamps, with highlights of green or red from the traffic light at the top of the alley.

"The others left for the train station already. I'll walk you to your car." Charlie gave her a lopsided grin.

She shook her head. "No worries. You need to catch the bus, right? Don't wait for me. I'm parked just up the street anyway. Totally safe."

"You're sure?" Charlie's brows drew together and briefly she flashed back to the way the mercenary's scowl had darkened his face. A fierce expression—not frightening so much as intimidating—and Charlie couldn't be more different. What she needed now was more than any of her friends or family could do.

"Yes." She forced her lips to widen in a smile. "Absolutely."

Another door opened farther down the alleyway, the venue's other back exit. Several men and women stepped out, all with the dark suits of the personal security her client had hired. Funny the way Henderson enjoyed flaunting his mercenary security, but they'd carried themselves with better polish and sophistication than the majority of the guests.

Speak of the devil. The man she'd spoken to and his colleagues must be heading home, too, wherever it was for each of them. She wondered if they called each other "colleagues" or something more...militant.

"See?" She turned back to Charlie. "I'm not even alone back here. Get going. And if anything happens, I'll shout to those guys for help."

Charlie eyed the group dubiously. "Men like those aren't safe to be around, Miss Cheng. I bet the women aren't either."

As if Charlie could do anything against them.

No, that was uncharitable. "Thank you. Really. But I'm sure I'll be fine. You get yourself on your bus or I'll have to drive you all the way home."

She made a shooing gesture to Charlie and after another moment's hesitation he turned, jogged up the alley to the street and headed for the bus station. She followed at a walk because trying to jog in heels this high was ridiculous. Plus she'd probably trip and break an ankle. An added embarrassment she did not want with those people, with him, behind her.

Maybe in an immediate emergency they'd actually move to action. Or they might just shout the name of a private investigator to her.

Not fair.

Shaking her head, she huffed out a laugh at herself. She was in all sorts of a mood this evening. And who would blame her? But being temperamental wasn't going to convince anyone to help her, and she needed help. She'd take every moment of frustration and rage and swallow it if it could get An-mei the help she needed faster. What Maylin had to do was be constructive, figure out next steps. There was always something else to be tried. Somehow.

And sometimes it seemed like every street in downtown Seattle was uphill. So no one would judge her if she took a breather up at the top of the alley and maybe stood at the corner a minute longer than necessary. If anyone did, she'd blame it on the crosswalk signal changing sooner than she thought she could cross.

Honestly, she needed to build up better cardio.

Screeching broke through her thoughts, the sounds of tires on wet pavement. She turned to her left and instinctively threw up her arm against the glare of insanely bright headlights.

"Down!"

A wall slammed into her left side, taking her to the ground and rolling with her until what was left of the air in her lungs was forced out in a whoosh as they hit the side of the building.

How? How had they rolled away from the street? And…what…?

Tires peeled.

"Are you okay? Hey!" The words boomed in her head from far away, like someone shouting through a fog.

Too many lights swam across her vision, images burned on her retinas blending with the streetlamps overhead. Her throat contracted and her lungs burned.

Breathe.

She gasped and cool air rushed in, clearing away some of the fog.

"That's it, sweetheart. Take another breath nice and slow. Slow." Strong hands patted her down, touched her with gentle purpose. "Does anything hurt? Your neck, your head?"

"The way you took her down, it's amazing her skull isn't splattered all over the sidewalk." Another man's voice floated over from some distance away. Or was it a shock thing?

Maybe she was in shock.

Did people's feet get cold at times like this? Only her left one.

"Your left foot is colder because you lost a shoe when I shoved you out of the way." A thread of amusement ran through the original speaker's voice. She liked the sound of it. Kind humor, like what she heard in his words, was the sign of a good man. "I'm going to help you to a sitting position, but if anything hurts at all, you let me know right away and we're laying you back down. Understood?"

"Yes." She said it out loud on purpose, because she was pretty sure she'd been talking out loud anyway so it'd be good to know if she could do it when she actually meant to.

The same big hands she'd taken note of before took hold of her, one sliding under her neck to give her support as she came up to a sitting position.

"Slow," her caretaker admonished.

His choice of speeds was frustrating.

"Had to be a DUI." The owner of the other voice had returned. "Driver ran up one curb and down the other all the rest of the way down the street. Got a couple of letters off the license plate. Lizzy and Victoria are securing the immediate area and calling it in to 911. Ambulance en route."

She turned her head to peer up. Blond hair, tanned skin, suit. One of the private security guys, the one who'd been snitching fried shrimp all night. She remembered Charlie coming to her nervous about whether to tell the guy the food was for the guests, but she'd laughed it off and made sure they kept the supply of that dish hot and ready. Fried shrimp were always popular anyway. Then what the man had said caught up to her.

"No ambulance. Really. I'm not hurt." And she didn't need to spend all night in the emergency room for a couple of scrapes and bruises. She hated hospitals with a passion.

"They're on their way." Her rescuer didn't leave room for argument. "They can look you over first, then you can decide."

His now authoritative tone, colder and clipped, sounded much more familiar than she'd initially thought. She peeked up at him through the escaped strands of her probably insanely messed-up hair.

Of course. She always had a special kind of ironic luck. The very man who wouldn't help her earlier was now kneeling beside her, shielding her from the night breeze with an arm around her shoulders.

"By the way, Cinderella, one of my teammates found your shoe. Victoria says shoes this expensive matter to a lady." The other man held it out to her. "Sorry, but I think it was a casualty. My name's Marc and this is Gabe, but I gather you two already met earlier. Lizzy and Victoria are sweeping the area to see if there's any security cameras we can mention to the police for possible footage of the car."

Fantastic. She reached to take her shoe, planning to mourn the heel hanging by a few stitches later, but Gabe took it instead.

"Hey, I could get that fixed." She hoped.

Gabe raised an eyebrow and tucked the shoe, careful of the barely attached heel, into his suit pocket. Most guys like him left the freaking temporary stitches in the pockets so nothing could go into those. "Your purse isn't big enough for it. I'll hold on to it until the medics get here and look you over."

What was she supposed to do, leave her other shoe on? Maybe he'd pocket that one, too.

"No serious injuries. I'm sure. Just some scrapes and bruises, probably." She tried to return his intense gaze with an assertive one of her own. "And my name is Maylin."

He might have saved her—and she was thankful—but as knights in shining armor went, he lacked any sort of courtly charm. Not a big deal. No need for princesses or fairy tales here. Those had been An-mei's favorite stories, not hers.

"Pretty sure your head hit the pavement when I took you down." A pang of regret there, she was sure of it. "We should get you checked for a concussion."

She thought about how they went to the ground and the strength it must have taken for him to roll both of them away from the street. Admittedly, his size probably helped him. He had a lot of height and weight on her. But he and his colleagues had been several yards behind her, even if they had been catching up to her on the way out of the alley. How fast was this man?

Sirens. The ambulance, most likely. And if she didn't string her thoughts together more coherently, they might decide she really did need to go to the emergency room.

"I'm also not sure that was a DUI, so why don't you tell me more about your missing person and why someone might not want you to find her?"

She stared at him wide-eyed and took in the grave expression, sharp eyes hidden in shadow, and the angle of his jaw. Tall, dark and seriously impressive as this man was, why did he believe her now?

His colleague crouched down on the other side of her. "What are you saying, Gabe?"

"I'm saying I'm fucking sure as hell that car was idling on the street. It was waiting for her."

Chapter Two

"You didn't have to see me all the way home. Honestly. The only reason I drove my car tonight was because of all the extra catering stuff I wanted to bring with me. Otherwise, I could have walked."

Gabe followed her with an armload of cooking gear in the early morning hours before dawn. None of it looked like anything he'd ever used in a kitchen, and he did know how to cook. If she'd brought all this in the first place, he wasn't sure how she'd managed to carry it all and still see over it to walk. In hot stiletto heels no less. One of which was poking a hole in his side, still in his jacket pocket. Thing could've been a murder weapon.

"I figure it's the least I could do since I did give you a bump to the head." And didn't he just feel like shit about that. Mostly because she hadn't gotten mad at him in any way and it'd even been a scuffle getting her to let him carry the damned box. Not to mention how it'd taken him, his team and the paramedics combined to convince her to be seen by a doctor. She was a trooper, even after hours in the emergency room stressed and obviously not wanting to be there. "Besides, like you said earlier, I'm one of the best—personal security, private military contractor, pack mule."

The laugh he hoped for wasn't forthcoming, but she did glance back with a soft smile on her face. Ah well, he wasn't much of a comedian anyway. Actually, he was shit for small talk.

He wondered if she'd realized she'd clung to him on the ride there in the ambulance or if she'd tucked herself against him instinctively as she came down from the shock. The woman wouldn't have gone at all if he and Marc hadn't backed up the paramedics with the recommendation to be checked over.

He hadn't minded her soft little form pressed against his side, though. It'd been reassuring. She'd come pretty close to turning into road pizza and he was shouldering some guilt over not agreeing to listen to her in the first place.

His stomach churned as he considered it, another reason why he'd come home with her. A hunch. Anyone who'd known to wait for her on the street after the event would probably know other things about her, too, like where she lived.

"A mild concussion is a small price to pay since things would've been a lot worse if you hadn't gotten me out of the way." Maylin jiggled her key in the deadbolt before succeeding in turning it, then struggled similarly with the doorknob.

Deadbolt and lock on the doorknob. Good. Too many people were complacent in upscale apartment buildings like this one. Considering the location and the security, actual issues inside the building were most likely unusual, but the parking garage probably had its share of incidents. No live security and not enough camera coverage.

"Might want to talk to the concierge down in the lobby

about those locks. Maybe you need a new key made up."
She was more aware of her surroundings than most civilians he'd met, but a person could never be too careful.

"Key usually works fine. I've never had to fudge with
it before. Not even a little." Fine lines had formed between her brows when she turned to look at him and
weariness showed in the smudges under her eyes. His
mood darkened at the sight of them and a protective surge
washed over him. She should get some rest, but he was
about to make her night even longer.

"Let me go in first." He set the box down in the hallway and took his sidearm from its holster.

She opened her mouth to protest, but fell silent under
his glare. Good. They could argue about it after he made
sure there was nothing to worry about.

As he entered the apartment, he visually confirmed
the main living area was clear. The place was neat. Pillows artfully arranged on a modern-style couch and
throw blankets neatly piled within reach. Several. Unless she liked to build forts in her spare time, he couldn't
imagine why she'd need so many.

Nothing looked disturbed. Maylin seemed to be in
the habit of leaving at least one light on while she was
away. He'd confirm with her later. Either way, it gave
him enough to see by.

Stepping away from the entry wall in measured steps,
he paused between each to scan the area inside the apartment from floor to ceiling before proceeding further
around the corner in a wide arc. The technique was re-
ferred to as "pieing the corner" and it was a strongly ingrained survival habit to negotiate turning any corner. It
gave him the best chance to spot a threat and take action
accordingly. In this case, though, he found nothing. But

that didn't mean there wasn't anything to worry about. There was something off about this place.

The entire apartment was dead silent. Either it was empty or her intruder was very good at hiding.

As soon as he had a clear line of sight down the hallway he advanced past the breakfast area and kitchen, careful to check reflections in the glass to give him added visuals behind the counter.

Finally, he cleared the bedroom. Again, the room was tidy, with no obvious sign of search or invasion. She seemed to like a whole hell of a lot of pillows on her bed, too. He wasn't sure there was even room for her to sleep on there.

An image of her burrowed in her pillows, curled up and sleeping, popped into his mind.

Banishing it immediately, he knocked a few to the floor to be sure there weren't any unpleasant surprises hidden among them. Not the time to be distracted.

Nothing seemed to be out of place, so he lowered his weapon and returned to where Maylin waited for him at the door, her phone in hand. Smart girl.

He lifted his finger to his lips and motioned for her to come inside. He retrieved her box of cooking supplies, too, and set it on the counter in the kitchen before conducting a second sweep. This time he checked every appliance, every light fixture.

Well, damn.

He could take her out into the hallway but he didn't want to remain exposed for longer than necessary. Once they left the apartment—and he intended to be sure she left with him—he'd want to be on the move immediately.

She was still standing in her entryway, pale and swaying on her feet. He stepped close to her, wrapped his arms around her. Her shoulders and back remained stiff in his embrace for a minute before she relaxed a fraction. He lowered his head to whisper into her ear. "Your apartment's been bugged. Do you have any family in the city?"

She shook her head, her face brushing into the hollow at his shoulder. A sense of purpose solidified. *Protect. Defend.* It'd started when he'd recognized the threat earlier and dove to get her out of harm's way. It'd only intensified since.

He wasn't about to leave her here.

He kept his voice low, his lips brushing her hair as he gave her his next set of instructions. "We're going to go into your bedroom. I want you to pack a bag with what you need for a couple of days."

Her head tilted up, her forehead bumping his chin and knocking his teeth together. "Where?"

Good thing she'd matched his whisper, but ouch, she had a hard skull. "I'm taking you anywhere but here. We'll figure out next steps after we get to your car and get out of the area."

"But…"

"There's too many red flags here. Even if you go to a hotel for a night, you can't stay at one indefinitely. Too accessible." He tightened his arms around her to stop her argument. "You are not safe and I want to know why. We can talk more about it on the drive."

Hours ago he hadn't wanted to have anything to do with her. Now, rage burned through him as he held her trembling form against his chest. Almost flattened by a not-so-drunk driver and the privacy of her home violated. Someone was investing a lot of effort into hurting her and it didn't make sense.

Puzzle pieces were floating around them, and no private

investigator had the means to help her fit them together before somebody took her out of the game.

Thing was, what was anyone like her doing caught up in any kind of game?

She raised her hand and slid it between them, flat against his chest. He thought she was going to push him away, and loosened his arms so she could step out of his hold if she wanted to. But her hand fisted in his shirt instead and she pressed her face into him. A moment later, hot tears seeped through the fabric to his skin.

"It's okay." He murmured the reassurance, not sure she even absorbed what he was saying. "I'll help you."

A promise. It wasn't a small thing he was giving her, whether she understood or not. What mattered was he recognized it for what it was. It'd been a long time since he'd been willing to make one like this. He intended to see it through. Maybe he'd think about why he was doing it later.

Hopefully, this wouldn't bite him in the ass the way his last mission had. That one had turned him bitter on the human condition in general.

Her shudders were the only sign of her being upset. He rubbed a hand up and down her back, hoping it was comforting. Crying women generally weren't his thing—he avoided them like the plague—but he couldn't bear to put her at arm's length. Not when she obviously had no support anywhere nearby.

Noiseless, she pressed against him for another minute, maybe two at most. Not a single sound to give her away to the invisible listeners in her home. Then she was taking a deep breath. When she stepped out of his arms, he might not have known she'd been crying at all but for the hint of bloodshot in the corners of her eyes.

She looked him in the eye and nodded.

Okay then.

He led the way to her bedroom, watchful for anything he might have missed the first time, any cameras especially, but it seemed all they'd done was install audio. He hoped he was right.

She approached her closet with hesitation, taking a long look at the open door. He stepped towards her but she shook her head and began to move with brisk efficiency. A duffel bag came out of a corner and clothing went into it, rolled tight to take up minimal space. When she turned to a drawer by her nightstand, he looked away politely when he caught a glimpse of lace and satin.

Oy. The drawer had been a rainbow explosion. She liked her underwear colorful and he was all sorts of interested in seeing more. Absolutely the wrong line of thought to be following at the current moment. Probably ever.

He shot a glance back in her direction and caught sight of a satin emerald bra. Maybe not never.

Maylin focused on drawing in air through her nose and letting it out slow, willing away the shivers threatening to take over her entire body. She wasn't in shock anymore. The emergency room doctor had cleared her. And yet, she couldn't stop shaking.

From the edge of her vision, she watched Gabe settle into the driver's side of her car and turn his head in her direction. He didn't say anything, though, only turned up the heat and set the fans to blow on high.

Her trembling had very little to do with being cold, and she'd bet he knew it. Still, the warm air chased away the clammy chill of the late night. It was late spring but the nights still had some bite to them, especially after a good rain.

"Where are we going?" If she wanted to pay this man and the rest of his team to help her get her sister back, she didn't have the funds to spare for a night in a hotel. Not one. And she wouldn't, couldn't take her focus away from An-mei, even to consider how long it would be before her own apartment was safe again. "Any hotel, either downtown or on the outskirts of the city, is going to cost too much."

One crisis at a time. It was the way to navigate through every mess, and she'd find a way through it all. Had to.

"No hotel. Even if you wanted one, we've got a tail, so wherever I put you someone is likely to find the room not long after I leave." Gabe didn't sound worried. How in hell did he not?

It was probably too much to hope he might be mistaken. "Somebody's following us? How do you know?"

He glanced up at the rearview mirror then turned his attention back to the road in front of them. "Same car's been behind us since about a block away from your parking garage. It's harder to tell at night, but the headlights are the same shape, and whenever we turn I confirm the car color. They're being smart and staying back with a car or two between us. On the plus side, it'll make it easier for me to lose whoever it is."

She hunched her shoulders and resisted the urge to shrink down in her seat. Fear twisted her stomach into a pretzel. "You're pretty confident you can lose them, I guess?"

"Do you get carsick?"

Oh, this was getting worse and not better. "Yes."

"Keep talking to me, then, and don't look out the windows. Try not to pay attention to where I'm driving and concentrate on conversation instead." He took one hand off the steering wheel and engulfed her hand in his, giving her a gentle squeeze. Warmth spread through her chest at the gesture, but he released her hand every bit as quickly and had both of his on the steering wheel again.

Swallowing hard, she tried to find her spine. "Notice how the minute you're supposed to strike up a conversation, you can't think of anything to say?"

He barked out a laugh.

The awful knot in her belly eased at the abrupt noise. He didn't seem gentle or nice. And neither of those were what she needed right now. Strange what comforted her at the moment. Of course, what finally came to mind to ask probably wasn't likely to keep her calm either. "Is all this because I've been looking for An-mei? How long do you think someone's been listening to me?"

"Not long. Maybe not at all yet. Impossible to tell exactly when unless we ask a few questions and put together a likely timeline."

Comforting thought. He hadn't answered her first question, though. She decided to tuck it away for now but when she was out of this car with her feet steady under her, she planned to press the issue. As much as he'd already helped Maylin, An-mei needed him and his team.

"I guess you're accustomed to those sorts of invasions of privacy?" Possibly not the best question to ask, but she was curious.

A pause. "I've had to find and get rid of a lot of that sort of equipment."

"Have you ever placed it?"

"Yes." Terse. Guarded. He spoke as if she might judge him for it.

"To be honest, it is good to know." She swallowed hard. "Knowing a mercenary team is the best based on a person's opinion and seeing them in action are two different things. You've saved me twice in one night."

He didn't answer.

"Not that I'd set something like this up just to test you all." The words came out in a rush as they braked hard. God, she hoped he didn't think she had. The urge to turn in her seat to look behind them popped into her mind and she thoroughly squashed the idea. Facing backwards in a car would only make her car sickness worse, and potentially tragic, the way he was making free with the acceleration and sudden deceleration.

"You didn't. We're good enough to know a setup when we walk into it." The amusement was back in his voice. He must enjoy it when she babbled like an idiot.

"Okay." She got the acknowledgment out in a small whisper.

The car swerved as he took a hard turn and accelerated enough to push her back into the seat. "Try to look far ahead or close your eyes. This won't take long."

"Okay." She glued her eyes shut instead and held on to the conversation.

"I'm guessing they put the listening equipment in when they learned their driver didn't take you out. It was quick work and means a lot of things." His voice had a gravelly tone to it and his words filled the close space of her car.

"They knew who I was and where I lived. I'm getting that. I don't want to. But I am. I must've left my name, phone number and even mailing address on at least a dozen voice mails while I was calling around trying to get information on my little sister." She swallowed hard. "I might need chocolate cake before this all sinks in as real."

A pause followed by a quiet chuckle. "Cake?"

"Double chocolate. I have a special recipe." She chewed on her lip and wondered if she liked the abrupt laugh from earlier or the softer one from just now. Either one gave her butterflies to chase away the anxiety. "Actually, I'll make cupcakes and share."

"Sharing is good."

And her brain hit a dead end again. She doubted he wanted to listen to her babble about Guinness-infused cupcake batter and ganache spiked with Irish whiskey. He would probably rather drink either. So who could blame her when her thoughts circled back to the bigger elephants in the car?

"Who are they? Why would they be out to squash me flat?" She hoped against common sense that he had answers for her. He'd only met her tonight and still didn't know even as much as she did about her sister's disappearance.

Still, she had several more interrogatives lined up for him whether he had the answers or not. They were jumbled up inside her head, bursting to be let out on someone. Anyone. But preferably a person who could help her.

"The hit-and-run wannabe wouldn't have made a pancake out of you. It would've been a sort of smashed and broken kind of mess…which I'll stop telling you about right now. The point is whoever wanted you dead probably got a look at me and my partners." He glanced up at the rearview mirror again, then cursed under his breath and made another sharp turn, then another. "They might've withdrawn to reassess and get a better idea of how much protection you had before attempting a second attack. That's a good thing."

"Oh." Not sure how it was, but she'd opt for believing him since he was currently driving her away from harm.

"Hey."

She looked at him, responding to the sharp command in his tone.

"You're under my protection now. Centurion Corporation isn't about to give them another opening to get to you." He turned his head and his gaze burned into her for a long moment before he turned his attention back to the road. "We've lost your tail and I'm taking you out of the city. The rest we can start on in the morning. It's going to be okay."

His words sank in, and for the first time since she'd gone to the airport to pick up her little sister—and not found her—Maylin started to hope.

"So you're going to help me find my sister?" It was a tenacious thing, this feeling, and she held her breath waiting for his answer.

He sighed. "I'm going to listen to what you know about your little sister's disappearance. I can't promise you'll find her."

She fell silent and stared out the window as the city lights gave way to the darkness of highway. Trees were huge shadows beyond the sides of the roads. She knew exactly what she wanted to say this time, but the majority of it was nasty, bad-tempered and definitely ill-advised considering how much he'd already helped her. Plus, his actions had only convinced her more that he and the Centurion Corporation were the help she needed.

"You're not going to recommend a private investigator

in the morning, though, are you?" And there was only a minimal amount of snark there. Honest. She'd tried.

"No." His tone had gone flat.

See? Not wise. At all. And not even a leftover fortune cookie stashed in her purse to help her get back to firmer ground.

"I'm sorry." Sincerity was the best she could dredge up. "I'm not sure how to give you the information you need, and I really want to present it in the most convincing way possible."

"We're going to want to hear out your whole story when you're better rested." His words had defrosted a bit. "You'll be able to think clearer and won't be as likely to fumble any details. My entire team will be asking you questions—not just me—and we'll need to do some research."

"But time…"

"I'll be using what little we have left of tonight to find out what I can about your new friends. They're the most immediate link to what's going on and probably connected to your sister's disappearance. I will not be wasting time."

So much confidence, assurance. She wanted to believe him.

"I really want to say you should get rest, too. But I want you to get closer to figuring out what happened tonight and how it relates to An-mei more." She cleared her throat. "Wherever it is we're going… I don't have a hosting gift. Does it have a kitchen and can I make you breakfast as a thank-you instead?"

He laughed again and flashed her a grin.

She was unreasonably giddy in response. "So do you like omelets? Or eggs Benedict?"

Chapter Three

Gabe pulled up next to the guest cabin and put the car into Park.

The last twenty minutes of the car ride had been quiet, peaceful even, as the twilight gave way to dawn and the events of the night had finally taken their toll on Maylin Cheng. She sat slumped in the passenger seat, her head tipped far to one side as she napped.

Impressive. As a soldier, he'd learned to nap anywhere, but she looked damned uncomfortable. Considering the best way to make sure she didn't fall on her face the minute she got out of the car, he opted to disembark and walk around to the passenger side. Opening the door, he spoke quietly, trying not to scare the bejeezus out of her. "Maylin. Hey."

She woke with a start, sitting bolt upright and pinning him with a wide-eyed stare.

So much for not scaring her. He held up his hands to show he meant no harm. "Remember me? Gabriel Diaz."

Her eyes remained wild for a moment before recognition eased into them. "Ngh."

He wasn't sure she'd spoken coherently in any language.

"Let's get you settled in to the guest cabin." He took both her hands in his and helped her out of the car.

She bumped her head on the way out.

"Whoop. Careful there." He sucked at this. If she ended up with a second bump, he had no good excuse for letting it happen. Thank god she didn't have a concussion.

Her eyelids shuttered closed. She was asleep on her feet. Literally.

"Hey, c'mon."

No dice. Her eyes fluttered open and she focused on him for a moment before her lids were too heavy to lift again. He led her forward a couple of steps and she stumbled with him, blind.

Okay, fine. She was exhausted. He could understand that. And he should not have let her bump her head again, however lightly. She didn't have a drop of energy left in her.

Giving up, he let her stand for a second. He bent over and gently put his shoulder into her midriff, hefting her over his shoulder. He could've been chivalrous and shit about carrying her in his arms but then he wouldn't have a hand free to get the door to the cabin open.

Either he was going to regret having met Maylin Cheng or she was going to hate him. One or the other.

"It's not like you to bring home strays." The voice in the dark wasn't angry or malicious. In fact, Lizzy had a way of maintaining the kind of completely neutral tone that left a man wondering if he'd see the dawn.

"Safest place for her, for now." Gabe rubbed his jaw. "Everyone in for the night?"

"Yup." His teammate stepped out of the shadows of the surveillance room and into the dimly lit hallway. Her hair was tied back and she wore a simple black T-shirt and jeans. Still wore her holster since she was on night watch. Even though she'd come out to greet him, she kept her gaze fixed on the security displays inside the room. "You were saying it wasn't any kind of drunk-driving hit-and-run. I was thinking the trajectory of the car was straight as an arrow, heading towards the girl and on its way out of range. The girl all right?"

He shook his head. "Got to her apartment, found it bugged. Some fairly high-end audio surveillance. The team will need to head back to do a full sweep."

One man trying to conduct that sort of search was definitely going to miss something. It was better completed as a team.

Even in profile, he could see Lizzy's brows draw together. "Lot of effort invested in keeping tabs on a single woman. Wasn't she part of the catering crew? Manager or something? Not usually the type to rate that much effort."

He nodded. "Makes me wonder what is going on with her missing sister."

Maylin Cheng didn't seem the type to be involved with drugs or the black market. Outside of those, there wasn't a lot to draw enough attention to a person to rate surveillance and assassination attempts. Mafia, maybe.

"You put her in the guest house?"

"At least until we decide on a safe house or secure hotel where she'd be more comfortable. Something we can look into in the morning. I checked over her car back at her parking garage. No obvious signs of tampering or tracking devices." Course, he and Maylin had only been upstairs in her apartment for a very short time and he'd parked her car in full view of two different security cameras. There hadn't been sufficient surveillance in the garage, but he'd made sure not to park in one of the blind spots. His mind moved on to the line of investigation he had for tonight. "If you can run queries on An-mei Cheng's disappearance and background checks on both the Chengs while you're on watch, I'd consider it a favor."

Lizzy raised an eyebrow. "Any reason you're not making it an order?"

As leader of their fire team, he was commanding officer. But they weren't active duty military anymore. They didn't have to live rank and position twenty-four seven. The structure of Centurion Corporation was more a hybrid of military and corporate organization. The corporate influence was especially apparent back at HQ in DC. His superiors at HQ oversaw contract acquisition and decided on resource allocation, sending squadrons made up of four to five fire teams, each all around the world.

For the most part, Gabe kept it simple. He commanded his fire team when they were actively on a contracted mission. Otherwise, they were more casual about their interactions within the bounds of earned respect.

He shrugged. "We're not on official contract and I haven't decided if we're taking the job yet."

She nodded. "Fair."

Lizzy was more than familiar with the way he operated, so her response made him pause. He wasn't committing to the job yet. "I'll be in my room, but call me if anything comes up."

"You got it."

Centurion Corporation Training and Recovery was a five-acre property tucked into the northwest corner of the Cougar Mountain Regional Wildland Park just east of Seattle. Heavily wooded, the acreage didn't offer any clear line of sight for potential onlookers, but hidden cameras were installed all over the property in addition to the more obvious perimeter fence and no-trespassing signage for normal passersby.

The men and women stationed at the training center and barracks were responsible for surveillance over the main perimeter and training grounds. The recovery cabins were set apart and to the edge of the property to give people on R & R space. Almost always having returned fresh from hot spots overseas, the Centurions staying there were operating on a high level of awareness, so they maintained their own second-layer surveillance of their section of the perimeter. Mostly for the structure of scheduled watches and for peace of mind.

It did a person a lot of good to fall into a familiar routine.

Lizzy would see any intruders long before they got anywhere near the guest house or main building. He'd have plenty of time to get to Maylin if there was trouble, and she'd be surrounded by the rest of his team, too. None of them were heavy sleepers, if they slept at all.

He didn't. Not much anyway.

The kitchen in the main rest and recovery house was dark, but indirect lighting came on as motion sensors detected his entrance. A quick search of the commercial-sized refrigerator scored him some leftover Beefaroni and stir-fried broccoli. Not a winning combination, but it'd do.

Damn. He should have made her eat something. Slight build like hers, she probably burned up calories just thinking too hard. But there had been no waking the woman, even as he'd carried her into the guest house and laid her on the bed. She'd probably have slept through him trying to force-feed her. As it was, he'd removed her shoes, spread a blanket over her and left a note next to a bottle of water for her, letting her know to come up to the main house when she woke. Hopefully not too creepy.

Gabe headed down a second hallway, past the kitchen and a couple of other rooms. He nudged the door to his own open with his foot and took a good look before entering. In the middle of his safe zone, where the chances of an intruder were slim to none, and he still couldn't relax.

Nobody would blame him. His teammates didn't ease down from the heightened state of awareness they all lived in either. It kept people alive overseas. He'd done three tours already, two on active military duty and one as a private military contractor. He planned to go out on a fourth as soon as his team had enough time to rest and recover. That's what the Centurion base in Washington State was for: training new recruits and recovery for teams recently returned. It was a good setup.

Setting down his dubious meal, he opened his laptop and jabbed the power button. While it booted, he shrugged out of his suit jacket and pulled his tie out of his pants pocket. Belt, shoes and socks came off next. He sighed. Something close to heaven when the damned dress socks were peeled off. He had no idea why the things were so uncomfortable. They didn't breathe.

He snorted. Tough Gabe Diaz, luxuriating over the chance to wiggle his toes. What. The. Fuck.

He sat down and shoveled a mouthful of Beefaroni before logging on to his laptop and bringing up the VPN. Once he was on Centurion's private network, he quickly scanned his email for urgent messages. One from headquarters caught his eye. The subject read "Safeguard Project" but it wasn't marked at high priority so Gabe flagged it to look at later and focused on the task at hand.

He shot out a couple of inquiries to see who might be

active in the area. Mercenaries followed the jobs, and people in his line of business tended to bump into each other again and again. Somebody he knew probably had an idea of who was after Maylin or had gotten wind of the job involving her.

One net cast, he started the first of the information searches he had planned to catch other fish. Lizzy would verify Maylin was who she said she was and that her sister really was missing.

Not that he didn't believe her, but Maylin was emotionally compromised. Too close to the situation to think clearly or evaluate circumstances objectively. Even if he wanted to believe her, he needed to confirm the veracity of her story via third-party sources. Meanwhile, he wanted to get an idea of what this missing person looked like.

An-mei Cheng was a fairly easy-to-find person, at least on the internet. First-generation Chinese American, born and raised in the Seattle area. Her father's family was from northwestern China. Her mother had been from Beijing. She was a few years older than the little sister he'd pictured from the way Maylin spoke about her. Regardless, both sisters looked young in the way most people of Eastern ancestry managed, with smooth skin and ageless eyes. He was betting a lot of people mistook them for way younger than they really were. Maylin's maturity came from her air of competency and the confidence she exuded. At least, when she didn't have to deal with assholes like him.

Water under the bridge, Diaz. You're helping her now.

Still, this was the last kind of job he wanted for him or his team. This kind of job sucked a person in, made them care. It was the kind in which only a sociopath could avoid getting emotionally invested. He'd been there and been burned, bad. Nothing about this was going to end well.

But he'd decided to help Maylin, at least far enough to ensure she didn't end up dead in the near future. And who the hell else would be able to? Nobody in the Seattle area had the resources Centurion had.

His smartphone rattled on the desk with a notification. There wasn't much point setting them to vibrate when the vibration could be heard across the damn room. He picked up the phone and gave the screen a swipe.

Lizzy had completed her search already.

He pushed away from his laptop and headed back up the hallway to the surveillance room.

"Lizzy."

She didn't turn from the multiple monitors this time either.

"Search didn't take long." Lizzy reached for a pile of printouts. "To be honest, I was curious after tonight's fun so I started a basic background query on Maylin and her sister before I settled in for surveillance. Finding out how An-mei Cheng disappeared was quick because there's not much out there to find."

Curiosity and paranoia worked hand in hand, mostly to their benefit. Lizzy would have given him a heads-up right away if anything about Maylin's situation set off red flags. Gabe took the printouts from her. "You're a freaking goddess."

"Basic" for Lizzy was more detailed than most background checks run for standard employers. There'd probably be more in there about Maylin and her sister than they knew about themselves.

"Yes, and how about you stand night watch for me next

time I need to switch shifts?" Lizzy sounded cold but a small smile played on her lips. "This missing person—police haven't done more than contact the authorities in China. They're sticking to the exact letter of standard operating procedure. The US Embassy over there has an alert for if she comes back to the embassy over the next couple of days, but there's no active search for her. Again, standard procedure. They're assuming she went off to party or sightsee, maybe lost her passport. They're waiting to see if she contacts them."

The same basic runaround Maylin had been getting. So far, her story was turning out to be accurate.

"What was she doing over there?"

"Our person of interest is some sort of übersmart person. A PhD in gene therapy and genetic recombination. She wasn't just attending a scientific research conference, she was a guest speaker. Not the sort who'd go on a drunken binge and miss her flight home. Profile isn't a match." Lizzy's face remained neutral. Her arms were crossed and she tapped a finger on her bicep the way she did when she was chewing on inconsistencies. "Both women are bilingual, too. They speak Mandarin, so it's not like An-mei Cheng couldn't ask for directions to get to the authorities or the embassy."

Not like she couldn't call for help.

"Seems to be a high-profile person, though." Gabe wondered why the authorities were so laid back if an important researcher, a guest in the country, hadn't turned up yet. Not as big a surprise that they weren't responding to worried family members like Maylin. Unless you had clout on the international scene, there was little a person could do so far away from the country in question.

"Not that high profile. She's got a thesis and some

promising research, but she's still up-and-coming in the academic world as far as I can tell." Lizzy tipped her head to one side. "'Bright future' and similar commentary popped up in any newsletters related to the conference. She's at the beginning of her career. Not important enough to make big waves now that she's missing."

Gabe nodded. "No ransom request either."

"No." There, Lizzy's tone edged into regret. She recovered, though, and returned to a brisk tone. "I left a few search strings running. I'll keep you updated if anything new turns up."

No ransom meant An-mei's kidnappers had taken her for other reasons, and the likelihood of finding the young woman alive was headed towards the minuscule. Maylin's extraordinary green eyes came to mind. An-mei had the same unusual color. Bilingual, attractive and possessed of a striking feature to set her apart. Human trafficking was a strong possibility.

"All right, I'll look through the background." Gabe was dog tired. He was going to need to think of a plan of action before Maylin woke later in the morning. Least he could do was call in a couple of favors over at the Beijing embassy. He'd place a video call in while they were still up and working.

"Your girl is clean, no shady history. Nothing to tie her to other reasons for tonight's attempt," Lizzy volunteered, still not looking in his direction. "But she's alone. Her and her little sister lost their parents. Mother died ten years ago in a plane crash and father died of a heart attack a few years back. Stepmother doesn't seem to have anything to do with them."

Didn't that make everything a little more awful? Lizzy was already invested. No way was the rest of his team going to walk away from his girl once they got a look at this intel.

His girl?

Ah, well shit. He was in denial and swimming upriver.

Chapter Four

The front door was open.

Maylin resisted the urge to lean in and call out a hello to the silent house. Mostly because she half suspected an alarm would go off, complete with sirens and bars dropping around her as an automated voice barked at her to remain where she was.

As she stepped inside, a jovial male voice called out to her instead. "Come on in. Kitchen's just down the hall. Gabe will meet you there."

Okay then.

A quick glance around the foyer revealed no shoe rack. She'd grown up in a household where you took off your shoes as you came in the door. Force of habit to check and she couldn't ever quite shake the feeling she was tracking in dirt as she walked through a home no matter how thoroughly she'd wiped her shoes on the doormat out front. It wasn't just an Asian thing, either. She'd had plenty of friends with parents who wanted to keep the carpets for as long as possible.

All grown up now and memories of childhood and school days clung to her. She'd dreamed of her sister and her parents. They'd been a family, doing normal family things. Routine. And now, none of it was there for her to find solace in.

Past the foyer and the sitting room, she wandered down the long hallway. A door was open on the left, presumably where the earlier voice had come from. As she passed, she got a glimpse of monitors. There were rows of them, set up three high and several wide. Multiple laptops sat on a tabletop and there was a familiar-looking man sitting there with his feet propped up, a tablet in his lap. He glanced in her direction and gave her a quick wave before returning his attention to the monitors.

"Right down the hall. Keep going. And good morning!"

"Thanks." She'd meant it to come out just as hearty, but to her ears, she'd sounded like a mouse. Ah, she'd have to pull herself together better than this. Strength, confidence were what she'd need to keep these people helping her and her sister.

First, she needed to find Gabe.

"You're up early."

She squeaked, then scowled. *"Tā mā de!"*

And there he was, filling the previously empty hallway and standing not a few inches from her. He'd come out of nowhere.

Gabe's eyebrows rose and a slow smile spread across his face. "But maybe not awake yet."

Probably not. Coffee could fix so many things and she was not going to wonder how he could look so good first thing in the morning. Well, late morning. It was well past her normal wake-up time but they'd been out very late and she couldn't remember arriving. Giving him a glare, she drew herself up to her full height. "Don't even try that. You like sneaking up on people."

If anything, his smile grew broader and a dimple made an appearance. A really cute…

She shook her head. "I was directed down here because there's a kitchen?"

Gabe stepped to one side and gestured for her to continue down the hallway.

Gathering what dignity she could muster under the circumstances, she marched past him. A few more steps and the hallway opened up to a surprisingly large kitchen area. The marble surfaces were clear of anything but the most minimal countertop appliances. All wiped down to a shine. Good, clean work area.

There was a restaurant-grade cooking range with eight, *eight*, gas burners and two ovens. A dual sink sported a handy pull-out kitchen faucet. Plus, the refrigerator. Oh, the kind of catering she could plan with a refrigerator that big. *This* was a great place to cook. So much better than the small utility kitchen at her apartment.

"There's coffee." Amusement spiced the suggestion and she tried to ignore the little shivers Gabe's voice sent down her spine.

He was standing inside her personal space and she pointedly ignored him. Only, it was very hard to overlook the way he loomed over her. Not in a scary way, no. Leaning back into his very solid chest was incredibly tempting and she had no idea why the urge to do so was clouding her brain.

Cooking. Yup. And coffee. He'd mentioned coffee.

"I promised to make omelets." She glanced around for cooking tools, at least a spatula. Maybe they were in a drawer. Her box was sitting on the counter of a sideboard. Oh, good. But those were all specific to Chinese cooking, and she didn't need them just to make omelets.

He stepped away and the space he'd occupied cooled in his absence, or maybe she imagined it. "You don't have to make them, but if you're hungry anything in the refrigerator is fair game."

Determined to stay on track, she strode to the refrigerator to see what they had in stock.

If she had high hopes based on the appliances, there were no words for the desolation of the interior. Looked like Mexican, Chinese and pizza either delivered or were within quick driving distance, based on the neatly stacked take-out containers occupying the bottom shelf. One drawer contained a few packages of deli meats and cheeses all on the verge of expiring. There was also a random jar of olives. The rest of the cooled space was wiped down and pristine. A lone carton of two-percent milk and several dozen eggs sat waiting on a middle shelf.

He must've gone out to get those while she'd been sleeping. The realization sank in as she closed the refrigerator. When she peeked into the freezer, all she found was a random loaf of ciabatta bread that must have come with some large order of takeout. She took a closer look at the cooking range. Barely used. The cabinets probably didn't have much besides ready-to-eat cereals. Call it a guess.

"Doesn't anyone living here actually cook?" She immediately bit her lip. Way to go, coming into the man's home and being rude.

"These are temporary quarters." Gabe didn't take offense. If anything, the amusement was threaded back into his voice again. The same tone she remembered from last night. "The kitchen is here in case a chef is brought in to help out or if someone staying likes to cook, but no one currently here does."

A mug appeared at her side. Did the man ever make any noise? At least she hadn't jumped and made a fool of herself again. Instead, she took the proffered coffee and considered the kitchen. "I was thinking about what additional information I can give you to help find An-mei. Where's the rest of your team? Is the man in the computer room near the front going to join us?"

Gabe hooked a stool with his foot and pulled it out from under the breakfast counter in the center of the kitchen. "They'll be along shortly. And like I said, you don't need to cook."

"Can they hurry? Are they far away?" More questions threatened to tumble out of her mouth, each one sharper than the previous. Instead of letting those loose, she took a sip and tried not to grimace. "You all use those instant coffeemakers with the individual cups, don't you?"

"It's decent and quick. Easy cleanup." He shrugged. Then he jerked his head in the direction of the hallway. "Marc is on surveillance right now but he'll join us when Lizzy and Victoria come out of their rooms. We're all in this building."

She debated asking him to check on them. But her sister needed this man and his team. Teams? She needed to give him the best answers possible, which meant she needed to refrain from antagonizing him and do her best to get her brain moving.

She bit back her request to go get Lizzy and Victoria, whoever they were, turning back to the refrigerator instead. She pulled out the milk and the eggs, feta cheese, plus a container of what looked like leftover salsa verde, then the remains of a spinach salad. When she placed her armload on the center island, she was caught by his stare. She blinked and swallowed. "Anything is fair game, right?"

His brows drew together in a scowl. Intimidating, yes, but not frightening this morning. Not compared to how angry he'd been the previous night. "We need you to concentrate, tell us every possible detail."

She met his glare with a steady stare of her own. "There's only you here right now and I focus better if my hands are busy cooking. Honestly."

This was how she worked best, multitasking.

"Can't hurt to let the woman cook. Some of us actually enjoy breakfast." A dark-haired woman with olive skin stalked around the corner from the portion of the hallway that went past the kitchen. Eyes so dark they were almost black pierced Maylin with a sharp glance. "I'm Isabelle, but the team calls me Lizzy. We sort of met last night for a few seconds before they tossed you in the back of the ambulance."

"I'm sorry, I don't remember." And Maylin wasn't sure how anyone could forget Lizzy after meeting her. Intimidating wasn't a strong enough word for her.

Lizzy shrugged. "You got flattened into the sidewalk. No worries."

Maylin didn't know what to say to that. Despite the impact of the initial introduction, Lizzy seemed to be satisfied with leaning her forearms on the counter and just...hanging out.

After a moment, Gabe sighed. "Skillets are in the lower cabinet to the left of the stove."

Oh, good, she hadn't been sure they had much in the way of actual pots and pans. Being in motion helped steady her, and organizing her thoughts on what she was going to make pulled other thoughts into more logical order, too. Like what information they'd need to find her sister.

"Anyone have an issue with green in their omelets?" She'd assume no one was allergic since it wasn't likely they'd keep those all on the same shelf. Usually anything someone was allergic to would be segregated.

"We all eat anything," another female voice called out, and when Maylin turned, a lovely pale blonde was leaning on the counter next to Lizzy. They made a striking pair side by side, Victoria's ivory and gold a perfect foil for Lizzy's dark tanned complexion, but the contrast was in basic appearance only. Both women had an air of ready competence. "And it is lovely to have someone ask what we might prefer in any case. I heard something about omelets? I'm Victoria, by the way. The team calls me Vic."

"Maylin."

"We know." Victoria gave her a friendly smile, maybe a little on the feral side. "Gabe and Lizzy gave us a little on your background. Hope you don't mind."

What kind of information had they gathered? Did it matter? She was nobody. Her sister was nobody. And still, people were exerting a lot of effort in regard to both of them.

Maylin tipped her head to the side. "Will it help convince you to find An-mei with me?"

No commitment in either Victoria's blue eyes or Lizzy's dark gaze. It was Victoria who answered her, though. "It means we're here to listen."

"And have breakfast." The man from the surveillance room, Marc, walked in and took a seat on a stool near Victoria. He grinned expectantly. "Seth is covering me while we have this chat. I promised to bring him back some chow."

A laugh escaped, bubbling up from her belly in a release of tension. Maylin decided to roll with it because any more stress would make her snap. At least they were all here now. "Breakfast it is, then. So do you all like sweet omelets or savory?"

She considered her ingredients. Could go either way.

Marc's eyes crossed in a comic expression. "Who likes sweet omelets? Is that a thing?"

Victoria shrugged. "I didn't know it was a thing."

"I think she said 'almonds.'" Marc didn't sound sure, though.

"No, she said omelets," Lizzy interjected. "And there's no almonds in the pantry unless someone bought trail mix."

Marc waved a hand. "Unless it's one of those sweet omelet rolls off a nude Japanese woman, I'll pass."

Gabe growled. Perhaps he thought she'd be insulted.

But Maylin had spent her share of time around rowdy people. Maybe not as dangerous as these, but definitely uncensored. This was nothing. She kept her expression politely inquisitive. "Does she have to be Japanese? Or just nude? If you're only worried about body temperature, I don't think ethnic background is a prerequisite to maintain sushi at optimal serving temperature."

Lizzy barked out a laugh. Victoria gave her a nod.

Shouldn't please her so much to see Gabe's dimple reappear, but really, she liked his smile. It was rakish, like he was daring her to do naughty things. It was fun speaking out around him. Fun to surprise him.

"What do you need to know from me?" Pulling out a good-sized skillet, she blew through the other cabinets for something to serve as a mixing bowl and started re-creating things from leftovers.

It was Gabe who gave her the first prompt, his presence to one side an anchor already. "We know your sister was at some sort of genetic research conference. How did she become a guest speaker? Did she propose a topic or was she invited?"

"Invited." It was reassuring, actually, to hear what they'd already found out overnight. Encouraging. "She was incredibly excited to be invited to speak on her research."

"Did she seem worried at all before she left?"

Maylin paused in beating eggs and frowned. "Stressed over getting her presentation just right. Aside from defending her thesis, she hadn't had much experience in public speaking. But not worried about the actual trip. She was really looking forward to visiting China for the first time."

Victoria shifted on her stool. "She'd never been?"

"Neither of us had." Maylin set a skillet on the stove, bending to watch the flame as she set it to the height she wanted it. When she straightened, she figured more information was better. "We're first-generation Chinese American and Mom always meant to take us when we got old enough, whenever that was going to be, but she died. And then Dad remarried and his new wife didn't have much interest in us, so we never went."

Daddy's new wife had only been interested in climbing the social ladder of the local Chinese society. The woman had shown no enthusiasm for Maylin or An-mei when neither would play her matchmaking games. They were leftovers to her, disappointing and little better than old baggage after their father died.

But they'd both kept up on their Mandarin, planning to go on their own.

Maylin bit her lip. "When this opportunity came up I didn't want her to give up the chance to go just because I couldn't take the time away from my catering business to join her. I'm the owner and I haven't trained up a senior enough assistant to leave things in someone else's hands for that long."

Guilt washed over her, combining with her worry. For a few minutes, there was silence as she poured egg into the pan and carefully created layers.

"The invitation came from the conference coordinators, then?" Gabe's voice came to her, gentle but insistent.

She spooned salsa verde across the surface of the omelet and sprinkled in baby spinach, giving it a chance to wilt just a little. "Actually, a colleague in the same academic circle extended the invitation. He's a chair on the programming committee."

"Do you remember his name?" Lizzy's question was sharp.

Carefully rolling the omelet, Maylin slid it out onto a plate and turned off the flame. Picking up a knife, she studied its edge. "Porter van Lumanee. He hasn't returned my calls, but according to his out-of-office email notification, he should have returned at the same time An-mei was supposed to."

Perhaps he was missing, too. But she doubted it. More than one scientist unaccounted for would have bothered the police more.

She cut the rolled omelet crosswise, serving the slices out onto small plates so the spiral of egg and green showed. To one side, she arranged fresh-cut apple slices.

As she placed a plate in front of each of them, she caught sight of Lizzy's suddenly blank expression.

"You know something about him." No need to make it a question.

Lizzy picked up a fork. "His name popped up in the search, but he's not missing."

Lizzy was watching her, and Maylin blinked, then put the knife down.

Deliberately taking a bite out of an apple slice, Lizzy chewed before answering. "He's on record as the last person to see your sister. He said she went out sight-seeing, possibly to meet up with some new friends for some end-of-conference celebration before heading back to the States."

"That's not like An-mei." Maylin wiped down the counter, unsettled. "The sightseeing, maybe. But she'd have sent me a text about it. She loved to share those things and I was getting multiple texts through the day on everything she was experiencing. She didn't mention plans to meet with anyone there."

"People do make new friends," Victoria said gently.

It'd do no good to get defensive. Maylin took a bite of omelet as she considered how to explain best. The salsa verde was sweet with a touch of spice to it, and the feta cheese she'd added took the omelet roulette over to the savory flavor profile she'd been hoping for. Complex but not over the top. Not bad for leftovers. "An-mei is mostly introverted. She prefers the privacy of a lab, her own apartment. Her idea of a wild night is staying up all night online playing a game app we both have installed on our smartphones."

"She chats online in a video game?" Marc started chuckling.

The concept of video games wasn't all that unusual, but An-mei's games weren't the type people usually thought of when someone mentioned staying up playing all night.

Maylin shook her head. "This game has no chat functionality, just a simple message inbox, and she doesn't answer in-game messages from people she doesn't know. She only accepts friend invitations based on rank so she can use the person's monsters on her teams to defeat stronger dungeons."

"Huh." Marc popped an entire omelet slice into his mouth and chewed. "So I'll look into this Porter guy's story. If he's back in the States and not answering you, probably best to check out his office in person to see if he's ignoring just you or everyone. This…whatever it is… is incredible, by the way."

Maylin smiled. It was why she'd built a catering business. Cooking for people made her happy. "You had good supplies in the refrigerator."

Lizzy snorted. "We had shit for leftovers. I don't know how you managed to put this together from all that."

"What was the last you heard from your sister?" Gabe placed a cleaned plate on the counter next to her. He'd eaten every bit.

Her stepmother would've been insulted. Some Chinese felt an empty plate was a silent criticism indicating not enough food had been served. It wouldn't have mattered to her stepmother that American custom considered cleaning one's plate a good practice and a compliment to the chef.

Maylin wondered if he'd liked it or if he'd only eaten out of politeness.

"We used a free voice mail and texting service so she could send me texts without using an international data plan. As long as she was in the hotel or somewhere with free Wi-Fi, I got texts almost every hour she was awake." She gathered the dirtied plates and bowls in the sink.

"Leave the dishes. House rules are if someone cooks, someone else cleans." Gabe placed his hands on her shoulders and eased her back to face the rest of the team.

Left with nothing to keep her hands busy and flustered by the unexpected zing his touch sent through her, Maylin grabbed a dish towel and wiped down the counter. "Most of the texts were about what the hotel looked like or what she had to eat."

"She send pictures?" Marc was still grinning.

"Text service doesn't allow for pictures. She just wanted to reassure me she was eating." Maylin might have been nagging her a little. Okay, a lot. "She always forgets to eat."

"You said *most*—what was unusual?" Lizzy hopped off her stool and brought her plate to the sink, where Gabe was making quick work of washing the dishes.

Maylin backed up so she could see them all, leaned back against the refrigerator and started twisting the dish towel in her hands. "A few texts. She said her presentation went well. Then there was a text that someone made a job offer but she wasn't going to take it. Then she said she wanted to come home. Now."

Anxiety rose up, her heart starting to beat harder. Something was wrong, wrong, wrong. In a way that she hadn't been able to explain to the police. But she had to get this right here, with these people. And to convince them her gut feeling was real.

"Only one or two texts after that, along the same lines of looking forward to coming home. No updates about getting to the airport or confirming when her flights were. She'd have checked with me to make sure there were no schedule changes so I could pick her up from the airport." And that was an awful twist in her stomach, too. Because Maylin had always been so busy, she hadn't been reliable. Even if An-mei had been on the flight home, An-mei would've checked to be sure Maylin hadn't got caught up with something work related.

"This text service, you access it via a web browser?" Lizzy asked quietly, wiping dishes as Gabe handed them to her.

"Yes."

"Will you share it with us so we can take a look through the texts?"

Maylin nodded. "I'll give you my password for the account. And hers."

"You know her passwords?" Marc dropped his forehead into his hand.

Maylin shrugged. "An-mei was a little absent-minded, so she asked me to remember them for her after I told her not to put them on a Post-it note. She doesn't know mine, though."

"Well, it'll help if we can take a look through those texts—and her recent email, too, if the passwords you know access that." Lizzy tossed the towel she'd been using on the counter. "Is that it? You didn't hear anything else?"

Maylin sighed. "The only thing that happened next was me sitting at the airport, waiting for her for hours. No one at the airport could tell me anything but that she hadn't boarded in China. The police said to wait a few days. My calls to the Chinese embassy said the same. I was researching private investigators and contractors with international affiliates when my job last night came up. Your corporation's name came up in my research and was on the list of vendors as private security. The best of the best. That client doesn't hire anything less. So I figured if anyone could help me, you could."

"It's not our usual type of mission." Gabe crossed his arms, leaning back against the counter in front of the sink. "Our fire team is a part of a bigger squadron and we usually go in to cause a lot of damage and get out. Extraction is not our primary objective."

"Not usually, no." Victoria tapped her lips. "But not unheard of."

Gabe nodded in acknowledgment. Maylin's heart jumped. Hope. They were listening to her.

And she wanted to know about them, about what they might be able to do. "How many of you are there?"

"I lead a fire team of four soldiers—me, Lizzy, Marc and Victoria. We're one of four to five fire teams in a particular squadron. Depending on the contract, fire teams can get moved around in the squadrons based on the needed skill sets for the mission at hand." Gabe's jaw flexed, as if he was chewing on the inside of his cheek. Bad habit, or maybe the echoes of an old one already given up. Her dad used to chew tobacco and did that for years after he'd quit. "Our entire current squadron is back on US soil, but only two of the fire teams came west for recovery here in Washington. Otherwise, we'd be at the corporate headquarters in the DC area."

She couldn't help looking back over the others. None of them looked injured. In fact, every one of them looked more fit than anyone she'd encountered either at work or walking on the street. It was in the way they stood, the way they moved smooth and soundless. There was a potential for action there, keeping Maylin on edge even before she'd thought to put a definition to it.

"Dislocated shoulder." Lizzy tapped her left and gave her a feral grin. "Not fit for the kind of rough and ready duty we usually do, but more than fine for the simple bodyguard duty we were doing last night."

"Broken thumb. Doesn't seem serious, but you need your thumb to operate a lot of equipment." Marc scowled as Victoria snickered. "Look. If the other squadron leader hadn't seen me fumble my weapon on the way into the pisser, he'd have never known."

"We were already headed here anyway," Gabe interjected. "No reason to hide it, and better to get it splinted and taken care of."

"Ah." Maylin didn't know what to say.

Was Gabe injured in some way? They all had looked at him, to him, to follow his lead in how much to share. She might not be supersecret military, but she could recognize at least those signs.

"Regardless, we're all mended and more than capable of investigating your sister's disappearance." Lizzy cut the air with her right hand.

"And you have a contract for the hiring of your services?" Maylin could grasp the formalities, and they were there to protect all involved parties. She'd learned that the hard way running her own business.

"Caleb can draw one up. He's the squadron's ops person back at HQ." Gabe didn't sound worried.

"For investigation into her disappearance and…extraction? Is that what you call it?" Maylin pushed because none of them had committed yet. And she needed it, in writing.

Gabe pushed away from the counter, then hesitated.

She lifted her chin and refused to look away from his considering gaze. Finally, he said, "One step at a time. There may be no one to retrieve."

Not a single one of their faces gave her any encouragement.

Fine. She'd have enough hope for them all. "If she's out there and we find evidence she is, will you help me get her back?"

She watched as Gabe exchanged a look with each of his people. There was nothing she could read between any of them. But she waited anyway. There were no other options.

"If." Gabe ran his fingers through his hair and sighed. "Fine, *if*. Then yes, we will talk about what it will take to get her back for you."

There were too many unknown variables.

Gabe watched Maylin continue to chat with his team. Considering the way they were already warming up to her, a lot of the investigation work could be done pro bono. If asked, his team members would likely say it was better than being bored.

It was what he would say, too.

His fire team might be out of rotation, on leave in the US while they healed up from their latest mission overseas, but eventually they'd cycle back and rejoin a squadron for their next contract. The Centurion Corporation had several squadrons deployed around the world, how many and where depended on the contract and the nature of their clients. Where there was conflict, there was a need for private military contractors.

As much as his team needed the rest, every one of them, including him, had been itching to do something after the first couple of weeks hanging around Centurion Corporation's Seattle base. That was when Gabe had suggested to their leadership that they take on the lighter duty, local bodyguard contracts. Didn't require as much physical activity and kept them all sharp.

It'd made sense. Then he'd encountered Maylin.

He watched the woman as she made yet another omelet for Marc and Seth, demonstrating how she made layers of cooked egg and rolled it.

His team was already getting engaged, attached to their client. Maylin wasn't some aloof wealthy personage hiring them for personal security. She was a warm, genuinely nice, dangerously likeable person with a talent for feeding hungry people.

And she was good at what she did. He'd seen her in action last night. She'd managed her catering team with cool efficiency. Her people came to her with issues and she was calm, decisive in handling anything brought to her attention. Always smiled for the guests, never broke a sweat. And the entire time she'd been worried about her sister and recovering from the craptastic rebuff he'd given her.

Yeah. He'd been slick. A real pro way to handle a situation.

And he might choke on the sarcasm of his own thoughts. Hell.

He sighed and placed his hands on the counter. His team stopped the chatter almost immediately, all of their attention turned to him. Maylin followed their cues, her green eyes wide. Hopeful.

"For starters, we'll head back to your apartment and try to get some intel on exactly who is after you."

She frowned. "An-mei is the one who's missing."

He nodded. "And for some reason someone tried to run you down last night and took the time to bug your apartment. Unless you're involved with the Chinese mafia or some other illicit activity, is it safe to say that sort of thing might be related to your inquiries about your sister?"

Her lips pressed into a tight line and her cheeks flushed pink with either embarrassment or anger. Considering the spark in her eyes, he'd guess both. And damn it, he didn't like it.

He looked to his team. Every one of their faces was carefully blank. They'd never voice their disagreement in front of a client. They respected him too much to undermine his authority. But the carefully neutral expressions they'd all put into place told him enough. He was being too much of a hard-ass.

He really hated these heart-string contracts. They always ended up a complicated mess.

"Look, it's the best lead we have, and it'll take the entire team to sweep the apartment." See? He could be reasonable. Nice even. "We stand the best chance of getting good intel the sooner we go."

Maylin nodded, a determined look taking the place of her earlier embarrassment. "Let's go."

Chapter Five

"All right," Marc began. "We know there's audio surveillance in the apartment. What we need is to confirm whether there's video. We also need one or more samples of those devices."

The team was stuffed into an SUV, which normally would be comfortable for a group of four plus Maylin, but somehow seemed a tight fit for Gabe's group. It wasn't as if they had a lot of gear or that anyone was particularly bulky in build. Each of them had a strong personality and carried an indefinable sense of pent-up energy. Gabe was driving, while Lizzy had shotgun and Marc and Victoria rode in the back. They'd insisted Maylin ride in the middle row, making her a part of the conversation. She was grateful for it. They didn't have to but it went a long way towards easing her nerves.

"I didn't see signs of video surveillance in the usual places," Gabe interjected. "But there was only me looking."

"What would it look like?" Maylin thought Gabe had taken a long time looking through her apartment, but she'd been tired at the time and confused about what he'd been doing.

"There's all sorts of possibilities," Marc answered.

"It's close to impossible for a single person to do this sort of sweep and find even most of the devices present, much less all of them. That's why our whole fire team is going in to look. Even if we only acquire one or two samples, we want to take note of the placement of every one we can find. Do you have a sound system, Maylin?"

"I have a small set of speakers in the kitchen and the bedroom." Startled, Maylin fumbled for her phone. "I hook them up to my phone for music."

Marc nodded. "When we go in, Maylin, once it's clear I'd like you to come in too and turn on some music. Not anything superdynamic with loud booms and quiet lulls, but music you play normally with a steady amount of sound. It'll allow us to have quiet communication without them being able to make out what we're saying."

"Hand me your phone, love." Victoria held out her hand. "I'll look through your playlists and pull some songs together that would be suitable."

Maylin passed her phone to Victoria gladly. "But if there's video surveillance, won't they know we're all there?"

"Yes. Not optimal, but you've been gone long enough they have to know you found somebody to stay with overnight." Marc nodded. His lips pressed in a thin line. "But we'll go in taking measures to hide our own conversation. They might have most of us identified from when they tried to run you down anyway. We were all there. It's not giving them that much more information to see our faces on video surveillance. It'll be even more frustrating if they can't figure out what we're saying."

Made sense.

Most of them wore baseball caps, though Victoria had opted for a fedora. Studying them for a minute, Maylin realized their faces would be hard to see from most security cameras set at ceiling level. Their hats went with their casual attire, so it didn't seem all that out of place in a public area.

If anything, she stood out from the rest of them. When they all got out of the car, they kept her between them and she decided a hat was going to be the least of her worries. She matched their pace and walked with confidence. This was her parking garage and her apartment building. She belonged here, knew exactly where she was going, and there was no reason to be afraid.

Or every reason to refuse to show how nervous she was.

They headed up to her apartment, and she gave Gabe the key when he turned and held out his hand. She watched in fascination as they each readied themselves for some surprise, keeping her around the corner from her entryway as Gabe unlocked the door and let them inside.

Gabe and Lizzy went in first, clearing the apartment while Marc and Victoria waited outside with her. Once it was clear, Lizzy returned and motioned for them to enter.

Marc indicated she should proceed with definitive gestures to the speakers she kept in the kitchen as Gabe drew the curtains across all the windows in her apartment. She set up her phone with the playlist Victoria had hastily created and hit Play.

Music filled the apartment and they began to spread out. Victoria and Marc began in the living room while Lizzy started in the kitchen. Maylin followed Gabe into her bedroom.

He leaned close to her, his breath tickling her ear. "Don't touch anything but look closely. Does anything look different, out of place? Is there any disturbed dust, or a place that looks like it's been dusted more recently than the last time you cleaned? Look especially around the level of about five feet, anywhere someone would be standing at bookcases, picture frames, lamps, any kind of fixture."

"Why five feet?" she asked in a low whisper.

Gabe shrugged. "Fairly optimal to catch conversation for people of average height."

She was so going to regret bringing this up. "Would the person placing these things in my home take into account that I run somewhat shorter than average?"

Hello, she had to arch her back and tilt her head to look up at Gabe when he got into her personal space. Which he did kind of often. Whether she minded or not was something to think about later.

The corner of Gabe's mouth lifted slowly. "We'll check in a range give or take six inches and lower areas around places you'd be seated or laying down. Why don't you update the others on the team and join me back here? Stay away from the windows, even with the curtains drawn."

She pressed her lips together. The minute she turned her back, he was going to have the biggest grin on his face. She knew it. Couldn't prove it. And for no good reason, she wanted a picture of it.

So not the time to be obsessing over the range of his facial expressions.

The sooner they found one or more of these bugs, the sooner they had their hands on physical evidence of whoever was trying to keep Maylin out of the way. More than likely, they were the same people responsible for An-mei's disappearance, and Maylin wanted answers.

She cautiously headed back to the kitchen and passed her message on to Lizzy. Lizzy only nodded. "I always check. You and I are around the same height. Stick with Diaz and I'll pass the message on to Marc and Victoria."

If someone was actively listening in, Maylin guessed they'd be able to monitor multiple frequencies, maybe including whatever channel Gabe's team was using. So it made sense for them to pass the verbal messages on this way, in low murmurs behind the music. It still felt like playing the telephone game or some other school time thing.

As she reached Gabe again, he kept her with him, his tall frame always between her and the windows and well away from them. He had her look carefully at all of her knickknacks and keepsakes, picture frames, and even her pillows. She stared at each item hard. Conflicted. On one hand she wanted to find something to help them. On the other hand, she was seriously hoping there weren't video cameras in her room or bathroom. Please, please not her bathroom.

Too creepy for words.

She rubbed her upper arms as a chill went through her. A moment later, Gabe draped one of her jackets from her closet around her shoulders. She smiled up at him in thanks and he gave her a solemn nod. His eyes were warm and, she thought, maybe held a bit of sympathy.

Minutes later, it was Gabe who found the first one. It was tucked into the corner edge of her headboard, not much bigger than a long grain of rice, and clear. She wouldn't have spotted it unless she'd gone into one of her insane spring-cleaning modes, and then she'd only have caught it with a cleaning cloth as opposed to actually seeing it.

He motioned for her not to touch it, marked it with a small colored sticky flag and resumed the search. As they stepped away from the device, he leaned close again. "We'll let Marc handle taking it. He's our communications expert."

Her throat had gone dry, so she only nodded. When he stepped into the bathroom, he turned on the shower. Presumably to create similar noise interference as the music in the kitchen.

It was a small space, so she stood back and watched him check the clear light bulbs and light fixtures. He also checked the fire alarm. When he placed a sticky at the corner of the bathroom mirror, she shuddered, hoping it was an audio device and not video.

Please no video.

It was a violation. Her home wasn't hers anymore. Someone had snuck in and made it theirs to use against her. She'd have never known without Gabe.

When he was done, he handed her an empty duffel bag—not one of her own. "Grab some more clothes for yourself. A few things for any situation. Give them to me to check over before packing them. Once you've taken what you need out of the closet, I'll do a sweep of it."

She nodded in agreement. This process was painstakingly slow. Her nerves were wound taut and she had to deliberately stretch her jaw because she'd been clenching it without realizing. Finally, she was packed and Gabe was motioning for her to head back out to the kitchen and living areas.

Gabe led her to the foyer, tucked into the small space next to the door to her apartment. He then moved to Marc and Victoria, taking up a watchful stance as the other man headed to the bedroom. Presumably, he was going to get the two devices Gabe had located.

Moments later, Gabe caught Maylin's attention and pointed to his watch, then held up five fingers.

Five minutes. Maylin nodded.

He gave her a brief smile and her spirits lifted somewhat. Then his gaze moved past her to the kitchen where the floor-to-ceiling windows looked out over Elliott Bay.

"Lizzy, up and over. Now!"

Lizzy responded immediately, planting her hands on the kitchen counter and hopping up onto the surface. Her left shin was bloody. Shocked, Maylin looked around wildly.

Something had torn through the lower part of the curtains in two, maybe three places. Tiny shards of broken glass glittered on the kitchen floor. Lizzy came the rest of the way over the tiny breakfast bar, grabbing Maylin's phone off the speaker stand as she did.

"Shots fired. Shots fired. Alpha team, out now." Even as Gabe was issuing terse commands, Lizzy was rushing to plaster Maylin against the wall. Gabe motioned for Victoria to precede him. "Marc, I'll provide cover as you come past the kitchen."

Lizzy grabbed Maylin. "Let me go first, but stay right behind me, you hear me?"

"Yes." Maylin choked out the agreement as Victoria caught up to them, grabbing up the duffel bag of Maylin's clothes.

Lizzy led the way, a small handgun out and ready as she checked the hallway. Once she motioned *clear*, Victoria hustled Maylin out and down to the far end of the hallway where the three of them hustled through the fire door to crouch in the stairwell. Victoria took a guarding stance as Lizzy holstered her gun and pulled a few lengths of bandage from a pouch on her utility belt. "Shit. Gabe saw it happen before I even felt it."

"Bad?" Victoria asked.

"Nah. Minor graze. Stings is all. I'm fine." Lizzy finished tying off the quick bandage.

"Is there something I can do to help?" Maylin asked belatedly. Everything was happening fast and she was not keeping up.

"Keep doing what you're doing." Lizzy took out her gun again. "Do as we say, no hesitation. You're doing fine."

There was a sharp rapping at the door to the stairwell in a broken staccato pattern; then Marc came through, followed by Gabe.

Even in her panic, Maylin realized Gabe had been waiting to be sure all of them had gotten out first. All of them.

Victoria gripped Maylin's upper arm. "We're going now. That wasn't a lot of noise, but if any of your neighbors got concerned, someone's going to check your apartment and find the broken glass. Best for everyone if we're away from here so no one else gets caught up in this."

Back in the car, the silence was killing Maylin. She'd huddled low in the middle seat of the SUV as they'd left the parking garage and only sat up once Gabe had given the okay.

They were out of the downtown area and on the highway before anyone spoke.

"No sign of a tail," Marc reported from the backseat.

"Roger that." Gabe's acknowledgment came out harsh, angry.

The entire car was quiet again after that. Maylin watched

mile markers go by, the tension inside her winding tighter and tighter. This wasn't the way they'd come into the city. Maybe Gabe was taking them on a more roundabout way home.

She couldn't sit still anymore. Reaching for the big, soft cooler bag she'd packed this morning, she tugged it up onto the seat next to her and started digging inside.

"Maylin, dear. What are you doing?" Victoria didn't sound displeased but her tone was gentle, the way one would talk to somebody fragile.

Maylin wasn't fragile. She was practical. And silence the whole car ride home was a waste of time.

She pulled out a sandwich wrapped in wax paper and held it out to Victoria.

The blonde mercenary blinked. "What?"

"It's been hours since any of us ate. I made muffuletta sandwiches just in case we got hungry." Maylin wiggled the package in front of Victoria. "There's salami, ham, mozzarella, provolone, and olive salad. I raided the bigger kitchens over on the training side of the complex earlier this morning."

"Seriously?" Marc snagged the sandwich out of Maylin's hand. "I'm starving."

Maylin quickly grabbed another wrapped sandwich and handed it to Victoria, who accepted it with a smile. Two more went up front to Lizzy and Gabe. Once everyone had a sandwich, Maylin took out one for herself, unwrapped it halfway and took a bite.

Savory, salty flavor burst across her tongue as she chewed. The olive salad had just the right punch and she loved the combination of the Italian meats. It wasn't just a sandwich, it was a meal, and every bite should be packed with flavor and interesting.

Immediately, the atmosphere in the car edged away from icy tension to more relaxed.

Gabe paused in eating his sandwich. "Lizzy. Status?"

"Minor. Just a graze." Lizzy took a minute to chew and swallow. "Shots came in a low spread across the kitchen. I'm thinking they saw vague movement through the curtains and took a chance they'd hit to injure."

"Looks like they're trying to wound our genius cook here, rather than kill her," Marc said around a mouthful of bread and olives.

"Don't get me wrong, I'm glad whoever it is isn't trying to kill me, but why?" Maylin took smaller bites in case something one of them said might make her choke. It'd been that kind of day.

"Couple of reasons come to mind." Victoria licked olive oil from her bottom lip. "If you're injured and an ambulance is called, it'd be easy to intercept and snag you before you ever made it to the hospital. No one at your apartment would think to look for you at the hospital for quite a while, am I correct?"

Victoria was right. Maylin swallowed hard. "Everyone would assume family or friends would meet me at the hospital. None of my neighbors know me well enough to know An-mei's missing or that she's the only family I'm in touch with."

"Easy way to catch you off guard and whisk you away, then." Victoria took a hearty bite of the sandwich. "This really is delicious, dear."

Maylin smiled.

It was a kind of relief to know someone wasn't trying to kill her. Only a marginal one, though, because being kidnapped was a close second on the scale of things that freaked her out.

"Well, we've learned a couple of other things about our mystery friends." Marc took the napkin Maylin held out for him with a nod. He'd inhaled the sandwich. "Those devices are completely enclosed, tiny, and custom made. Probably limited range, so we're okay now that we've put a few miles between us and their receiving device. But I won't feel completely good about it until I can take what we've got apart and disconnect whatever power source they've got. I'll try to do that while we're on the move, before we get back to our base of operations. I'll know more about any signature the maker might have once I take them apart, but those details alone are telling."

Gabe looked up into the rearview mirror so he could see Marc. "Lay it out for us."

"First, the clean and enclosed packaging means whoever did this had these ready for this specific purpose or for regular use. Either way, the maker put a lot of tech into tiny devices, which says to me some deep financial pockets. That kind of work isn't cheap."

Maylin put her half-eaten sandwich down. She wasn't sure how she was going to counter adversaries with such money at their disposal.

"The smaller a device is, the shorter range it has, so the listeners had to be close." Marc cleared his throat. "They were close enough to have eyes on the apartment, and even with the curtains drawn they could see enough shapes to take a shot at someone in the kitchen. I'm going to propose they thought it was our Maylin here, since anyone who's observed her for more than a few hours knows she tends to hang out in there."

A grunt came from Gabe up front. "Go on."

"Once we get back to Centurion Corporation facilities, I'll take these apart. I'll be able to tell us more about their make. Power supply design, battery type, parts and mode of assembly should give us a few leads. One or two of the parts might even be 3D printed." Marc sounded excited to dig in and find out more.

"Anything else?" Gabe's words were still short, but there was a hint of amusement there. Or maybe Maylin was imagining it.

Marc didn't comment on it. "Didn't find any video devices. Not surprising, because it's a crazy effort to rig the place for both audio and video when they already had such a clear view of the apartment. Those were some big windows. Not too many places hidden from view if the curtains were left open."

And obviously, they could see at least shadows with the windows closed in the late afternoon to evening. Maylin shuddered.

"Was that big cooler just for these sandwiches?" Lizzy spoke up.

"I brought more." Maylin dove back into the cooler and came out with small mason jars of layered graham cracker, cheesecake and fresh fruit. "Dessert?"

"Pass it up here." Lizzy accepted hers enthusiastically. "This is way better than pain medication."

"Get it looked at once we get back anyway," Gabe admonished. "Maylin, can you hold on to mine till we get back? Can't drive and enjoy that at the same time, and I don't want Marc to eat mine."

"Hey, I haven't even got mine yet," Marc protested.

Maylin laughed and passed him his serving.

Victoria was just finishing up her muffuletta and accepted one of the cheesecake jars, too. "You pack a wonderful picnic."

"I figure it's what I can do to contribute." Maylin drew

in a breath. "Anything I can do to keep everyone fueled up and ready to find An-mei is completely worth it."

Up front in the driver's seat, Gabe took another bite of his sandwich and chewed. Maylin watched him and wondered, was it all going to be enough?

Chapter Six

Gabe started and swallowed half a dozen suggestions to move along as he walked Maylin from the SUV back to the guest cabin. She wasn't moving fast, but he figured she might have a lot on her mind and she was reasonably safe here on Centurion ground. He decided to rein in his hyperawareness and let her take her time. She stopped to study the wooded area around them—the worn path between the main building they'd just left and the cabin, even the freaking leaves of a random shrub.

"Look." There was something he should clarify. He'd get straight to the point and it wasn't going to get any better if he dressed it up. "We're going for one goal at a time. Find your sister first. It's very possible she's going to be irrecoverable."

Maylin turned to face him, her eyebrows raised. "You mean dead."

Yes.

"Or worse." And wasn't he the biggest ass out here?

Her face became a porcelain mask. "I don't want to believe that."

No one ever did. But it was better to face the possibility than operate under delusions of happy endings.

He started to say…something. Not sure what, but she lifted a hand.

"No. I get what you're saying. I do. I'm also saying I don't want to." She looked down for a moment and then back up to him. "Is it possible to be realistic and hopeful at the same time?"

He rolled one shoulder in an attempt to ease some of the tension across the back of his neck. "In my experience, planning for the worst hurts a lot less in the long run."

She laughed then, and it was so sad it cracked his carefully built wall a little. "So what would you say this is? Giving me the hard truth?"

When she made it sound like that, he reached for a better fit. "More like managing expectations."

And wow, way the hell more awkward.

"*Liáng yào kǔ kǒu*. A good medicine tastes bitter." She huffed and turned away to study a tree trunk. "Thanks for the medicine, but you sound more like a guy trying to set boundaries with his girlfriend."

Oh, even better.

"I don't do relationships." He gritted his teeth. This conversation had jumped the tracks. "And what's with the Chinese proverb?"

She shrugged, traced a random pattern in the bark. "Every interaction with every person is a relationship. What kind is up to what each person makes it. And I grew up with random proverbs tossed at me whenever they seemed most likely to teach me an intended lesson. Some of them fit and some of them get lost in translation."

Didn't everyone have one of those sage personalities in their families? At least one whose advice was like a repeating track on an overplayed music list, and maybe one whose comments were the kind that stuck with you for life. He was guessing from the bitterness in her tone she was remembering the former.

"You mean from Chinese to English?" He'd heard enough of both Mandarin and Cantonese to recognize the languages apart from something else, like Japanese or Korean. But he didn't know enough of any of those languages to actually understand even the simplest phrases. Most of his language skills were based on his more recent deployments in the Arabic and Balkan regions. Each language had a cadence to it that helped him separate and identify as opposed to trying to pick out familiar sounds or words.

"I mean from the one culture to another. What seems suitable based on the situation might not be, depending on the perspective." She chuckled. "And to be honest, having been born and raised here I might not use all of them in the right moment either. I very much loved my parents, but there were a lot of awkward moments through the years. I grew up on a lot of proverbs and I take the sayings I like to heart, but I apply them my way."

"And the ones you don't like?"

She lifted her chin. "I prove them wrong."

He liked her. Hell, he'd appreciated her looks since the night before and approved of her resilience after the scares she'd had. But here, talking directly to her was comfortable. He'd settled into it without thinking. And he couldn't remember the last time he'd conversed with anyone beyond a specifically business-related exchange of information. Not a detail worth tracking down. It'd been a long time.

It only made this job harder. Even if they did find her sister, depending on where she was and who was holding her—assuming she was alive—the effort to extract the girl could be incredibly expensive. Maylin wouldn't be able to afford it.

But, following his own advice, one step at a time. If the girl was someplace they could infiltrate as a single fire team, there was a chance to keep costs reasonable for Maylin without making his superiors at HQ squawk.

"We can't change everything that isn't the way we want it." He'd watched people try. Demand he make it so. "My team isn't going to create a miracle for you."

She nodded. "That's fair. And thank you for telling me the truth."

"Not many people thank me for truth." They cursed him. Screamed at him. Blamed him. Or shot him in the back.

"Well, I'm at least one." There she went, practical again. No snark in her tone or mocking. "You don't seem to have had enough in your life and I'd think you've done a lot to deserve gratitude."

The memory of his last client's wife's catty attitude was so fresh in his mind, he almost added it to Maylin's words inside his head. Only it wouldn't have been fair to Maylin. She might be one of the most straightforward people he'd met. Ever. "People tend to remember the bad."

"And take the good for granted?" She whispered her question and tipped her head to the side. "I can see it. My experience isn't the same, but never good enough was a recurring theme for a long time."

If she was going to be fair to him, he should make an effort to do the same for her. "It's a lot of the reason I didn't want to take on this mission for you in the first place. You, your sister…you're family. Everything about this is personal and emotionally driven. You aren't going to remember anything about this but the outcome, and the outlook is not as good as you want to hope."

There was a long silence. Yeah, he was harping on the realistic outcome of this whole thing, but it was damned hard to find neutral in all this.

"What kind of jobs would you have preferred?" Her tone was carefully measured.

He'd upset her and he didn't want to. Ultimately, it might be for the best. She shouldn't like him and definitely didn't have to. Course, here he was getting to know her better. And there she was making a postcard moment out of every time she paused to look at a piece of greenery. Picture-perfect beautiful without even trying.

He cleared his throat. "The best contracts are the business-driven ones. Escort cargo from point A to point B, for example. Easy. Straightforward. Harder ones are when there's a need for a team to infiltrate or take down an enemy site. But it's still impersonal and if we can manage it with good planning and optimal timing, no body count."

"But sometimes there are casualties." Her very serious gaze met his and he didn't look away.

"Yes." Most of the time. In truth, any well-guarded facility was going to have somebody on duty at all times. And there were other contracts, other missions he didn't want to talk about. Those were the kind of thing a person could only understand if they'd been there, too.

"I started looking online for other cases of missing loved ones and kidnappings when I first tried to figure out how to find help." Maylin started to wander through the trees alongside the trail. She wove in and out of them as if being a little lost would help her talk through her worries. "The things I read about… I didn't want to think could happen. At the same time, I truly believe they happen every day. We're lucky we grew up here, in this country, where to us, it's all the stuff of action movies. Only, our father isn't alive to rescue her with a very specific set of skills. There's only me."

Movies and television. She really did watch a lot of it.

"Your father didn't have the skills for this." Shit, that came out harsh. Not what he meant.

Maylin swung around a tree trunk to pin him with her startlingly clear green gaze. "No. You do. Even if Daddy was alive, I wouldn't have gone to him for help. My stepmother would've said it was An-mei's fault for putting herself where she'd be vulnerable. Would've said to leave it to the proper authorities."

And her father would've ceded to her stepmother. Okay. No wonder Maylin was so independent. And alone.

"This kind of job is full of emotional baggage." He laid it out there since it seemed like she'd eventually get into it, struggling to present it in a rational way. Reasonable. Trouble was, he didn't like to think about why it stuck with him as much as it did. "Bodyguard jobs always end up messier than they're supposed to be. If something goes wrong, it's not goods or property lost. It's a person."

"A loved one," she whispered.

"Somebody's loved one." He'd give her that. "The last mission I was on, I went personally to the home of the person I'd failed to protect. I figured it was the least I could do. Give them the news face-to-face that I'd failed to get him out alive."

Maylin waited, motionless. No judgment in her eyes even after he'd admitted failure.

He shook his head. "His wife was ready to hand him divorce papers when he got home. She'd been cheating on him while he was overseas and even while he was being held prisoner. When she found out he was dead, she was relieved. No messy divorce. And then the bitch tried to sue Centurion Corporation for emotional damages, playing the bereaved widow after she'd pulled herself together and put on the front the public expected to see."

People were shit to each other. Scavengers.

"Cào bī." Her face reddened and her hand flew to her mouth. "Okay, that one was pretty bad. But seriously, she's an awful person."

He'd been okay with her original statement, no translation needed. It *sounded* right. He'd bet she could curse a blue streak in English if she got over the idea of curses being unacceptable in polite company. He wasn't polite. "I didn't stick around for all of it. I had follow-up surgery on my back and was laid out in recovery by the time she tried her nonsense."

"Follow-up?" There was real concern in her eyes.

His walls cracked more. And damn but he didn't even mind somehow. "I got shot in the back during the mission. When I went down, the man my team had gone in to rescue was killed. My team got out and dragged my sorry ass with them."

But they'd been betrayed by several of their own. And he really wasn't ready to share those details.

"So you're all in Washington State." She reached out until her fingertips touched his chest. "I'm very glad you were here in this part of the world last night."

His brain turned off. Yup, just like that. It'd been one thing to look, listen to her. She'd had to go and touch him. He took her fingertips and ran his thumb over the tops of her knuckles, enjoying the electric connection from the barest skin to skin contact. When he stepped into her space, she didn't back away. He liked it about her, the steel in her spine and the spark in her eyes. Challenge.

She swallowed.

"Run out of words?" Maybe he should go to hell for how much fun he was having with her in this one moment.

Her delicately arched brows came together and the spark in her gaze flared to temper. "I didn't realize I was supposed to have something to say."

"You're full of questions." He brushed her hair off her shoulder because he liked to watch the light play when her hair moved. It was literally a black cascade. Gorgeous and silky. "I like listening to them."

And she had about a hundred questions piling up behind those very kissable lips of hers. He wanted to push her into a flood of them.

"What are you…?"

He kissed her. Shouldn't have. But her lips were every bit as soft as he imagined and her words tumbled into his mouth. Her hand tightened around his, her fingertips still caught in his grasp. And she didn't pull away. Didn't slap him.

So he wrapped his other hand around her waist and pulled her slender body close.

She melded against him, soft and pliant and he couldn't keep his hands from wandering. Especially since her own were tracing their way across his shoulders and up the back of his neck. No resistance. So he lost himself in the sweet, tart taste of her mouth.

He'd discovered a lot of contrasts in her so far. Different from the women he'd been with in the past, sweeter and genuinely kind. Soft. But with an underlying strength and flexibility. Her ability to adjust each time something went insane was nothing short of amazing. And as he bent her backwards a bit, enjoying her mouth and soft little moan, he wanted to see just how bendy she could be in other ways.

When she gasped for air, he let his grip on her loosen. She might not be ready for all that...yet. He straightened, bringing her with him. But when she looked up at him through her long eyelashes, there was a storm of want waiting for him. He could give her time and let those feelings smolder some.

Instead he stepped back a fraction, making sure she was steady on her feet. "Thank you."

She blinked rapidly. God, she was cute. "What?"

He leaned in and stole another kiss. A little one. "For that.

Maylin shut her mouth before it remained open for too long. She had no idea how to respond. None. Not at all.

Gabriel Diaz had kissed her and she'd lit up like a living flame. And now he was stepping away and thanking her like they'd stepped off a dance floor.

Bet he was a good dancer too. Maybe.

And why was she thinking all these things?

Why had he kissed her?

Why...?

"I'm betting your head's still full of questions." His amusement was warm and friendly, a secret shared between them.

"Yes." She tried to pull her face to some semblance of proper seriousness and glare at him. "But not any of the right ones."

His eyebrows rose. "Last I checked, there weren't any wrong questions in this world."

Well, maybe so. Again with the maybes. She smoothed her hands on her pant legs, trying to dismiss the lingering heat from touching his skin. And that was just his hands, his neck. The idea of running her palms over the flat planes of his chest and abs…

"Let's say a higher priority question would be what are we doing next to find my sister?" Because she was here for a reason.

He nodded. "And the best people are on it right now." He tapped his chest. "I will be joining them as soon as I see you safely back to the guest cabin and make sure you're comfortable."

She opened her mouth to protest but he touched her lips with his finger. She resisted the urge to bite it.

Humor sparkled in his eyes, giving his normally grim face a lot more charm than she'd thought possible. "There's a lot of research in the beginning. It's damned boring to watch. It also sucks to be the researcher with someone breathing over your shoulder. You wanted us to do this. We will. Right now the best thing you can do is stay out of our way."

She blew out a breath in frustration. Temper tantrums wouldn't do any good here. "Is there anything constructive I can do?"

He nodded. "Get out a piece of paper and a pen, or sit at a computer if that'll work better for you. Blank your mind. Then start recording every single thing you know about your sister's disappearance. List it all out. If there are relations, draw them. Any odd detail, no matter how insignificant, could be a thing. You gave us a good start, but random things pop into people's heads later on, when they aren't under pressure to talk."

Okay. She settled back on her heels. Those were things

she could do. And she did see the sense in what he had to say. "How often do you do this for your team?"

"What?"

"Take the client aside and set them to some constructive, or even not so helpful, task to get them out of the way?" She looked at her feet. If he hadn't given her something to do, she really would've been hanging over their shoulders. "I'm betting some people get pretty irate."

Everything had been a series of doors shut in her face so far. To finally have help gave her new energy and she wanted to drive them forward, make things happen. It was frustrating to have to wait again.

Gabe's hand came into her field of view, taking her chin and gently coaxing her to lift her head. When he spoke, his voice was kind. "You're not irate, though. And you're a big help so far. I've had clients screaming and spitting with no useful information whatsoever, expecting us to work internet magic to solve their problem. They've gotten violent, hysterical, any range of emotion you can think of. You, so far, just seem to think a lot—which I personally like."

She risked meeting his gaze and her cheeks heated again. *Like.* "Is that why you kissed me?"

Oh, good, she'd gotten her question out without stuttering. Points for her, because she was all sorts of flipped out internally.

One corner of his mouth lifted in a lopsided grin. "Yeah."

Not a lot of explanation there. She bit her lip in frustration. "Care to add some detail?"

He ran his thumb across the line of her jaw, sending heat and electric sparks along her skin before he released her. "It seemed like a good idea at the time. I do things in the moment and I don't always have a lot of thought behind why. Too much thinking makes you miss opportunities."

He paused, watching her watch him, and she almost looked away, but didn't. He was too fascinating, too magnetic.

After a minute, he placed a hand on her shoulder and squeezed, then gently turned her in the direction of the trail. "Let's get you back to the cabin. You can think all you want there. Maybe I'll bring you some honey."

She huffed but couldn't come up with a good response. Overthinking was her issue and he knew it about her already.

Chapter Seven

"Seriously? You're going to be gone two weeks?" A man's voice cracked over the smartphone's speaker as Gabe returned to the guest cabin. Did she have her call on speakerphone?

It'd been an hour and Gabe wanted to give her an update on their progress. Standing on the porch with her back to him, Maylin sighed without bothering to hold her phone away from her face. It wasn't on speaker. No wonder she hadn't heard him coming. "At minimum."

Didn't she take vacations from work once in a while? Granted, two weeks was a solid chunk, but maybe mainstream did things differently from what he'd thought. Gabe hadn't ever been a civilian, seemed like.

"What are you going to do with yourself? I mean, of course you're not going to be doing anything with yourself, but…"

Must be one of the employees from her catering company, probably the kid who'd helped her with cleanup. Gabe snickered in silence. Where did the kid think he was going with that? And why was Gabe so happy Maylin didn't seem to get where the boy's thoughts were coming from? Pfft.

"Look, Charlie, I'm going to find An-mei." And there

was the steel in her voice. Dauntless and determined. All that resolution contained in a tight, tempting figure. Gabe's admiration was growing for her in a whole lot of ways. Oblivious, she continued, "I've got the right help now and I can't just sit by waiting for news."

"You're sure?"

"Absolutely." So much conviction in her tone. He and his team had only agreed to locate the girl. They still needed to work out the details of extracting An-mei once they found her—and those were far from trivial—but Maylin seemed sure she'd overcome one challenge at a time. He suffered a pang of guilt letting her continue as she was but he was hoping there'd be a workable solution. "Genevieve can handle the small parties scheduled over the next two weeks with you and the others to support her. I've already sent her an email with all of the details and gone over them with her. You get to break the news to the rest of the staff. You'll all be fine."

"We've all been working towards the day when you would trust us enough to take some time off for yourself." She froze. Charlie's statement startled her. "I only wish it was for a happier reason."

Gabe wondered how much Maylin buried herself in her work. Obviously far more than she'd realized.

"Me, too." So much regret in the one statement. "I should've taken the time off and gone with her in the first place."

"You can't blame yourself. That wasn't why I said it." Charlie's voice cracked with frustration.

Okay, at first it'd been unintentional, but if Gabe continued lurking behind this tree he'd be a certifiable creep. Besides, listening to Charlie pour out his concern was grating on his temper. Making an effort to step on a couple of twigs here and there, he walked into the open.

"I need to go now, Charlie. I'll try to check in when I can." Without waiting for her friend's response, she ended the call.

Good. Bye, Charlie. Don't wait up.

Her peripheral awareness wasn't half bad, all things considered. And she stood fairly calmly waiting for him to cross the rest of the distance between them. No deer-in-headlights look. Another plus.

To be honest—and he hated that it was true—it was awkward for him to be around civilians. Hard to respect someone who hadn't ever been punched square in the face and come back swinging. They'd called it the warrior ethos back in Basic. Mostly it was an attitude and a perspective a person either had or didn't. Maylin's quiet strength wasn't a fit for either category. She wasn't made for combat, but she wasn't a sheep lost away from the herd either.

He didn't know how to act around her. At least, not when he had time to consider his actions. The kiss had been hot as hell and he wanted more. But then he'd gone back to all business again and she'd obviously been left off balance. He'd kept himself apart from the mainstream for too many years to be any good at true interaction anymore.

Generally, he preferred to glower at people and intimidate the hell out of them.

"Any news?" Those green eyes were every bit as brilliant in the light of day. She wasn't even wearing makeup.

Sugarcoating would be a waste of time. Besides, she wouldn't thank him for it. "Not yet. I took a look through the consulate emails you forwarded me. You're not likely to get any further with those."

"The responses were too polite." She pressed her lips together in a thin line. "Didn't seem like the consulate representatives put any thought into it at all."

Probably hadn't. He lifted a shoulder in a half shrug. "Too easy to dismiss an email as not a real person. A voice across a phone call isn't much better. And the people answering those inquiries don't actually know anything."

Her posture sagged for a split second before she squared her shoulders and lifted her chin. "Then I need to get to the nearest Chinese consulate and talk to someone face-to-face."

She had steel strapped to her spine. He liked it every time he saw it. "Not the nearest. Those are San Francisco and L.A. For the kind of clout you're going to need, it'll save time to skip the general consulates and go straight to the embassy. Anyone at the consulates would probably send a message to the embassy anyway for it to be routed overseas. If information came back, it'd come back through the central point of contact first."

She blinked then gave a slow nod. "Okay then, I'll go to the embassy."

He admired her determination, as single-minded as it was currently. Still, someone walking in without an appointment wasn't likely to make much progress. Though, considering what he'd seen of her drive, she might make it further than most on force of personality alone. Her fluency in Mandarin would help her. He might be able to arrange for a little something to help give her some clout. And while she had attention on her, he'd tap a few contacts of his own.

"We won't make most of the morning flights out, but

we can head to the airport this afternoon and catch a red-eye tonight. It'll give you time to pick up any toiletries or whatever at the airport." He leaned back, made an effort not to loom over her, but she was petite. And not the type to back down. It'd been why he couldn't resist tasting her earlier. Dangerous ground.

He needed to keep his hands to himself, at least until they had a better idea of how this would all play out. If his team beat the odds and found her sister, maybe there'd be something to explore. It'd only make it harder for Maylin if he muddied the waters before this mission was complete, though. Experience—and he had the pain in his lower back to remind him—advised proceeding with caution and keeping it simple. No further complications. No matter how tempting she was without even trying.

"Not a lot of time to book the flight." She bit her lip.

Besides, plane tickets cost money and cross-country flights weren't cheap.

There was the hesitation he'd been expecting. One thing to hire a man for a specific mission and another thing to fly to the other end of the country. "You can stay here. I'll go and report back any news I find."

"No." Her voice took on the edge he'd heard the night before. "I'm going. I just need to know what flight and I'll reserve my ticket."

He ought to argue with her. Generally, it was easier when he worked alone, even stateside. If he left her here on Centurion Corporation grounds, she'd be safe. She'd be at higher risk out running around with him. Not immediate, because Gabe had plans to confuse whoever was trying to take her out. But eventually they'd unravel the trail and locate her.

It'd been Lizzy who'd asked him if he was leaving Maylin with the team. None of his people seemed to mind. But they'd all gotten a measure of Maylin at breakfast. The minute he left the property, she'd be after him whether the rest of the team let her go or not. They could stop Maylin, but they might have to restrain her to do it. And none of them wanted to go down that path.

This course of action went with the flow of her choices and provided opportunity to flush out her enemies without her waiting here as bait.

"I'll take care of it." He almost flinched under her suddenly piercing glare. "Expenses will be tallied at the end of the job but for the time being, I don't want to wait on someone else's funds to get where I need to go to find what I'm after."

"I'm going to need to take a close look at that contract you owe me." Anyone else would've sounded insulting, but her? No. Somehow it was politely chilling and definitively uncomfortable.

"It's in your inbox. Once you've sent it back with your e-signature, we are all sorts of official. Take this afternoon to review it, send it back, and zip up your travel bag. We leave at seventeen hundred hours. Leave your smartphone and laptop here with Marc."

"A red-eye leaves that early? And why leave my phone?" The second question was asked at a slightly higher pitch.

Would she start twitching if she was separated from her phone for too long? He chewed on the inside of his cheek to keep from smiling. She wouldn't appreciate it right now.

"The personal electronics stay here with Marc until he can verify they are clean. I've got a temporary phone for you in the meantime. As for the leave time, I figured I'd get you something other than omelets or takeout for dinner before yanking you clear across the country." He paused. "Unless you want me to do a grocery run so you can stress-cook again?"

She laughed. The sound was a mix of surprise and pleasure. "I eat other people's cooking once in a while, especially when it's better than what I can cook myself."

Considering the way she'd whipped up culinary art out of their meager supplies this morning, and then a mobile lunch for them later in the day, he was figuring there weren't too many in Seattle who could do better than her. "Not sure if it'll be better, but I have a nearby place in mind."

She gave him a smile then, a real one, if small. "I look forward to it."

He sincerely hoped he could take the shadows from her face. Soon.

"Mister Reyes?" Maylin hissed at Gabe as the elevator smoothly rose. "Welcome to you and your *wife*?"

Maybe she was still groggy from the red-eye flight and a morning driving around DC waiting in the car while Gabe made a few discreet stops, but this was one of those things he could've warned her about in advance. Luckily, the concierge thought she'd been surprised by the hotel they were checking into. As opposed to the sudden change in marital status.

Gabe shrugged. "I could have said we were newlyweds, but special occasions stand out too much."

Maylin struggled to keep her voice somewhat close to calm. "You warned me we'd be arriving in DC under assumed identities. Okay. And you even coached me on my temporary name. I appreciate the instruction. You *didn't* tell me we'd be sharing a name."

"Does it bother you?" He wasn't mocking her, but he didn't seem overly concerned either. Mostly, he sounded infuriatingly neutral.

And yes, it did. But not for any logical reason she could think of, so why was she making a fuss about it again?

She'd think about it later.

"And what is a classic suite, anyway? It was nice of them to upgrade us for no charge, but what were our sleeping arrangements going to be in the first place?"

"When I looked into this hotel, the classic suites had a wall partition between the bed and the sitting area where there's a pull-out sofa. I figured it'd give you a little privacy." The corner of his mouth tipped up a tiny bit.

She drew in a breath and blew it out slow. Hard to make a thing of it when he was being so considerate.

His arm settled around her shoulders, a solid weight but not too heavy. She froze.

"Easy." For his part, he didn't even look down at her, his gaze on the display showing the increasing floor numbers as they rose. "Security camera in the upper corner over there. We're your normal, cuddly couple."

There was an edge to the word *cuddly*. Not the tough guy mocking tone, but more a bitter something. Like he had a bad taste in his mouth when he said it. She didn't reply, but tucked herself snug against his side.

Leaning into him came naturally, and it was all a part of the pretense, wasn't it? Absolutely reasonable, and comforting, too. From the minute their plane had landed, she'd been a bundle of nerves as she followed him through the airport to the car rental, and even on the drive to the hotel. His solid strength calmed her, settled the jangling anxiety. She could do this.

"Yes, you can." Gabe's quiet comment surprised her and she jerked her head up to stare at him. He chuckled. "Is this where you ask if you used your 'out loud' voice?"

She blinked. "I've never thought to ask quite that way, but yeah, I guess I must've babbled."

"Not really." He gave her shoulders a squeeze. "It was just a few thoughts under your breath. You're doing great."

"Pfft. Sure. I've seen TV shows like this. I'm about to try for a graceful exit and trip over my own two feet." But the idea of him catching her, maybe the two of them falling to the floor… Oy. She'd been watching too many dramas in the kitchen over food prep.

His chuckle was low, sending shivers down her spine. "One of those moments where your skirt flips up and we find out you're wearing panties with cute bunnies printed across your bum?"

"M-maybe." Spluttering only made him laugh harder. She pressed on. "You've watched anime, haven't you?"

He dragged his fingers through his short-cropped hair. "Caught. Your scenario would've been a classic fan service moment."

A pause, then he continued, "When you're overseas you watch *anything* in your downtime to burn up the hurry up and wait. One of my squadron mates had a hard drive full of those cartoons."

"Most of those are not kid's cartoons." She'd watched quite a bit through school. Still had a few favorites tucked away on her computer.

"Which is why I opted for watching them over a

bunch of ponies running around learning about lessons on friendship."

"Ah." She nodded. "Well, if we find ourselves in a wait situation, I have other guilty pleasures for us to check out."

His entire body stilled at her side.

Tā mā de. "I… I meant stuff to watch."

Oh, and that sounded so much better.

"Dramas. Chinese dramas." She chucked it out there before he had to go for the awkward professionalism discussion. "Consider anime a gateway drug to all the great Asian dramas out there. One of my favorites has been made into a live action drama in Taiwan, Korea and Japan."

He relaxed against her. "Which is your favorite version?"

"The one from Taiwan." No doubts about it.

"Because of the language?" The elevator dinged and he stretched a hand across the threshold to hold the elevator for her.

"No." She chewed on her lower lip, thinking on it as she stepped out. "I don't mind reading subtitles, so those wouldn't be a factor. The story line is closer to the original manga they were all based on and I just like the actors better. Plus, the soundtrack is cute."

He huffed. "Soundtrack?"

"Yeah. The actors who play the main hero and heroine are both in music groups." Smiling, she rose up on her toes and pressed a light kiss on his jaw, for the benefit of the security camera, of course. "Thank you."

Then she scampered out of the elevator as fast as she could.

He'd had no trouble catching up with her. None at

all. As he fell in behind her, he settled his hand on the
small of her back and gently herded her down one hallway. Changing gears, she wondered whether he danced.
A strong lead could guide his partner with minute pressure in the small of his partner's back. It was similar to
what Gabe was already doing.

But he was still on their earlier topic. "Hmm. Smart
marketing."

It was a miracle he'd been able to track her thought-
hopping for as long as he had.

"Guess so." Maybe it was because he didn't seem to
mind. An-mei hadn't either, but she switched topics even
more often. And she was the better dancer despite the
both of them having been sent to dance classes. An-mei
hadn't enjoyed dance as much as studies on the piano,
though. It'd been Maylin who couldn't get enough of the
dance lessons.

"Hey."

Maylin stopped short, the space on her back where his
hand had been had gone cold in its absence. Heat filled
her cheeks as she turned to see him waiting by a door.
He must've stopped and she'd kept right on walking.

He raised a single eyebrow, slid the card key into the
reader and opened the door, then held it for her to enter.

"Why don't you settle your things in the bedroom
and take a look at the room service menu." Gabe proceeded ahead of her, his gaze sweeping the room as he
opened the closet and flipped the curtains. The realization hit her a moment later. He was checking the room
for other people.

Had she ever thought to do the same when she'd stayed
in hotels in the past? No. Should she?

"It's been hours since you last ate, and a quick to-go

sandwich at the airport on the way to pick up a rental car is not a real meal." He edged around the doorjamb and took a good look in the bathroom. "You might want to take advantage of the shower, too. Hot shower to wake you up before we head to the embassy."

"I want to ask them about An-mei as soon..."

He pinned her with a glare. "You take the time to get food in your belly and your head on straight. Polish yourself so their impression of you is at your best. You'll get a better response."

She swallowed angry words and absorbed what he'd said.

An embassy was full of people who made appearances and perception an art form. If she rushed in there bedraggled and halfway to fainting, they'd dismiss her. He was right. And if she'd been thinking with the professionally savvy part of her brain, she'd have anticipated it, too.

"Thank you." And she meant it.

"Don't thank me yet. We're only getting started." He set his small duffel on the couch and opened it up.

She hovered in the doorway. "I must be very silly to you."

He stopped, straightened, then turned to face her. "No. You're incredibly driven. And focused. Too focused. Your thought process hasn't strayed from your sister for longer than sixty seconds since I met you."

"She's important." Anger and frustration welled up inside her, boiling up from her belly.

He nodded once. "Yes, and you're too close to see your way clearly. In this kind of situation you need to learn to step away and look at other things. Let your mind go off on side trails. That's when we'll find the things no one expects."

As she stepped into the bedroom, she chewed on his advice. Mulled it over as she unpacked her hastily balled-up dress suit and put it on hangers.

"Did you have anything you needed ironed?" she called out into the living room, not sure where he was. The man made almost no sound moving around.

"I've got a dress shirt." After a moment, he was at the doorway with shirt in hand.

She took it from him. "I'll take it into the shower with me."

His eyebrows rose.

"What?" She might be grumbling, but really, it'd been a long...day? Night? Not days yet, but things were going by in a blur. "The steam will help the worst of the wrinkles fall out and make ironing easier."

Silence.

Already halfway into the bathroom with the hangers of clothes and her toiletries bag, she halted and leaned back to see him still standing in the doorway. "Something wrong?"

"Not particularly. You're going to leave them in there with the water running?"

"No!" She huffed. A lock of hair fell in her face but she didn't have the free hands to tuck it back where it belonged. Irritated, she continued, "It'd be a waste of water. I hang them up during my shower. If you're taking a shower right after, I'll leave them in here. Otherwise, I'll take them out and start up the iron to take the rest of the wrinkles out."

One corner of his mouth turned up in a lopsided grin. "Waste not. Good practice."

She hesitated. "I guess you don't need to steam or press your uniforms much overseas."

He leaned against the door frame, somehow closer than he'd been when he'd handed over his shirt but without having taken a step inside the bedroom. "Well, there's a balance we tend to find between not looking like a piece of sh—crap and not being too much of a *princess* either."

"Okay." And she should spit out her real question instead of waffling and keeping them both lingering in doorways. "You're going to be out there, then?"

"I might go get ice down the hall."

"Oh." Perfectly reasonable. Why was her stomach twisting in knots thinking about it?

Gabe's gaze grew sharper, the weight of it something she could feel on her skin. "I can wait until after we're both finished showering."

Her anxiety eased a little. "I'd...appreciate it."

"No problem. I'll be out here. Relax. It's almost lunchtime over at the embassy and they won't open up to see people again for a couple of hours." He stepped back out of the doorway, pulling the door closed between them.

Chapter Eight

What was wrong with her? She bustled through hanging up the clothes and turning on the shower. It wasn't until she was rinsing shampoo from her hair that she realized she was listening for the sound of doors opening and closing. He'd said he wouldn't go anywhere. And she believed him. But part of her was wary of someone sneaking up on her.

Afraid.

With Gabe out there, it wasn't as bad as it might have been. And earlier at the Centurion Corporation property, she'd felt insulated and secure. Surrounded by people who made it their business to protect people, among other things. But she hadn't stopped moving along the way to let things sink in.

Her apartment had been violated.

If it hadn't been for Gabe seeing her home, someone would have heard—and maybe watched—everything she'd have done on returning. Taking a shower. Going to sleep. When would they have taken advantage and come to finish what they'd started with the attempted hit-and-run? And who were they? What did it have to do with An-mei? The questions had been hovering in the back of her mind, on continuous repeat, all day.

Hot water scalded her skin as she tried to scrub away the worry.

Overthinking was a danger. Thoughts born of fear wouldn't be constructive. She needed to change her line of thought. Gabe was right.

And what about him?

Fitful naps on the red-eye might count as sleep deprivation. Why else would her thoughts scatter at the sight of him? It'd happened repeatedly throughout the day as he returned from the car rental counter or from some random building at one of their multiple stops. Plus her heart rate was definitively erratic—both earlier and right there in the shower. Maybe she'd had too much coffee. She'd stopped counting cups after they left the airport.

Or she could be honest with herself and admit he was the most attractive man she'd ever encountered.

Turning off the water, she pushed aside the shower curtain and reached for a towel. The mirror was steamed over, showing only the softest outline of her reflection.

How did he see her?

When they'd met, he'd thought she was propositioning him. Heat burned her cheeks. Not the strongest first impression she'd ever given. And it wasn't as if she spent much time interacting with men outside of business anyway. Night clubs and bars weren't her thing. Cooking classes were fun, but most men signing up for those were already part of couples. The few men her stepmother had initially tried to match her with had all been completely wrong for her. Dating had been sporadic and without any sort of…spark to rate pursuing a further connection.

And here was Gabe. The man was a force of nature, so completely different as to make any other man she knew pale in comparison. Overthinking could be impossible with him. Mostly because he was capable of derailing any thought process simply by standing there, or sitting next to her, or brushing near her.

And that sounded perfect.

She patted herself dry, her hair still damp and falling loose down her back. Then she wrapped her towel around her torso and stepped out of the bathroom, careful to close the door behind her to keep the steam in with the hung clothes. Padding across the carpet, she opened the door to the bedroom before she reconsidered what she was about to do.

The whole point was not to.

"Did you need anything?" Gabe stood facing away from her by the sofa bed, having pulled it out and made it up.

Yes, please help me stop thinking.

But she couldn't say the words. Couldn't figure out how not to sound like an idiot. And couldn't stop staring at him. The muscles across his back flexed as he moved, showing through his thin T-shirt. Broad shoulders, strong arms. She remembered having those arms close around her, carry her, support her. And she wanted more.

What the heck was she supposed to say? If she hesitated much longer, she'd hide in the bedroom and not come out again until it was time to go. And the whole point was to not think at all. Change direction. Do something *different*. "*Need* might not be the right word."

Gabe turned towards her then, caught sight of her and froze.

But he didn't say anything.

Taking a few steps towards him, she came to a stop, her gaze glued to his chest. She couldn't quite manage looking him in the eye yet. But she took the leap anyway.

"You don't have to leave your stuff out here. I mean, you could…join me, if you want."

There. She'd said it.

Please don't let this turn into one of those things I'm going to regret for the rest of my life.

Gabe put comprehension on hold for half a second. All he could process was the sheen of golden skin wrapped in nothing but a hotel towel. His libido had barely been restrained while he'd been imagining water running down her skin as she'd been showering. Now his pants were painfully tight and she stood too close for her own safety. He balled his hands into fists. He couldn't help looking, though, following the curve of her bared shoulder up to the place where it met her neck, exposed while her hair was slicked back and still wet. He wanted to lick her shower-fresh skin, kiss and bite her—right there. Her face was even more defined with her hair back, her lips a perfect kissable bow shape and her dark eyes hidden under delicate lashes as she kept staring stubbornly down or to the side or anywhere but at him.

Join me, if you want.

Those words were an invitation. And to hell with his earlier intention to keep things simple, he wanted to take her up on them. Hours of watching her doze fitfully on the plane had wound him up tight with a mix of concern and desire. On his recommendation, she'd come with him across the damned country. Every step of the way, she'd absorbed his instructions and asked intelligent questions.

She was stepping up in every way and it only made him want her more.

But he'd misunderstood her the first time they'd met,

so he didn't want to mess up again. Her looking down and away wasn't what he wanted.

He reached out, insanely glad when she didn't flinch but instead seemed to lean into even the slightest touch of his forefinger under her chin. Exerting gentle pressure, he coaxed her to look up at him. When the full force of her gaze hit him, a cacophony of nervousness and determination and desire, he almost took her mouth right there. But he had to be sure he was reading her right. "Are you inviting me to have sex?"

Her cheeks flushed with heat and her tongue darted out to wet her lips. "Yes."

Instant erection. Actually, he'd already been straining inside his pants but he was about to bust his fly open at this point. He'd better act fast. He could see doubt and second-guesses piling up in her eyes and she was starting to pull away from him. Nothing else he was going to say was going to come out right.

He kissed her.

She parted her lips for him. He tasted, explored, as her tongue danced with his. God, he'd wanted this. Craved the taste of her again ever since he'd kissed her the first time.

Her needy whimper set him on fire. He gripped the nape of her neck, deepening their kisses, and kept his other hand at the curve of her back to hold her against him. She was warm, pliant, molding her body against his. He wanted to rip the towel away and explore every inch of her, but damn it, she'd started this and he didn't want to rush her into changing her mind. This had to be her lead.

The level of control it was requiring might kill him.

Letting them both up for air, he tried for words. Communication was good. Important. "I agreed to help you. Don't do this if you think it's some kind of payment."

He didn't want her lowering herself to that.

Her eyes widened and she shook her head. "No. I just... I don't want to think anymore. And every time you're near, there's you. Just you. And the questions go quiet and I want that. Please. I want to do this in the moment. With you."

Couldn't argue with his own words. Damn if he couldn't remember a single reason for why this would be a bad idea. "Do you still want to go to the bedroom?"

To hell with simple. Especially after he'd been laid out with a bullet hole in his back, he was all about living.

She pressed her face into his chest, her breath hot through his T-shirt. He needed to get rid of it. The shirt. He wanted her lips on his skin as he moved inside her. When she placed her hands on his torso and fisted the fabric of his shirt in her hands, he groaned. She tugged, stepping back towards the bedroom, and the message was enough for him.

Bending his knees, he wrapped his arms around her thighs and straightened, hoisting her slight form up against him. When she squeaked, he laughed and a part of him came undone. This woman. Having her in his arms fit perfect and unlocked so much want. He couldn't wait much longer.

In a few ground-eating strides he reached the bedroom, slowing and stooping carefully to make sure her head cleared the doorway. She clutched his shoulders and he took the opportunity to nuzzle her. Her fingers dug in and he took it as encouragement. The towel was coming loose and he couldn't wait to taste his prize.

"Lights," she gasped. "Turn out the lights."

He wanted to see her, but paused and freed a hand to swipe at the switch on the wall anyway. The daylight behind the curtains gave him enough to see by and if she was more comfortable with the room lights out, he'd make it happen.

Her small hands framed his face and a few damp strands of hair fell around him as she leaned to fit her mouth against his.

"Thank you." Her lips brushed over his with her whisper.

He buried his face in her chest and inhaled. She smelled of fresh soap and rosemary and mint. God, even her shampoo must be infused with herbs and he wanted to eat up every part of her. He planned on it.

When he laid her out on the bed, she gazed up at him with anticipation. Her hands were folded over her chest, clutching the towel. He eased back to give her time if she needed it, even though every part of him wanted to pounce on her. "You can say stop. Anytime. I won't get mad."

Tension flowed out of her and she smiled. Then her expression turned to mischief as she bit her lip and parted the towel, leaving herself exposed. His mouth watered. He was a freaking beast. But the sight of all her smooth skin, her perky breasts and flat belly, and oh, sweet Jesus she was smooth down below.

He bent over her, reverently kissing her navel first. It was like a feast and he was about to partake. The only question was what to taste next. And for that, he waited as Maylin arched under his mouth and sighed. When her fingers ran through his hair, he moved higher and ran his own hand up her side to cover one breast. Placing kisses along the underside of her other breast, he reveled in the softness of her skin. Then he teased her already taut nipple with the tip of his tongue. She gasped and he chuckled. Absolute perfection.

Her curves just filled the palms of his hands and he paid attention to the way she reacted to every touch and lick. Her fingers tightened on his scalp as he started torturing her in the best of ways, enjoying her needy whimpers interspersed with gasps and sighs as he alternated suckling her breasts.

She clutched at his shoulders, pulling at the fabric of his T-shirt. "Off."

Yes, ma'am.

Straightening, he pulled off his shirt and tossed it. Maylin sat up with him, her nimble fingers undoing his pants. He looked up at the ceiling and reached for control as she freed his cock. Gentle fingertips wandered over the length of him and he almost lost it right there.

That wouldn't do. Her first.

He pressed her back down on the bed, pausing to give each of her breasts a fun squeeze and teasing suckle before kissing his way down her belly. Her hands fisted the sheets on either side of her as he coaxed her legs apart. Once he had her exposed, he blew a hot puff of air on her most delicate flesh. She twitched in response and he gripped her thighs just firm enough to hold her without hurting her. Listening, he waited for her to breathe once, twice, then he leaned forward and tasted her.

She cried out and he chuckled again, enjoying every minute. Taking his time, he explored every fold of her. Alternating between quick, darting touches with the tip of his tongue and long, lazy licks, he learned what drove her crazy. And when she seemed at the very edge, he pressed the tip of his finger into her entrance.

Tight. Her hips bucked and he covered her clit with

his mouth and sucked as he carefully continued to tease her entrance with his finger.

"Gabe." The sound of his name almost broke his control. "I can't…can't…"

Raising his head, he looked up the length of her beautiful body and pressed his finger further inside her. She writhed. Her head was tilted back, her mouth parted as she panted. He whispered against her skin, "You can, sweetheart. You absolutely can."

Then he locked his mouth over her clit and sucked, pumping his finger inside her in time with his suction. Her hips lifted off the mattress, every muscle in her taut for a half second before she crested into orgasm. He kissed and licked her through it, using his finger inside her to stroke and lengthen the experience for her.

For a long moment after, she lay panting with her eyes closed, the most relaxed he'd ever seen her. And holy shit, was she incredibly sexy. He pressed a kiss against her lips. "Wait a second. I'll be right back."

He strode back out into the other room and ripped his duffel apart for his travel kit. Always prepared. Nabbing the condom packet, he got back to Maylin in lightning speed. It took no time to roll the condom on and toss the foil.

She'd gathered herself in the meantime, watching him with so much heat in her eyes his cock jumped under her regard. Climbing over her, he fitted his hips between her legs as she lay back, welcoming him with a murmur. He nudged the head of his cock at her entrance and waited for her gaze to lock with his. He asked because he needed to be sure. "You want this?"

If she said no, if even the slightest hint of doubt clouded her eyes, he'd get up without a word. It'd kill him and he'd need some time in the shower with his hand. But he'd do it. It was enough to see her come apart under his touch like that.

But her lips spread in a sweet smile and her arms lifted and curved around his neck. "Yes, please."

Thank God.

He pressed inside her, agonizingly slow as she stretched to accommodate him. So. Tight. So. Good. Then she wrapped her legs around his waist, tilting her hips to encourage the fit between them. He buried his face in her neck and groaned.

He was not going to last long.

"Gabe." She accompanied his whispered name with a nip on his earlobe.

Growling, he withdrew and slid inside her again. She threw her head back as he thrust and he increased his rhythm, desperate to get deeper inside her every time. Every sound she made, her pleasure amplified his a dozen times over and he savored every bit of it.

Her thighs, her inner muscles, gripped him with surprising strength. No fragile flower here. Her hands had moved to grab his lower back, tugging and encouraging. Rolling his hips, he plunged deeper and harder. She rewarded him by calling out in time with his strokes. Her nails pricked his skin as she unlocked her ankles and planted her feet on the bed on either side of him, lifting her hips to meet him. Her body arched and her muscles squeezed, milking him, until she cried out louder and jerked as her orgasm took her.

His balls tightened and he came hard, erupting inside her in a hot rush. He thrust deep one more time as he lost his damned mind. Shuddering in the aftermath, he lowered himself over top of her carefully.

Holy shit.

"Mmm." She nuzzled his neck. As she shifted under him, her insides squeezed him.

His cock twitched.

Whoa, down, boy.

He ground his hips into her one more time before withdrawing slowly, carefully.

As he rose from the bed, she gave him a happy and sated smile. Her eyelids were at half-mast and she looked about ten seconds away from a nap. Good.

It took less than a minute to step inside the bathroom and get rid of the condom. He grabbed a small hand towel, wet it and rung it out, then returned to her on the bed. Her eyes widened in pleased surprise as he helped her clean up.

"Thank you." She sounded embarrassed.

He kissed her. "Least I can do. Thank *you*."

She bit her lip. Adorable. "I know we have to get ready to go in a while, but will you lay with me for a few minutes?"

Tossing the towel to the floor, he eased down next to her and gathered her against his side. Immediately, she turned towards him and snuggled in close.

His heart thudded in his chest. He liked this. *Really* liked it. This had been different—she was different—from his past experiences. Some women were a hundred miles away even as they lay in the same bed. Others literally got up and left, their itch scratched. No hard feelings. No strings attached. And he'd never worried about it. However they wanted to move on, he'd been fine.

But having Maylin cuddled up against him, warm and happy, was all sorts of better than anything he'd imagined. Good. Better than he deserved.

"So we're leaving in a while for the embassy, then coming back here for the night?" She traced little patterns across his chest as she asked.

"That's the plan." He pressed a kiss against the bridge of her nose. He'd bet her questions were slowly filling up the inside of her head again. He was glad he'd been able to help her reset her mind. Hoped she'd ask him to do it again.

"Whatever happens, I… I'm glad we did this." She pressed a kiss against his jaw in return.

Pleased, stupid happy kind of pleased, he wrapped his arms around her. "Me, too."

"And it's totally okay if this is a one-time thing. It won't be awkward, so I don't want you to think…"

He stopped her, capturing her mouth and drowning them both for a long minute. They were gasping when he lifted his head. "Not sure what this is yet. But I want to figure it out. I don't want it to be a one-time thing."

She smiled and his throat tightened. Wow. She was lighting up his world.

A minute later, her light dimmed.

"What is it?" He brushed a stray hair from her cheek.

"An-mei," she whispered.

Ah, hell.

"No guilt. Don't. Not for a minute. I don't want to distract you and I'm going to focus on what I set out to do," he reassured her. "We can set this aside for now. Then once we find your sister, we'll find our way back to here."

"Here?"

"Not this hotel, unless you want to. But this chemistry." He pressed his hips into hers, making sure she could feel his already half-cocked erection. "Because trust me, this thing between us isn't a one and done. You okay with that?"

She nodded, and this time she was the one to pull him down for a kiss.

"You know," she whispered, twining her legs with his. "I'm not sure how you thought you'd fit on the sofa bed out there anyway."

He chuckled, tucking her close. "Glad I don't have to try."

Chapter Nine

Gabe kept his pace easy, his stride adjusted to more of a student's swagger. Wouldn't make sense to slouch with his build. But there were enough physically fit students walking around the university grounds surrounding the embassy for him to blend with them. Carrying a backpack helped his assumed image, too. Everything he was wearing was non-descript, something any person could've been wearing in this area. And in the backpack, he had a spare shirt and pullover in case he needed to rapidly change his appearance.

With Maylin safely inside the embassy making legitimate inquiries after her sister and the status of investigation surrounding An-mei's disappearance, he was free to look into other sources of information. The both of them might have to exert some pressure to get a response, but his kind involved less noble tactics. To be honest, it gave a corner of his awareness some peace to know she was inside and out of harm's way. The rest of his mind was focused on the task at hand.

His target was about twenty yards ahead of him, easy to keep in sight and not moving like he was in a rush. When the man stopped at a bus stop on the other side of the embassy, Gabe figured himself lucky and hung back until a bus came into view. Catching his man exiting the embassy was so much easier than having to go in to find him and get him aside for the chat Gabe had in mind.

Timing his pace, Gabe hopped on the bus a person or two behind his target. He slid into a seat behind the man as the bus rolled forward.

"Andy Li, it's been a long time."

Li jumped, but recovered reasonably quickly without turning around to look at Gabe.

Good practice even though most of the seats around them were empty. Not surprising in the middle of the afternoon. The few people who'd boarded with them were scattered and absorbed in their own private bubbles. Just about everyone had earbuds, even, listening to their own entertainment.

All to the good as far as Gabe was concerned. Chatting on a bus was far less conspicuous than pulling the man aside in a building. Less likely to be overheard. "Taking a long lunch or are you done for the day?"

As a freelance translator, not attached to any specific dignitary, Li tended to take odd shifts and his schedule varied every few weeks. Convenient, really, because no one ever questioned his being in the embassy building and his employment history wasn't scrutinized as closely as employees with hands-on access to documentation. Freed the man up to be where he needed to be, when he needed to be, to hear the choicest bits of information in English, Cantonese, Mandarin, and even a few Southeast Asian languages like Taiwanese or Malaysian. A lot more than Chinese came through the embassy on various visits, and selling those pieces of overheard intelligence was more than lucrative enough to offset the inconvenience of rearranging one's sleep schedule.

"Diaz? Didn't expect to hear your creepy voice sneak up on me anytime soon." Li's own was low, not likely to be overheard by anyone more than a seat away, even with the current lack of company.

"You're getting lazy." Gabe pondered for a minute. Creepy? Maylin didn't seem to think so. At least, hopefully not. "Don't tell me business has been getting slow?"

Li shrugged. "Not a lot going on in my neighborhood in the last few months."

Lie.

The man's posture was relaxed now, but his tone was all off. Too laid-back.

"That's a shame. I'd think you'd be worried about your livelihood."

"Ah, well. Gotta let the luck come when it will." Li laughed, a touch too high-pitched. "Besides, I heard about your incident overseas. Didn't expect you around…at all."

Ever was more like it. It'd been touch and go there, getting out of that hellhole and then recovery afterward.

"You know rumors." Gabe leaned forward, turning his face as if he was looking out the window. "Greatly exaggerated."

And to his benefit in any situation. There was an edge to being underestimated in his line of work. Element of surprise tended to work to his advantage when he managed things properly.

Li shifted in his seat, giving a barely perceptible amount of ground. "My information is gold because of its accuracy, man. You took a shot in the back from the person you were supposed to be protecting."

Yeah, wouldn't that just suck? The reality was a hundred times worse. Li's precious information was inaccurate, but Gabe wouldn't hold it against the informant. The truth behind the actual shooting was locked in a need-to-know file and only Gabe's commanding officer needed to know. Even Gabe's team didn't know yet.

"Not enough to take me out." Of course not. Gabe didn't bother trying not to sound surly about it. Being shot hadn't tickled.

"Some say it was enough to take you out of the game."

"Those people are wrong." Gabe bit off each word.

And why did Li seem disappointed? Damned informants. Rarely friends. What mattered more was whether Li had gone from neutral to biased in favor of one of his other clients.

Li let loose his nervous laugh again. "Don't get me wrong. I'm happy, real happy, to have one of my best friends back. Of course."

"Of course." Sure. And Gabe might go back to wearing tighty-whities tomorrow. "In honor of our *friendship*, why don't you give me some insight?"

"On what?" Li sounded genuinely puzzled. "Like I said, there's no news recently."

"Not looking for jobs or background on any of the diplomats in-house." Gabe tapped the metal rail along the back of Li's seat. The urge to shake what he wanted out of the man was pretty strong. Still, Gabe would learn more if he nudged Li into babbling instead. "There might be some effort to sweep a few things under the rug, though, maybe a missing person?"

"People go missing every day, especially overseas. Police have more data on those reports than the embassy does." Too glib. Rehearsed, even. Definitely something there.

"I'm not talking about a kid on the side of a milk carton. And the embassy is the link to the authorities overseas." Gabe let his tone drop lower. "I don't want to have to dig for this. Don't make me."

"C'mon, Diaz. Shouldn't you be recovering? Might be too early for you to be up and out in the field." Li dragged a shaking hand through his hair.

It was. He'd been on light security recently because it let him stay reasonably active, but he wasn't cleared yet for serious duty. The long plane ride back to the East Coast had left him stiff and aching, a reminder to proceed with caution this trip. Course, caution might have evaporated when Maylin had ambushed him earlier.

No warm, cuddly thoughts right now. Gabe glowered to make sure they didn't show in his expression.

"You'd like to think so." He was done with being nice. "But here I am. And my recent experiences don't leave me inclined to give anyone the chance to betray my trust again. Is that what you're trying to do?"

"No, no." Li clutched his saddle bag, but didn't reach inside or otherwise make any motions to pull a gun or a phone. ——

Not like a gun was going to help the man at this close range. Gabe could have him disarmed and break something before Li could disengage a safety.

"I'm guessing your stop is coming up soon." There were more ways to mess with a man's livelihood than breaking things. "But you wouldn't mind me getting off with you, right? No one to care if I'm seen with you."

Li gulped. "It's been weird lately, Diaz. You know? Nobody respects an objective observer anymore."

"So I see." Playing the sympathy card. Going straight to the jelly for a spine. "What's the world coming to? Giving info on dirty diplomats doesn't eat at the soul the way other things do. Like covering up the disappearance of a young woman, maybe?"

Li froze.

Gotcha.

"An American citizen, with family looking for her. I can show you her face."

"No!" Li wiped sweat from his forehead. "I didn't do anything. Just deleted a few emails and let a couple of calls get lost on hold indefinitely. That's all."

Probably true. Li supplemented his translating engagements with temp work as a low-level administrative assistant. He had access to a lot of random information—the kind that wouldn't be valuable unless it was pieced together by someone with a broader perspective—but not a lot of power to do anything with it.

Gabe leaned harder on the back of Li's seat. "Helped make a young woman disappear is what you did. What happened to her? Sold? You know what they do to pretty girls? You been making it into a new line of business? How many other people are you making disappear?"

"Nothing like that, no no no." Li broke and started babbling. Being implicated in human slave trade was too big a deal for an information broker like him. The slave trade business sucked a man in and didn't let him back out alive. "She's some sort of genius. She won't be hurt. Not at all. They took her to do science for some big company. Cutting-edge stuff."

"Do science? That what they call it nowadays? And what if she won't do the research they want? What if she doesn't produce the results they're looking for? You think about that? She'll end up sold to make up the investment any way she can." Because Gabe was thinking about it.

"No, no." Li actually squirmed in his seat. "The company is legit into research. They take the latest and greatest and apply it to military tech."

"You're drinking the Kool-Aid, my *friend*." Gabe figured he'd twisted the knife long enough. "Who arranged for this girl's disappearance?"

"I got no names. You know how I work, mostly emails and avatars. No real identities. People can be anyone on the internet." Li dragged in a ragged breath, struggling to keep his voice down. "Only a couple people come find me in person."

A choice few.

"Porter van Lumanee." Gabe let the name drop like a rock.

Li's hands shook. "There's a name. Dunno if it's real. But he's someone attached to your missing girl. He's a chair on the programming committees for a few scientific conferences. He keeps an eye out for talent, scientists of interest to his sponsor. Other than that, he stays out of the messy activity. Probably doesn't know more than me."

Gabe would pay the man a visit just to be sure.

"Guy had some bad dumplings or something last trip," Li continued. Best thing about informants, if you scared them enough they vomited their guts until you let them go. Kind of like sea cucumbers. "He's back in the States but hospitalized for food poisoning. Could be a while before he's up to returning to work."

Maybe Gabe wouldn't be following that lead after all. Sounded like van Lumanee had outlived his usefulness. Maybe became too visible since he'd turned up on the police report as last to see An-mei. He'd have Marc check into the hospital records before any of them made the trip.

"So. There's a name you knew after all." Gabe uttered

a disappointed grunt. "I'm beginning to believe I can't rely on your information anymore."

"Look, Diaz. I don't want to cross you. I don't." Li dropped his forehead to his hand and muttered a few curses in Chinese. Funny, Maylin sounded a lot cuter when she cursed.

"You might think whoever asked you to do these things is the scarier person," Gabe crooned. "But you don't want to be in a position to make either of us prove it."

"Look at it this way, man, it's like a goddamned high school reunion. I don't want to be in the middle of a battle of the exes."

Gabe sat back. Well, damn. "She's nearby?"

"Pops up out of nowhere. As bad as you." Li was almost crying.

"All right." Gabe didn't want the man dead, after all. "You keep on riding and you keep on doing what she tells you to do."

Li nodded.

"But if you give me a heads-up on what you've been asked, I'd consider it a favor, between friends." Gabe stood as the bus rolled to a stop. Didn't matter where this was, so long as it wasn't Li's stop. And best if Gabe got off as soon as possible.

A favor was a lot to give the man, but he was the best lead they had to An-mei.

Gabe scanned the area as he left the bus. No watchers in the few shadows afforded by buildings and trees midafternoon.

Pulling out his smartphone, he dialed up Marc.

"Lykke," Marc answered after three rings.

"Diaz." Gabe didn't waste time with pleasantries.

"Porter van Lumanee is in the hospital. Check to see if it's worth it to try to have a talk with him."

"On it." The sound of fingers tapping keys came across the phone. "Didn't happen to get the name of the hospital, did you?"

"He's stateside, if that helps." Gabe wasn't worried. Marc would find the man. Besides, Gabe's gut told him Porter van Lumanee was a dead end, possibly literally. Still, best to follow every lead. "Pull up the latest we have on Jewel's activity, too."

Silence. Then Marc cleared his voice. "She's in this?"

"Looks like." Gabe wasn't thrilled.

"Van Lumanee's a dead man, then." Marc might grumble, but Jewel used to be one of their own. She wouldn't leave loose strings. "I'll see what I can get, stat."

"Thanks."

Marc wasn't done yet. "If Jewel's in this, will you be okay?"

It was a fair question. Gabe and Jewel had been a thing. They'd burned hot in their time together. Damned bad idea. Most times, mercs could indulge and go their separate ways, no hard feelings. Not him and Jewel. She'd ended them by leaving the Centurions in the worst way possible. Having her back in the game wasn't welcome news.

In all fairness, Gabe should cede this mission to another fire team. Bias. Conflict of interest. All sorts of ways things could go wrong if his judgment was compromised. But he had a handle on this and a clear head when it came to Jewel. He was sure of it.

"For now, yeah." Gabe paused, then added, "We'll play it by ear for now and I'll step back if things get complicated."

"Roger that." No questioning. They'd all learned to trust each other that way. And if there was any indication Gabe wasn't acting in the best interest of the mission and the team, Marc would let him know. The team was tight. "Porter van Lumanee was admitted to the Centinela Hospital Medical Center on arrival at LAX with a serious case of food poisoning. He was unconscious on arrival and in critical condition under the care of a Doctor Becker. He's been on intravenous fluids but hasn't come to yet. Apparently it hit him in flight and there wasn't a lot they could do for him until they landed."

Marc was fast.

"Vic and I will head out to see if we can get access to him. If he wakes up." Marc sounded dubious. "If you read between the lines, the prognosis isn't good. Doctor mentions it's the most serious case of straight up food poisoning he's encountered. They're looking for some sort of allergen or other slow-acting contributor to the issue."

Gabe scowled. "If the guy had a peanut allergy, wouldn't it hit right away?"

"Anaphylactic shock is the most dramatic, but according to Google, there's slower ways for allergies to present themselves. If it hit on digestion, it could explain why it took longer to show up." And Marc's Google-fu was near Jedi level.

If it was food poisoning due to something he actually ate. None of his team specialized in poisoning and neither did Jewel—they all preferred more directs means of confronting a person—but they'd worked with others who had. Jewel knew those names as well as Gabe did. Easy to induce the food reaction, and it looked completely natural. Travelers suffered from food poisoning all the time.

Course, if it *had* been a natural reaction to something the guy ate, it was very interesting timing.

No way for his team to know for sure right now.

"All right. Keep me posted. We want to know what this guy has to do with things."

"Roger that." Ending the call, Gabe decided to address next steps.

He'd dropped Maylin off at the front of the embassy, waiting for her to enter safely. Not likely to be much danger for her there, with all of the surveillance on property. Plus Gabe assumed whoever was tracking her had their attention on her phone, back at Centurion Corporation outside Seattle. Especially with Marc simulating normal activity on the phone, logging into email and apps as well as running predictable web searches.

But his ex was particularly good at remembering faces and recognizing family resemblance. If she was in the middle of all this, the embassy didn't seem so safe anymore.

Chapter Ten

"I haven't technically left the embassy." And Gabe wasn't there to hear her mumbled defense anyway. Nope. A good thing, too. Maylin stood just in front of the entranceway, still on the embassy grounds, with the late afternoon breeze clearing away some of the embarrassment and frustration she'd built up over the course of the afternoon.

Hours of wasted time.

Oh, it wasn't the cool reception when she'd first entered that bothered her. She'd been an entrepreneur for too many years to be intimidated by the formalities and the initial insistence that she make an appointment with some unspecified official who likely would be out of office anyway. She could and did handle those obstacles. The consultant badge associating her with the Centurion Corporation private military organization helped get her past the more difficult barriers when she might not otherwise have been able to as a random visitor. Subject Matter Expert had a much more valid ring to it than Desperate Client Who Almost Became Road Pizza.

And it wasn't the patronizing attitude either. It would be politically incorrect to claim it was cultural. But it would also be ignoring reality to claim there wasn't a social structure at the embassy, and she came in at the low

end of the pecking order as a supplicant, consultant or
not. It'd been a childhood survival skill to keep her frustration under control when her parents' Chinese friends
made social events a complex dance of backhanded compliments and thinly veiled verbal barbs. Besides, if she
took a step back and observed objectively, every culture
had a flavor of it. It was just the *way* they did it. Human
nature, maybe.

It was what had happened once she'd found someone
to help her. When they'd genuinely tried to run searches
and couldn't find any record of her emailed inquiries or
phone messages. When they had no record of her little
sister's visa.

When they'd asked her if she was sure her little sister
had gone to China at all.

To her shame, she'd been so incredibly frustrated and
angry, tears had threatened. She had to step outside to
calm herself despite Gabe's warning to stay inside the
embassy. It would damage any small respect she'd gained
if they saw her cry, and stepping away at all was an acknowledgment of her lack of composure. And that, in
itself, would set her back hours.

Time wouldn't turn back, and she needed to get back
to the person trying to help her before the nice man left
for the day and she'd have to start her story all over again,
going through the same searches. She pulled out her temporary phone to check her messages. For one thing, Gabe
might have texted her. For another, it would give her a
reason for having gone outside since there was no reception inside the building. She'd be able to save face
to some extent.

"Excuse me."

The unaccented, American voice was so close, Maylin jumped.

A blonde woman stood within inches, tipping her head to one side with a soft smile. "I'm sorry. I didn't mean to startle you. I couldn't help overhearing you inside."

Interesting. Maylin forced her brow to remain smooth, her lips to shape a return smile. The woman hadn't been anywhere in sight as far as Maylin had noticed.

"I'm afraid the aide had to leave for the day and the embassy will be closing soon."

Oh, no. Ice washed through Maylin's body and her smile froze on her face. She never should have left. Now she'd have to start all over again tomorrow.

"Perhaps you could tell me more about your little sister?" The woman was tall, leaning too close into Maylin's personal space. Her gaze was sharp and her smile reminded Maylin of a Cheshire cat. "I've worked in DC for years now and maybe I have a few connections who could be of help. Missing persons cases are difficult, otherwise, and I'm sure you've been running into a lot of red tape."

Every internal alarm went off inside Maylin's head. The woman had too much information for absolutely no good reason.

"Depends on your definition of help." Gabe's voice flowed through Maylin, washing away the tension. She wasn't alone with this stranger who knew too many things.

The woman stepped past Maylin in a smooth motion, the intensity of her focus completely transferred to Gabe where he stood outside the embassy gates. Without waiting for any signal, Maylin strode directly past the woman to join him. Might have been wiser to circle around the stranger, but what would she do on embassy grounds in broad daylight? Another place with less light and Maylin might have been more cautious. But for the time being, she was done losing face.

Once Maylin reached him, Gabe's gaze flicked over her in a lightning assessment before fastening on the woman following her. "What brings you here, Jewel?"

Jewel halted on the sidewalk outside the gate, facing them both. She and Gabe squared off, maintaining several yards between them.

"Gabriel." Sensuality oozed out of every pore and her posture became fluid, feline, an invitation. "It's been a while. Have you been taking good care of yourself?"

Why did the question sound more like an innuendo than a courtesy? Maylin tried to ignore the twist in her stomach.

"Why are you here?" More bite to Gabe's question this time.

Good. Maylin kept her own expression neutral. This was one of those times where she'd follow his lead but wouldn't spare a moment's guilt for slamming him with questions after they were alone. Timing and all that.

"I've got a job to do, obviously." The woman, Jewel, leaned her hand on her hip. "You being here makes things a little more complicated than expected. Of course, I'm sure we could come to an understanding of some sort."

"I'm not too fond of your assumption." Gabe's body language was aggressive and chilling at the same time. From the cold, flat look in his eyes to the thin line of his lips to the straight set of his shoulders. Anyone leaving the embassy would see a few people talking, but Maylin was caught up in the tension between them. Gabe could explode at any moment and she planned to be ready to duck if he said so.

Jewel still stood relaxed, with an almost lazy smile playing on her very red lips. "Well, I'm guessing you're not quite as fond of me since last we met."

Gabe had been shifting forward in small movements until Maylin realized she was leaning to one side to see around him. How did he do that? With the embassy gates at her immediate left and Gabe between her and this Jewel person, Maylin glanced around them, figuring this was too public a place for Jewel to try anything truly dangerous. There were people on the street. Heck, more people were walking up and down the sidewalks than when she'd arrived earlier in the day. End of the work-day, probably end of classes for many of the university students, too. Rush hour, university campus style.

"Where's her sister?" Gabe's question wrenched Maylin's attention back to their discussion.

Jewel widened her eyes and batted mascara-lengthened lashes. "What makes you think I know where she is?"

Gabe jerked his chin up and down in a short, small motion. "You didn't say you didn't know."

Maylin wanted to reach out and shake Jewel, demand the woman spit out whatever it was she knew instead of playing games. Probably not the best idea. She balled her hands into fists at her sides instead.

"Well, you *are* very good at reading body language, so I do my best not to lie to your face, Gabriel." Jewel studied her nails.

"But you'd put a bullet in my back." Gabe spat the statement out and Jewel's already pale skin turned a few shades chalkier. "Problem with a bullet when it doesn't go through and through is someone could dig that bitch out and work forensics magic."

Any worries about jealousy were fading with that bit of information. Dislike for the woman was slowly burning into an active hatred. Jewel knew important things about An-mei and had hurt her man. Maylin was going to wipe the arrogant look off Jewel's face someday.

"You sure you didn't lose too much blood in your last mission?" Jewel's comment came out flippant, her composure recovered quick as anything.

Too much hung in the air between the two and Maylin soaked it in, tried to commit every detail of the confrontation to memory. She was going to be thinking hard on it later.

"You owe me," Gabe growled. "Where is her sister?"

"No." The word dropped from Jewel's mouth like a stone. "You owe *me* for not taking a head shot on that contract. Anyone else would've taken you out permanently rather than risk having you come after them, but the primary objective was specifically to disable the team and ensure the target didn't make it out alive. I made a field decision and you're alive because of it. Keep that in mind." The Cheshire cat smile returned in the long beat of silence that followed. "Besides, your little friend here would find her sister far quicker with me. And she wouldn't have to fly to the other side of the world on a wild goose chase, either."

It was tempting to run towards Jewel. Scream at her. Demand. But Maylin bit her lip and stayed right where she was. In this situation, Gabe had the lead. It was important. And acting on any impulse would likely land her right in whatever Jewel had in mind. Maylin was not going to give the woman the satisfaction.

Without making a move, Gabe somehow loomed. His big, bad and dangerous unlocked without any visible effort on his part. "Walk away, Jewel. This is a Centurion Corporation job."

Jewel's smile faded a fraction. Her eyes darted, focusing on Gabe then Maylin then back to Gabe. "I'm with Edict now. There is no walking away."

Gabe stiffened, his broad shoulders and back frozen for a split second before he relaxed again into the ready-to-move posture Maylin always admired about him. This tightrope walking on the edge of action was exhausting her and she wanted to shout. Make something happen.

After a pause, Jewel flipped her hair over her shoulder. "Take the tiny woman back to wherever you plan to stash her and keep her under wraps. If she quits looking for what she's lost, she can go back to her life with no worries."

Oh, no way.

"Not likely." Maylin took a step forward, but Gabe's arm blocked her momentum. Anger burned away thought process and Maylin only wanted to get right up into Jewel's face.

Jewel laughed, a short bark. "Remember to look both ways before you cross the street, then."

Maylin opened her mouth to say something. A hundred questions crowded, jostling to be the first out. But Gabe was herding her to one side and into his rental car.

"Stay down," Gabe muttered before shutting the passenger-side door and striding around to the driver's side. Once inside, he kept his attention on Jewel as he started up the car and pulled away from the curb.

Scrunched up in the seat, Maylin fought a nasty internal battle with the part of her most likely to tell him where to shove his orders and jump out of the car. She could assert herself. Prove she was her own woman and go confront this Jewel person, try to make the woman tell her how to find her sister. But Gabe was a professional and obviously knew Jewel. The comments they'd tossed back and forth had too many layers of meaning, too many references to things unspoken. Too much history.

Besides, Jewel had wanted Maylin to go with her. Reason enough to follow Gabe's instructions. Call it intuition or instinct or questionable survival skill. Maylin didn't trust Jewel in any way, shape or form.

So she wasn't going to ditch Gabe to go with the woman. But she wasn't going to follow along blindly either. It'd been several long minutes and she was done with waiting for him to speak to her. "Are we far enough away for you to tell me why you stuffed me in the car instead of making that woman tell you where my sister is?"

"No." Gabe sighed. "Yes. I'm sorry."

A little of the resentment loosened inside Maylin's chest. He sounded sincere. It was hard to let someone else make the decisions, but Gabe kept proving he wasn't taking her acquiescence for granted. "Apology accepted."

And to be fair, frequent traffic light stops meant they hadn't traveled more than a few miles as yet. Washington, DC, and the surrounding areas were much more confusing to her than Seattle. The street layout didn't make it easy for her to picture a map of the area in her mind or get her bearings.

"You're lucky I got there when I did." Gabe's grip on the driving wheel tightened. "You weren't supposed to step outside the embassy."

Maylin shook her head. If he could apologize, so could

she. "I'm sorry, too. Could she have taken me off embassy grounds?"

Gabe took in a deep breath. "She was trying to coax you, get you to walk with her. Then, it wouldn't take much to snatch you off the street."

True. Maylin could picture it pretty readily. She closed her eyes and recalled several cars on the street. No black minivans or windowless work vans, but more than one had been an SUV or similar larger vehicle. Not hard to shove someone into one of those and drive away. She needed to take these things in more at the moment instead of in hindsight.

"But why?" The question burst from her and she took a moment to slow down, try not to sound panicked. "Why do they want me at all? If they were trying to silence me, stop me from looking for An-mei, I understand why they would try to run me over. But these other things that have been happening. They're trying to take me alive and I don't understand."

It didn't make any sense. And she needed for it to make sense or she was going to go crazy.

"You'd be leverage. Your sister is capable of conducting valuable research. But they can't beat her into doing what they want. They need her in reasonably good condition and able to think. That's where having you in custody makes sense. They can threaten you to gain her cooperation. It's a good sign because it could mean your sister is alive and resisting. As long as you're loose, we've got a better chance of getting to her before she fulfills their use for her. And you're turning out to be valuable." Despite his positive words, Gabe's tone remained serious. "They're going to try harder and harder to get to you. I want to say as long as you do what I tell you to, you'll be fine, but my team and I can't anticipate every move. We'll do our best, but your chances increase exponentially if you keep your calm and think clearly on your own, too."

"That's both scary and sort of encouraging," Maylin admitted. She very much hoped he was right about An-mei, though. Her sister was tougher than she looked. An-mei could hold on.

"It should be. You've got good instincts. We call it 'situational awareness.' You had a good distance between you and her. You knew where other people were around the two of you. Very good." His praise warmed her. "I was also glad to see you holding your ground, not taking the bait."

And Jewel had been baiting her. But why? Things had been happening so quickly and she'd been so focused on getting the Centurion Corporation team's help…she hadn't considered what value she had to anyone out there.

"I can't imagine what it'd be like to live this way all the time." Maylin gave in to honesty and the release of tension had her babbling. "You live in this state of constant vigilance. It's exhausting to watch. There's news articles about PTSD and how people live in a state of hyperawareness. I always tried to imagine what it was like, but until all of this, it never sank in. It's all the time. Everywhere. How do you not go insane?"

Gabe sighed. "It isn't a sudden thing that'll be cured by a session of therapy. It doesn't go away someday or get better. It's a shift in worldview, a change in the way you look at everything around you. The first time I came home from a deployment, fuck, I wanted so bad to change my state of mind. I did. But I ended up going back overseas because things made better sense to me over there."

His words were raw and yet his outward expression

was blank. She wanted to have this discussion somewhere private where he could let his control ease up and let his emotions show on his face. But this was where they'd gotten into the topic and this was where she'd learn. And to be honest, she didn't know exactly where they were. They'd driven on and off a combination of city streets and larger highways but it'd all been in a generally circular direction. At the very least, it was just the two of them. He'd have told her if someone was following.

"Did it help, going back overseas?" Not sure it was the right question to ask.

"It made more sense. It was simpler to follow the rules out there. There's a system to it. People have skills, have their role to play, and they do their job or everyone on the team could die." Gabe hesitated, then added, "I trust my fire squad. Lizzy, Vic and Marc. And I used to trust every member of my squadron. But when Jewel deserted, it left the entire squadron shaken up. The Centurions took a while to reassess every person in the squadron and the trust is still building. That's twenty active individuals all looking around, wondering if they can rely on their teammates."

To do their job, or everyone could die. Maylin swallowed hard.

"It wasn't until later the forensics evidence came back confirming the bullet in me came from her weapon. We decided to keep it under wraps until we knew where she'd gone and, hopefully, why."

"Edict?" She hoped she was remembering the organization correctly. Jewel had spat it out quickly, with such a tone of bitterness, Maylin wondered how she could stand the taste of it.

"Apparently." Gabe nodded with a grim smile. "I'm

still wondering about the reason. But I might not get that answer anytime soon. Simple answer would be better money, but with Jewel it's not always about the ready cash. She could have other reasons."

Or he hoped she did. It was unsaid and Maylin decided to let it lie for now. It wouldn't help to continue to poke at the sore subject when there was no way to find out more.

She wanted to dismiss everything that was happening as fantastical. It sounded like a television show. A book. Not real. But wasn't that the mistake people made? Her stepmother had told her if An-mei had disappeared, it must have been because An-mei had behaved irresponsibly going out on her own, and people didn't just disappear from science conferences. "Overly dramatic" was exactly what Maylin's stepmother had called her, and she wouldn't believe anything bad had happened.

But it had. It was reality. And so was the life Gabe led.

"Was Jewel really baiting me?" Maylin's hopes dropped to the floor at her feet. "Maybe she didn't know anything about An-mei."

Gabe tapped the top of the steering wheel with a finger. "Possibly. But then again, she doesn't lie straight to my face. I think she was telling the truth back there."

Which part was he referring to and where was the white rabbit? It was safer to latch on to the connection between Jewel and Gabe.

"I need a little clearer communication here. I got the impression the two of you were fine, what with the witty repartee, but I need a little more straightforward detail." Maylin paused. It'd been nerve-racking listening, watching, unable to *do* anything. "So if she was telling the truth, you mean she could've shot you in the head at some point?"

And was there a chance Maylin could end up with a hole in the head herself?

"Probably." Gabe's jaw tightened. "There's a history there."

"I want to say I don't need to know, but I'm running a little low on faith considering the way she oozed sex in your direction." And Maylin hated admitting it. Hadn't even acknowledged it herself until she'd said it out loud. She might not have done a lot of dating in her time but even she could see the tension between the two of them had been more than just former acquaintances or colleagues. "I don't even know where we're going right now. I need more information. About everything."

"We're headed to Centurion Corporation headquarters." Gabe's response was sober, which was good because if he'd laughed at her, the twisting insecurity she was struggling to control would rip something inside her. After a pause, he continued, "We were a thing. It was a while ago."

A thing. Did he consider what was between him and Maylin "a thing," too? Or did she not even qualify?

"Everybody has marks in their ledgers, sweetness. I'm not going to lie to you about this one." Gabe shrugged. "Jewel and I were together. Bad idea for squadron mates. A relationship clouds your judgment in a mission. But what we had was all sex, no messy sentimental baggage."

She should say something. He'd paused for her to respond in some way. "But you did care for her."

He made a strangled sound. "In a complicated way. We had too much respect for each other to jeopardize a mission if things went south for either one of us. And we were good together…physically."

Maylin shrank in on herself. She shouldn't compare.

The rational part of her mind was checking out, though, and what was left switched between raging jealousy and trembling embarrassment.

She'd come face-to-face with a former lover of his, a woman who'd worked with him as a mercenary with the skills to do all the things Maylin couldn't. This woman would've been able to go after her family without the help Maylin had come to the Centurions for in the first place. And she knew something about An-mei.

Jewel had a lot of things Maylin didn't and right now, it meant everything.

"Hey." Gabe's hand reached out, palm up, an invitation. She hesitated and then placed her own in his. His fingers closed around hers, engulfing hers. "What we have between us is a completely different chemistry."

"It is?" And wow did she hate how vulnerable her voice sounded.

"I'm not sure what it is yet, but you've got me unhinged in ways I've never experienced before." He squeezed her hand gently. "In a good way. And we have a promise."

Yes. Once they found An-mei. But in the meantime, Maylin needed to ask one more question before she could settle and process it all.

"Why did you two end it?" It shouldn't matter. There were more important topics. But trust seemed to be in short supply and this *did* matter on so many levels.

"She shot me in the back."

Well, okay then. Maylin couldn't think of a single thing to say.

"I told you before about my last mission, the husband whose wife was cheating on him. We were overseas, contracted to extract a military scientist and get him out safely. I'd gone in first, had the man with me, when our fire team encountered hostile fire. He'd picked up an M16, was firing to either side of me, scared out of his damned mind." Gabe delivered the story in a monotone. He was sitting right next to her, but she had the sense he was far away. "When I took a bullet in the back, we all thought he'd been the one to shoot me. When I went down, he took two to the chest. My team got me out, and him, too, but I was the one to survive."

It took a minute for Maylin to connect what he was telling her to the reason he hated getting tangled up in emotional missions. "But it wasn't him. It was Jewel."

And there was some messy emotion there having nothing to do with the dead client or his wife and everything to do with Gabe's lover shooting him in the back.

Maylin wanted to say something, anything. But she couldn't undo any of those things. Instead, she listened. Because this wasn't the kind of thing that was shared easily. She should absorb it, remember it with respect. And not hurt him by asking him to repeat it someday down the road.

"Jewel shouldn't have been anywhere near that engagement. Her fire team was assigned to a different position guarding the secondary escape route. After the mission, she and her fire team left the Centurions before I even woke up from surgery. They'd come to the end of their contract, and no one would've thought anything of it. But our medical team managed to retrieve the bullet from me and ran forensics on it. It was a five fifty-six all right, the right kind of bullet, but it hadn't come from an M16. It'd come from an AK, and none of the hostiles we encountered were armed with those. Hell, none of the other Centurions on that contract had been either. Just Jewel and her AK one-zero-one with an ACOG magnification mount, custom modified. And she'd checked in after the mission with her weapon in hand. She'd put the bullet in my back and only my Kevlar body armor saved me from worse damage when it hit. Otherwise, I'd be in a wheelchair." Gabe shifted in the driver's seat. It still hurt him, even if it was mostly healed. Maylin bit back concerned remarks because she didn't think it'd help to point out the continued weakness. "By the time the results came back, she was in the wind. This is the first time I've seen her since."

Hell of a way to break up with a lover. And no way was Maylin going to say it out loud. But she had to wonder what kind of unresolved issues it'd left behind. Could be an awful time to ask, but if not now then things could move too fast. There may not be a later.

"You're very quiet over there."

She jumped. It hadn't seemed like a lot of thinking, but maybe she'd chewed on it a lot longer than she'd meant to. "I don't know what to say. And…to be honest I don't know if I have a right to say anything."

"You can ask and I can do my best to answer." Gabe made the offer.

Hesitantly, Maylin went out on a limb. "Do you miss her?"

Hard to ask a question when you weren't sure you wanted to know the answer. But it was important to know. She wasn't good at communicating when it came to relationships, even if it was about a memory of good times gone by. Everything came out awkward and not quite the way she intended.

Gabe gave her question serious thought, his brows drawn together. "Yes and no. We had good times and we were good together back then. But it wasn't something

I craved after it was over. I think what I miss is the way we worked together. She was a good squad mate, excellent at her work. It's hard to find people you can work with out there. There's a sort of…easygoing confidence when you have good people at your back, and she is no longer one of them. Leaves an exposed spot. Does that make sense?"

"I'm sorry." This time she wasn't sure exactly why she had to apologize, but she wanted to.

"I am, too. I trusted her." Gabe ran his hand through his hair. "But the history is so you know who she is and what she is to me. It's over. And you and me, we're not sure what we're doing, but it's not a one-night thing. At least not to me. I want time for us to figure it out."

What to say? He made it sound simple. What did she feel? "I'm glad."

Stupid. Awkward. But it was what she was thinking. His story would take time to sink in and she couldn't figure out more on the spot.

The corner of his mouth turned up. "Good. Hopefully I can add to that a little."

Maylin blinked. "How?"

"Jewel's other truth." Gabe reached over with one hand and covered Maylin's knee. The heat of his touch seeped into her skin. "She said you'd find your little sister faster with her and you wouldn't have to go to the other side of the world to do it. An-mei isn't lost in China. She's here. In the US."

Chapter Eleven

"This…is a really slow elevator."

Gabe smiled at Maylin's neutral tone. All things considered, she was holding up like a champ. Some women would've flipped their shit meeting an ex. And Jewel made confrontations with women a sort of sadistic stress reliever the same way some people walked into bars looking for a brawl. Add in how very good Jewel was at hand to hand combat, the average jealous woman ended up mostly broken and sadly humiliated. He did not want Maylin subjected to similar treatment. Especially since it was obvious Jewel had planned to take custody of Maylin.

Over his dead body.

Which was why he'd brought Maylin with him to Centurion Corporation headquarters. The hotel might not be secure enough, and he wanted eyes on her as much as possible now that Jewel, and Edict, had made a grab for her.

"We got the elevator out of a decommissioned submarine." Gabe offered Maylin the tidbit of information. She rewarded him with an adorable expression, her delicately arched brows drawing together as she bit her plump lower lip. He could see the gears turning in her head as she tried to come up with reasons why they'd want to do that.

"Do all the buildings in the area have these?" she asked, finally.

Not a bad follow-up. "Other private military contractors might have made similar upgrades to their buildings, like this elevator and installing Thermopane or extra-thick glass."

"I'm guessing the glass isn't for energy efficiency." Her lips twisted into a cute, wry smile. "Does it prevent people from listening in with those laser beam things?"

Or something.

Gabe nodded, though. Surveillance technology, bullets—the thick glass was a deterrent for a lot of things. "Not a bad guess. The elevators are actually safe areas in case the building is caught in the shocks from a nearby explosion. There's safety mechanisms that clamp to the sides of the shaft, and extra shielding."

She craned her head to look up at him. "Common concern for people in your line of work?"

"Let's say we are potential targets and like to be prepared just in case."

Hypervigilance, or some might say paranoia, but private military contract companies like Centurion Corporation had a tendency to build up defenses against the types of incursions they were hired to do themselves. Call it practice or peace of mind.

"It was an American submarine." She was staring at the panel of buttons for each floor.

Gabe studied the panel. "Yes."

Whatever she was seeing, he was missing it. He'd never been in a Chinese sub, but he didn't think she'd ever been in either.

"Well, I can't be sure, but in normal elevators some floor numbers are skipped. Like thirteen." Maylin pointed to the buttons for twelve and fourteen.

"Yeah." Still not sure where she was going.

"In buildings in certain Asian communities, any floor number containing the number four would be missing, too." She pointed to the four button on the panel. "So this wasn't a Chinese submarine."

Huh. Learn something new. "The number four an unlucky number?"

She laughed. "A lot of people are superstitious. Pretty sure that's a cross-cultural thing. In Chinese superstition, the number four sounds like the word for 'death.' I don't consider myself particularly superstitious, but in an exceptionally tall building, going to one of those floors does give me a cold chill. Maybe I'm not quite as Americanized as my stepmother despairs."

Having knowledge of one's ethnic roots gave a depth to a person. He envied her. Growing up, his mother'd put most of her effort into making them the All-American family with little to no emphasis on where she or his father'd come from. After his parents died, he'd spent his time in the foster system with only the name Diaz and a mirror to tell him about his background. His identity had been built with his own two hands in the service, then with the Centurions.

After a moment, she shook her head. "Ugh. Speaking of my stepmother, she also thinks I watch too many of those police procedural dramas on television. She might be right, and I hate admitting that, but after watching those, the idea of having one of these elevators in your company building totally makes sense in my brain."

"You like watching those?" Along with Asian dramas

and Japanese cartoons. Funny how unreal those shows were, and yet reality could be even less believable. Then again, if the average public found the things he'd seen in real life entertaining then he'd consider the human race doomed. He'd seen some sorry examples of what people were capable of.

She had her eyes on the floor light indicator, watching the slow progression upward. "Sometimes. There's usually a marathon of one series or another going on and I like to watch while I'm experimenting with recipes in my free time."

The elevator finally came to a stop and the doors opened to an atrium of polished dark marble. No insignia marked the floor or walls. As they crossed to a set of glass doors, only a small removable plaque marked the office space as Centurion Corporation. "You messing with ingredients for your business or for home?"

It was fun to watch her in a kitchen. Always in motion, taking charge with a confidence he found irresistible.

The receptionist inside had seen them coming and the magnetic lock disengaged with an audible click. He reached out and pulled open the glass door, motioning for Maylin to precede him.

She answered as she walked by, her tone calm and still conversational. "I look for new recipes to add to my themed menus, but they're usually made to serve a small dinner party. Scaling up to catering for between fifty to a few hundred isn't always simple math. There's practicality in food prep to be considered and approaches to presentation. Plus, deciding whether it can sit out as long as it would need to for a buffet. And every once in a while, kitchen chemistry can be unexpectedly exciting."

He snorted as they approached the reception desk. "You make it sound like pots explode."

Out of the corner of his eye, he caught her shrug. "Not saying they don't once in a while. There's also the occasional fireball."

Huh.

"Hey, Diaz." The young man at reception looked to be about sixteen. In reality, he was in his midtwenties and had been deployed with the Air Force as an officer once before deciding to move to the private sector. Caleb was doing his training with corporate before coming out to the Seattle branch to train with his new squadron. Officer training in the military had given him polish; the Centurion Corporation would give him seasoning. "We've been expecting you. Just need your associate to present a valid photo ID and sign in."

Maylin gave Caleb a smile as she pulled out her real driver's license. From over her shoulder, Gabe gave Caleb a warning glance as he caught the kid trying to get a better angle as Maylin leaned forward to sign on the electronic signature pad. Seriously, it was both attractive and infuriating the way she was unconsciously tempting. At least Gabe had confirmation her effect wasn't exclusively on him.

Caleb snorted as he assembled and handed her a plastic visitor badge with a label affixed to it displaying her name and identifying Gabe as her escort, all business now. "Here you go. Wear this someplace visible at all times. It's only good for the day. Red hatch marks come up on it after eight hours."

His ability to do his job and remain unintimidated by the older Centurions without insulting anyone was part of the reason he had a good future with them. He knew his stuff, got along with everyone, accepted each of them with their relatively dangerous quirks. Good man.

Maylin nodded. "Got it."

"You don't seem surprised." Gabe guided her beyond reception and down a hallway past a standard gray cube farm.

She clipped the badge to her shirt. "I've done catering for corporate luncheons. Badges are pretty standard. Some of them have an expiration date and some of them have this sort of visual thing to show the badge isn't good anymore. Had these kinds of badges before but wasn't expecting this level of formality in an organization like yours."

"We do business with all levels of corporations and government." Gabe led her to a small conference room at the back corner. The entire wall was glass, so anyone could easily see in, but it had a white noise generator and the exterior window was thermo-glass. Normal in appearance, but a secure place to put her for the time being. "Can you wait here? I'm going to report in and probably bring someone to come talk to you. Caleb will probably stop by in a minute to see if you need water or anything. Restroom is right next door."

"Okay." Maylin took a seat. She didn't appear completely serene, but she wasn't freaked out either.

Not bad considering he'd only told her they were coming to corporate to regroup and consider next steps. Not nearly as much information as she deserved, but he didn't want to promise anything until he'd confirmed he had the go-ahead. She was putting a lot of trust in him so he hadn't wanted to give her empty promises. He turned to leave and paused.

Ah, hell.

She looked up, eyes wide in surprise when he returned to her. He brushed a stray hair from her cheek. "You're safe here. I want to be sure you know."

She swallowed, her shoulders relaxing a fraction. "Okay."

Her run-in with Jewel had hit Maylin harder than she let on. For all that her expressions gave away her surface emotions: confusion, surprise, anger—he really shouldn't enjoy anger as much as he did—she was incredibly good at hiding her worries and insecurities.

He was going to need to see to it that he took those into consideration. Might have been easier for the other people in her life to just assume she could handle all the things, but he refused to leave her struggling. Recent intimacies notwithstanding, he found himself wanting to see her smile real smiles more often.

It was good for her to be wary of Jewel—there was no doubt which of them would come out on top in a fight. Jewel had the training and experience behind her to best most women and many men in hand to hand. But he needed to do something to reassure Maylin about what was between them, that he and Jewel were done. That might take a while. For the time being, he could address Maylin's anxieties about what players were in the mix when it came to the kidnapping.

"And we're going to get help for your sister. Edict complicates things, but it's not a showstopper."

"You haven't told me much about Edict yet except that they're another merc—contract group." Despite her assertion, her words came out in a whisper instead of a challenge. And he couldn't blame her for thinking of mercenaries when it came to them.

It was a label. Most people had the worst meaning in

mind when they thought of mercenaries. But he was what he was and he still made his choices based on what he decided was the right thing. Labels didn't bother him much.

"There's not a lot to tell you yet besides that. We'll get facts here and as soon as I have them, I'll share them with you. Trust me a little while longer."

"Only if you promise to make the next long elevator ride more fun."

She might have meant it as a joke, but desire roared through him, taking him by surprise. The visual of her with her head thrown back as he took her up against the wall of the elevator took over his entire mind for a full minute.

Down, boy.

"Careful what you wish for." Wrestling as he was with the idea of the multitude of elevators he could take her to, he couldn't be blamed for how gruff his voice had become. Right?

Desire sparked in her eyes. "Let's table that for another time."

Of course she had to mention tables. This conference room was looking tempting, too, glass and all.

He watched her, wondering how he could be struck by how beautiful she was multiple times a day. Not as if he ever found her unattractive, but he just never got used to it. She took his breath away. And as he saw her own breath catch under the weight of his gaze, he had a hell of a time wrenching his mental processes back to the mission at hand.

"I'll be back soon."

"You look wound up tighter than a violin string." The man behind the desk stood immediately and came around to pull Gabe into a quick hug, pounding him once on the back. "You need to go get laid or something."

"You've got a way with words, Harte." And he wasn't particularly wrong either. Gabe just had a specific lady in mind and a mission to complete first.

Harte was one of those men who could head into a bar and walk out with his choice of women. He wasn't pretty, per se. He oozed charm, though, and cleaned up good. He could also carry off the day-old-scruff look and still have women hanging all over him. That said, Harte's advantage was his brown hair, brown eyes, slightly taller than average height stats. Anyone taking a description of him would get very little in the way of distinctive details to go on if they were trying to track the man down.

People instantly liked and trusted Harte when they met him, then couldn't quite remember a day later. A very nice talent in their line of work. Besides, Harte actually enjoyed speaking to people. It was why he coordinated what major contracts they took and negotiated the terms, most of the time.

"How's the missing girl job going?" Harte dropped into one of two armchairs arranged in a conversational grouping with a leather couch to one side of his office.

Gabe sat on the edge of the other, leaning forward so his elbows rested on his knees, and threaded his fingers together. "Good news and bad news."

"Always the way. Gimme the bad news first."

"We're going to have to go through Edict to get to the missing girl. And since it's Edict, they've got deep pockets funding them." Gabe watched Harte closely to gauge his reaction.

Harte didn't move but his expression darkened. "Professionally speaking, they get things done."

"True."

And private military contractors like Edict made the term *mercenaries* an insult to the rest of them. A big part of the reason Gabe had joined Centurion Corporation after he'd been discharged had been the ethics the Centurions held higher than money. Maybe not as noble as the US military branches, but simple and humble: do the right thing.

"It's how and what they choose to do." Harte stood and headed for the small bar setup. "You need anything?"

"Nah." It wasn't that Gabe didn't drink. He just didn't need one right now.

"Here's some rocks in a glass so I don't feel like an asshole drinking by myself." Harte returned holding the promised tumbler out. "What the hell is their acronym again? It's some long ass thing."

Gabe took the tumbler. "*Edict* is an acronym?"

Well, shit, he'd have to do some digging. Never occurred to him to look.

"Not officially. One of the boys came up with it one night after a particularly irritating scrape with them. I think we'd need to be shit-faced drunk to remember it." Harte took a sip of his scotch. "It was funny as hell at the time."

Not much humor in the current situation, though. "The added bad news is Jewel is working for Edict now and directly involved in this situation."

Harte stared at Gabe, took another drink, and stared at Gabe again. "Didn't she shoot you?"

"Yeah. But I got better." And he didn't plan to give Jewel the opportunity to do it again.

"She's not carrying around her AK, is she?"

Gabe shook his head. "Not unless she's got a creative way to hide it."

Jewel hadn't been dressed to seduce when she'd approached Maylin, but the mercenary had still been wearing a sleek power suit emphasizing all things female. Maybe it'd been intended to intimidate Maylin, but as far as Gabe could tell Jewel hadn't phased her. His girl had tread with a healthy dose of wariness once he'd arrived, but only because she'd been sensitive to his tension. When it came to self-confidence, Maylin was very comfortable in her own skin, and it'd take more than Jewel to shake that.

He liked it. A lot. Even if it would be safer if Maylin backed down when it came to confronting Jewel one-on-one.

"I'll have Caleb update the file on her and run a search on any additional info we might not have from her recent adventures." Harte leaned back in the chair. "With Edict involved, this is a bigger job than one or two fire teams can take. Especially with your members in recovery, you included."

It was important for a person to know his own limits. So far, this mission had been well within his. If they had to go head-to-head with Edict in a serious engagement, he might be more of a liability than a leader. He'd cross that bridge when he came to it.

"It's somewhat more complicated than what I had in mind when I recommended we take on a few smaller domestic jobs before heading back overseas." Gabe tried to keep neutral. Take his time. Harte was taking his temperature on the situation every bit as much as Gabe was assessing Harte.

"I liked the initial recommendation." Harte chuckled.

"There's an email sitting in your inbox regarding the idea in general, by the way."

"That the one with 'Safeguard Project' in the subject line?" Gabe struggled to remember. "I've got it flagged to read as soon as I catch a minute to spare."

"No worries. I'd want to see how all of this pans out in any case." Harte shook his glass. "What do we know about the funding behind Edict currently?"

"Not as much as we need." Gabe had Marc and Lizzy gathering intel but corporate headquarters might have more immediate information. "So far, the trail leads to a small biotech out in California. Apparently they've invited Miss An-mei Cheng to do research for them."

"Doesn't sound like the kind of company to have the funds to back Edict. What kind of research?"

"Need more details on that, too, but my contact had the impression her research had some creative military applications."

"What sort of research does this girl do?"

"Genetic. Maylin says her sister is at the forefront of her field in gene therapy and recombinant DNA, working with gene-editing proteins and how they get into human cells. Potential treatment for genetic disorders in live patients." And wasn't that a mouthful? Gabe had spoken to Maylin at length on the flight from Seattle to be sure he could say it all without stuttering. For a woman with a completely different career, Maylin had a far more thorough understanding of her sister's research than expected. Gabe had no doubt his girl was every bit as intelligent as her little sister.

Considering how many people trapped themselves in a miserable job because the job description reflected their intelligence level, Gabe thought Maylin was a whole lot wiser than most in choosing what would be right for her even if her family didn't respect what she did.

Maylin had built a challenging, fulfilling career for herself with her catering company and she was *happy*.

He could learn a lot from her.

"Considering the potential applications, I'm doubting this biotech company is so interested in the girl for humanitarian reasons. If they have her, they'll have some real security around her. Otherwise, it'd be awkward to explain to the US authorities if she somehow finds her way home. You're not going to walk into a research lab and find her there holding test tubes, chained to a lab bench. There's going to be layers of security and personnel to get past. Even if all we have to worry about is Edict, it'll be a challenge." Harte leaned forward and set his half-drunk glass on the low table between them. "Your girl can't have the funds to pay for the kind of operation it will take to get her sister back."

And here was the difficult part.

"No." It killed him to say it. But resources, ammunition, equipment, they all came with a high price tag. Maylin was not independently wealthy. "At the beginning I'd hoped once we found the sister, it would be something doable with a four-man fire team. The more we find out, the bigger this whole thing is looking."

Harte shook his head. "What made you take this on in the first place?"

"Someone tried to run her down right in front of me." Gabe clamped his mouth shut. Swallowed arguments that'd only waste time. This wasn't going well, and he wasn't going to be able to change Harte's mind if he came across like a man gone soft. Practical reasoning was what he needed.

Harte sighed. "Knight in shining armor syndrome. Every fucking one of us falls victim to it."

"It's why we work for Centurion and not Edict." It was petty to say. Gabe did anyway.

The difference between Centurion and Edict was a set of ethics. A moral code. The members of Centurion Corporation had one and were willing to sacrifice profit for it. They were also pickier about what contracts they took in the first place. It meant they suffered through some complicated decisions.

Edict kept things straightforward. Pay them and they got the job done. No matter how wrong it was.

"You hinted there was good news in here somewhere." Harte peered mournfully into his glass.

"Since the biotech sponsor does have offices in Tianjin, I initially thought we'd need to go there to locate and extract An-mei Cheng." Gabe sipped some of the melted ice water in his glass. "Our little run-in with Jewel included a slip of the tongue. Indicates the sister is actually in the States."

"No shit?" Harte raised an eyebrow.

Gabe nodded. "Worth checking out their facility in California and any other sizable holdings they have domestically before taking the search to the other side of the world."

"Keep me posted." Harte stood. "Can't give you additional resources right now, and I'm guessing you knew it walking in here. We're good men but we're running a business, not a charity. It's my job to keep us business-minded enough to stay well into the black every year when the books are balanced, even if I have to be the asshole."

There'd been a small hope. But the decision was made

and communicated. Gabe didn't waste time or emotion on disappointment. "Our team has decided to move forward with locating the girl. We'll renegotiate once the initial goal is achieved."

Harte nodded. "You do that."

Chapter Twelve

Gabe took himself out of Harte's office and strode down the hallway. He wanted to get outside and take a run or head to the nearest gym and pound a punching bag. Do something to take the edge off his temper when there wasn't anything he could do about the hard news he had to give. Neither of those was a good option at the moment, with limited time and Maylin waiting for him.

Still, he ducked inside a conference room at the other end of the suite and starting pacing. He wasn't ready to give the update to Maylin yet. Too many things didn't fit.

He'd have been fine if he'd never had to deal with Jewel again. Some part of him had known he would have to, though. The business of private military contractors had a high turnover rate but it was a small world. They'd have ended up on a multi-contractor job together—or ended up like this, set to go head-to-head. All things said and done, it was less complicated as it stood.

Still, a couple of questions were hanging out there and he didn't like letting them go unanswered. Jewel wasn't as good a distance shooter as Lizzy, but she could've made a head shot in that last mission. She could have killed him. He'd spent his recovery rapidly progressing through the shock and betrayal, setting those aside and dismissing the whole thing, assuming she'd decided leaving him crippled was worse than dead. He'd gotten good and angry then and used it to fuel his temper and get himself back on his feet.

Now? He wasn't so sure. She might not have adjusted her shot out of spite.

He and his teammates didn't pry into each other's backgrounds much. They had all met as they'd joined the Centurions. All any of them had ever needed to know about their teammates was who they were as Centurions: skill sets, abilities, anything lending to the completion of a given mission. Strengths and weaknesses were reviewed in terms of performance.

But none of those things gave insight into why people did the shit they did. Gabe wasn't particularly fond of psyches, but he saw the value in a therapy session if it helped a person get their head back on straight. With Jewel and her fire team leaving the Centurions, he'd assumed they'd made a simple choice: money.

Her having chosen not to kill him added a twist to the logic. And her showing up now mucked things up. Made it more difficult. Because he didn't want to wonder if she was going to take him out this time, or worse, kill Maylin.

Gabe dragged a hand through his hair and cursed.

He'd always been a no-strings-attached kind of guy. When he mixed it up with a woman, it was for mutual enjoyment and lasted only as long as convenient. No regrets when it came time to walk away.

He halted and planted his hands on the windowsill, looking out and not seeing anything. He couldn't walk away from Maylin the same way. It wasn't just about missing her. Even considering leaving her opened up a hole inside him.

No idea what it meant, but the thought of Jewel or her team doing anything to Maylin filled him with ice cold fear.

Fear slowed a man down, made him hesitate, second guess. If he couldn't see clearly, he was going to make a mistake. He needed to decide how to move forward with the least amount of damage.

His phone rang. Yanking it out of his pocket, he growled, "Diaz."

"Lykke here. You okay? You sound pissed."

Gabe sighed. "Nah. Just working through some reality over here."

"Ah." Marc probably had a good idea of what the reality was, but he'd wait until Gabe briefed the team. "Well, I got some bad news to add."

"Sure." Great. Fantastic. "Better now than later. Go ahead."

"Porter van Lumanee died. Diagnosis still indicates food poisoning as the root cause." Marc didn't sound too broken up about it. "I managed to find a few different email accounts for the guy in addition to his work email. An-mei Cheng was the first scientist he was tasked with approaching and acquiring, but if it had gone successfully, she wouldn't have been the last. There's one or two other emails with information on other scientists. None of them are missing."

"Yet." Gabe pushed away from the windowsill and started pacing again.

"I'll get an anonymous tip in to the universities they do research for and to the local authorities."

Gabe nodded. It'd keep any other players distracted. "Good. Anything else?"

"He had some interesting deposits to an overseas

banking account. I'm trying to track the source but it's going to take a while." Marc was typing away as he spoke. "Best I can tell you is that it wasn't the biotech firm—Phoenix Biotech—and it wasn't Edict."

"So we're looking at an anonymous sponsor." Gabe frowned.

"If we make some judicious assumptions, it'd be a good guess that the same sponsor is giving the orders to Phoenix Biotech and Edict."

Gabe didn't disagree. It made sense. The biotech company would have a board of directors, but this sort of activity required a more direct line of decision making. "Take a close look at the board of directors for Phoenix Biotech. Could be one of them or a connection."

"In progress." Marc hesitated then added, "The email about An-mei is pretty concise. Just includes her photograph and bio, some instructions to invite her to the conference and offer her the opportunity to do cutting-edge research for a private organization. There's not even a mention of Phoenix Biotech. Definitely no information on who picked up the next part of the job. Van Lumanee's instructions left him in a silo, separate from other players."

So Porter van Lumanee was a dead end.

"Smart sponsor." And where did that leave Gabe and his team? "Keep digging, but proceed with caution. It'd be good to figure out if this is potentially a government program or a private interest."

They really didn't need to get mixed up in government activity. The US government had a different way of approaching its intellectual resources, more ethical. And a foreign government wouldn't likely have facilities on US soil where they couldn't have absolute control. So it wasn't likely, but it was best to confirm.

"Roger that." Marc ended the call.

Gabe cursed. They'd turned up information but weren't any closer to finding their missing person. And even when they did, they weren't going to be able to do anything about it.

He still had too many questions unanswered, and wearing down the carpet in here wasn't going to do anyone any good, so he headed back to Maylin. At least he'd gotten things organized in his head so he could address them.

As he rounded the corner of a row of cubicles, he had line of sight on Maylin, still sitting in the conference room and playing with the phone he'd given her. She was backlit, the light from the outside windows a bright contrast to her silhouette. Seeing every elegant line, every curve of her stopped him in his tracks. Damn, the woman took his breath away.

And he was about to tell her there wouldn't be enough help to get her sister back.

She'd waited long enough. He wasn't going to dodge giving her the bad news. So he got himself walking again and crossed the last few yards.

Maylin looked up as he approached, her face clearing as she caught sight of him. Hope shone in her eyes and he swallowed hard.

"What are you up to?" Okay, he was going to dodge for a minute. He just couldn't give it to her cold.

"Hmm?" She looked down at the smartphone in her hands. "Oh! I downloaded a game I play. I hope it's okay. Caleb got me connected to the guest Wi-Fi."

Gabe leaned forward and got a look at some cartoon-y dragons and a grid of spheres in multiple colors. "Once we return your phone we'll reset this one back to factory settings, so it's not going to matter much. What kind of game is it?"

"My sister got me into playing it." Maylin gave him a sad smile. "It helps when I get more worried about her than I can handle to jump in and play. It's mostly a pattern recognition–based game. Match up spheres of the same color, and the corresponding monster in your team does damage to the monsters in the dungeon."

"Huh." Okay then. He wasn't sure what to say. Video games weren't his thing.

"There's a simple messaging system in-game, too." She held up the screen to show him. "This was An-mei's last message to me before she disappeared. This is how I initially knew something was wrong. She wasn't logging in to play the game, and she logs in *every* day, multiple times a day. Any time she needs to reset her mind after being too deep in the research. The message freaked me out."

The message was simple…and weird.

Hey. Miss you. aTaaTaac aTGacTaT aTGaTGcc aTGTaaaa

"What is that?" He'd seen plenty of codes. This one? New to him, and he'd bet Marc would love to take a look at it.

She huffed out a laugh. "It's a silly thing we started doing after I went through high school biology. You know how kids like to send their notes to each other? This is like leet-speak, but for me and her."

"But biology-based?" Something familiar about it, but damn, biology class had been a long time ago.

"It's DNA bases used to indicate binary." She murmured

and pointed to the message. "*T* and *G* equal one, and *A* and *C* equal zero."

"Then you take the binary to create a message." He shook his head. Morse code, he had a chance of reading. Binary? Not his strong point.

"An-mei could read this just by looking at it." Pride filled Maylin's words. "I got out of practice after college so I need an online translator for the longer messages. This one, though, it's short and simple. It's how I knew she needed me."

DNA and binary. Generally not things a person saw combined. Maylin and her sister had some serious brain power between them.

He stared at the letters. "What does it say?"

"Here?" Maylin pointed to the four groupings of letters on the first line. "It says 'help.'"

Got it. Definitely alarming. "So it wasn't just that she wasn't logging in to play anymore."

"That's why I knew to look for her right away and not wait the forty-eight hours the police said I should." She paused. "I should have shown you and your team. But I didn't want you to dismiss me because of a kid's secret code in a game app."

Some kid's code. It was pretty complex from where he was standing.

"We're closer to finding her, aren't we?"

Her hope just about ripped him up inside. "We're narrowed down to the continent we're on. We'll see."

They'd take it one step at a time, and hopefully, he wouldn't have to tell her they'd reached the end of their resources.

Chapter Thirteen

"You can sleep if you want." Gabe made the offer as he guided his car onto the main highway heading out of the Seattle airport.

Maylin smiled in spite of the anxiety pushing at her. The trip to DC and back had exhausted her. She was still processing what she'd learned from her encounter with Jewel and what Gabe had shared with her. But she didn't feel any closer to finding An-mei.

Was it really likely that An-mei was still alive?

Was the situation better or worse?

What else could Maylin do?

Too many questions, and worse, every time she thought of the few hours she'd spent with Gabe in the hotel room she burned with embarrassment...and desire to do it again.

Oh, she didn't regret. Not at all. She'd made the decision to change her focus drastically and he'd given her every chance to consider a different option. He'd been an incredible partner and had been considerate since.

But she'd gotten a good look at Jewel. Completely different in physicality, demeanor and personality. If Jewel had been a match for Gabe, how could Maylin be anything but a passing interest?

And if Jewel was one of the people who had An-mei, Maylin needed to find a way through the woman regardless of what she might still mean to Gabe.

Maylin almost laughed at herself. Considering the confidence in Jewel's attitude towards Gabe and their common line of work, Maylin did not have the skills to get past either of them when it came to conventional means.

"Hey." Gabe's voice was kind, even a little teasing, maybe? He'd gone back to mostly gruff and neutral since they'd left the Centurion's corporate headquarters. Withdrawn from her and hopefully mulling over the challenge ahead of them.

"Mmm?" She kept her gaze on the passing roadside as the view changed from buildings to trees to buildings again. They weren't headed to downtown Seattle the way she was used to.

"I can almost hear the gears turning in your head." Gabe reached over and held out his hand, palm up.

She blinked, unsure of how much the gesture meant. A sneaky warmth bloomed in her chest and she placed her hand in his. His fingers closed around hers and gently squeezed. So much reassurance in his touch. When he rubbed his thumb lightly across the back of her hand, her breath caught and delicious shivers ran along her skin.

"You barely slept on the plane." Gabe accompanied the admonishment with a gentle squeeze to her hand. "This car ride isn't going to be long, and you staying awake won't get us there faster."

She glanced at the speedometer. "Do you always follow the speed limit?"

"Not always, no." He kept his attention on the road. "But I choose when to hurry."

It sounded wise but there was more. Or at least she figured there ought to be. "Okay, I'll bite. Why?"

"That a promise?" He shot her a playful glance and returned his attention to driving.

Reservations about comparing herself to Jewel evaporated, at least for the moment. She liked his kind of play. "Maybe. Depends on if you'll return the favor."

Not hard. But the idea of his teeth grazing her skin, gently pressing against her... Her breath quickened and her nipples tightened under her shirt.

"I'll be sure to remind you about this mutual promise." He continued to rub his thumb ever so lightly across the back of her hand. The sensation didn't fade or lessen in impact.

He gave her one more squeeze and released her hand. "In the meantime, I'll tell you why an experienced person doesn't hurry up just to wait in every situation. It's a waste of energy better spent when you actually need it."

"I can see how that makes sense." She considered for a minute. "You've been in situations where you had to do it. It mattered a lot."

"People's lives depended on it," Gabe agreed. "If I didn't have enough in reserve to do what had to be done—"

"You would have found it." Maybe she shouldn't have cut him off. Still... "I'm probably naive and I definitely don't know what you've faced overseas. But I can't imagine you not giving every last drop of energy you had to doing the right thing."

And she meant it. It resonated inside her. And maybe she was a little afraid of her own truth because she believed it so completely.

"I've failed." His hands tightened on the steering wheel. "Don't make me out to be infallible."

She was brushing off on him. He was far more educated than he'd seemed at first, with an extensive vocabulary. But she noticed, and liked, the way he only flexed his way with words around her. At least, as far as she knew.

"You're human." This time she reached out to him, tentatively touching his thigh with her fingertips. His muscles bunched under the fabric of his jeans. "And we make mistakes. But it doesn't mean you don't give everything you have."

Faith. She had it in him. At least to do the right thing and help her. But she wasn't sure about what would happen once they'd reached their currently mutual goal. Then it wouldn't be about doing the right thing anymore. It'd be a choice.

What she was hoping for, she didn't have the courage to ask.

Gabe sighed. "Don't make me a hero. I'm a man with a set of skills and eventually, I need to earn a p—"

Something popped. Loud. And the car's forward motion jerked. Instead of slamming on the brakes, Gabe cursed and kept his foot on the gas pedal. Or at least she assumed so since they weren't slowing down. As the car's forward motion steadied, Gabe let the car decelerate and flipped up the turn signal as they pulled over.

His expression was grim as he yanked up the parking brake. "Stay in here for now. Keep the window cracked so you can hear me and be ready to get down if I tell you to."

Ice shot through her. "What happened?"

"Could be a normal tire blowout." He unbuckled his

seat belt. "But in case it isn't, be ready to do what I tell you. No questions."

"Okay." Fear started to trickle in and she reined in the flurry of what ifs until Gabe could tell her what happened. Like he said, it could be a normal flat tire.

"While I'm checking this out, call the team." He opened the car door. "Whoever is on watch will answer. Tell them we've made an unplanned stop. They'll send someone out to give us support."

She fumbled with the phone and called the number listed as "Centurion-Seattle." It was that or "Centurion-DC" so she figured she'd picked the right one.

"Yeah."

The sound of Victoria's voice was all the trigger Maylin needed to spill the message. Victoria listened until Maylin finished.

Her response was succinct. "Sending Lizzy."

And then Victoria ended the call.

Maylin lowered her window a crack and called out to Gabe.

"Got it." He didn't even pause as he answered.

He had his gun with him. Actually he had more than one. He hadn't flown with them, but he'd taken the time to pull on his shoulder harness when they'd gotten back to the car. Maylin had wondered if he had a favorite and he'd gruffly told her she watched too many TV shows.

All of which were flashing through her very over-active imagination as he worked his way around to the passenger side. He was scanning the area around them, and Maylin looked out, too. They were isolated here. It was one of those short stretches of highway lined with trees, hiding the nearby houses and businesses from view. She wasn't familiar with this highway, though, so she had no idea how deep the stands of trees were. Could be a short walk before you'd end up in someone's backyard, or it could be surprisingly longer. Hard to tell as you got closer to the state parks and reserves.

He seemed satisfied for a moment and crouched down to examine the tire. He scowled.

"Out. Out of the car."

Maylin scrambled to undo her seat belt. It stuck. She took a deep breath and tried again. And one more time. It wasn't releasing. "I can't."

Fear filled her. She wanted to shout at him to get away and to help her at the same time. But mostly, she wanted him away. He could help An-mei.

He was on his feet and at her door so fast she didn't see him move. He yanked at her door but it wouldn't open. Both of them looked at the lock. It was popped up, appeared unlocked. Maylin tried the door from her side. It wouldn't open.

Tā mā de.

He cursed, too, out loud. It was weird to hear, calm and cold but still explicit enough to make her blink. "Get your window down as far as you can."

At least they both knew the window was working, since she'd cracked it when he first stepped out of the car. She pressed the button to lower it in a careful and deliberate motion, afraid it might jam or something if she hit it. Probably stupid, but hell. This was not the time to be breaking things in a rush.

The window lowered smoothly. As soon as he could get over it, Gabe leaned in with something dark in his hand. He pulled her seat belt away from her chest and hooked it with the thing he was holding—a utility knife with a seat belt cutter. The fabric of the seat belt parted easily. He did the same at her lap instead of wasting more time to pull it loose. So glad he hadn't had to use an actual open blade. What if she'd twitched?

"Just put your arms around my neck and let me pull you out. Watch your head." Gabe coaxed her to him and tightened his arms around her torso as she leaned towards him. As soon as he had her out the window and set her on her feet, he grabbed her by the hand and yanked her into a run.

She ducked her head and watched the ground. At this speed she didn't have much time to watch where she was going, but she did her best not to trip as they reached the tree line. Last thing he needed was for her to slow them both down.

He pulled her down behind the large trunk of a tree.

She crouched in the shelter of his arm, trying to make herself as small as possible. Her throat burned from sucking in air as they'd run. Her mouth had gone dry. She could blame that on either the run or fear. She'd settle on the former since the latter wasn't something she had time to contemplate. Instead, she worked on settling her churning stomach and hoped her heart wouldn't beat its way through her sternum. If they needed to run again, it'd be best if she could catch her breath.

Long seconds went by. Shivering against him, the rock solid strength of him anchored her, helped keep panic at bay. She'd expected something to have happened. Maybe a loud boom.

She lifted her head. "Wha—?"

BOOM.

The sound of the explosion reached them first. Cursing, Gabe tucked her close against him as a concussive shock wave passed right through the tree—and them.

She felt it deep in her chest, like being right next to giant speakers at a dance party when the DJ had gone crazy with the bass. Wildlife in the surrounding trees called out in alarm, and leaves fell all around them.

As suddenly as it came, it'd passed, and Gabe was easing up his hold on her. "Are you all right?"

She nodded. He scowled. She cleared her throat and gave him a verbal answer. "Yes. I'm all right."

He gave her a terse nod and then turned his gaze towards the car. Peering around the trunk of the tree, fear came crawling back up from the bottom of her belly and she tasted bile at the back of her throat.

It was like someone had gotten under the car near the front tire and shot a rocket up into the passenger side. Fire and smoke filled the interior and a hole had been blown through the roof of the car. Chunks of twisted metal and what might have been parts of the seat poked out through the new sun roof.

Her seat. She'd been sitting there, trapped by the seat belt.

Her lungs seized and her stomach churned. She turned away from the car, away from Gabe, and threw up.

Gabe's big hand was rubbing her back in soothing circles. He was helping her hold her hair back, too. She didn't care. She heaved and heaved again until there was nothing. Then her stomach cramped and she gagged on the taste of bile.

"Easy. Try to breathe in through your nose, out through your mouth. Go ahead and spit out the taste if you have to. We'll get you water as soon as we can." Gabe's voice as he spoke to her was soothing, low, but changed pitch to sharp and demanding as she heard him dial his phone and start talking. "Lizzy? ETA? Going to need cleanup."

Maylin couldn't hear Lizzy's response, but she couldn't stand bent over anymore. She straightened, using the tree trunk for support, and sucked in more air. She looked around the tree and saw smoke billowing from the top of the car. A few flames still licked the inside of the car cabin.

Thank goodness she had the loaner phone and wallet with her in her pockets. Her duffel bag was in the car. She was going to need more clothes.

The trivial nature of the thought caught her and a giggle bubbled up in her throat, gained momentum, and she clamped her hands over her mouth hard to stop herself before she escalated into full-on insane laughter.

Hysteria. Had to be.

"Meet us about a half mile north of current location. Track our GPS signal." Gabe ended the call and dropped his phone into his pocket.

"You can do that? Even on the way?" Maylin blurted out the questions. Too much adrenaline, no more filters.

Gabe hugged her to his chest for a split second. "With the right tech, yeah. It's why I had you leave your smartphone back with Marc and gave you the temp. C'mon, we're walking."

Walking was good. Way better than running. "Well, yeah, I figured you had to be in a sort of control room or central computer hub to do it, though."

He shook his head as he led her on a path parallel to the road, inside the tree line. "There's an app for that."

She choked out a laugh. "You didn't just say that."

"It's true, though." He glanced at her and gave her

a small grin before returning his attention to their surroundings.

"I don't remember you having this much of a sense of humor the last time a car tried to kill me."

"The last one was trying to run you over. This one just tried to launch you into the atmosphere."

One foot in front of the other. Putting distance between them and the smoldering car was a good idea. There was no use getting freaked out about him saying it out loud if she'd already survived it. "It's worse when you say it out loud."

"I didn't until we were away from it." His voice had gentled, a note of concern.

"I know." And she bit her lip. "I'm sorry. It's like I'm just saying anything crossing my mind right now. Words are just popping out left and right and there's no stopping them."

"Not a bad thing."

"Easy for you to say. You're experienced with this. Do you ever get used to it all?" She wasn't sure she wanted to know the answer so she kept talking, keeping her voice low even though he'd have told her if he needed her to be silent. "It happened and I saw where I could've been sitting. Only I'm not and I am very glad to be walking here."

"Absorb it all later," he advised. "Here. Now. You act. Listen to what I tell you to do and trust your gut. You've come through this great so far. Keep doing it."

"Really?" She had an inane moment imagining herself as the first victim to die in a bad horror movie.

"Yes." He paused. "Don't get cocky."

She smiled. And tripped.

His hand around her shoulders kept her from falling

flat on her face. She kind of wished she had, so she could hide her burning cheeks.

"All right? You didn't hurt your ankle, did you?" He didn't stop but he'd slowed down.

Last thing she wanted to be was dead weight. Ignoring the very minor twinge in her right ankle, she paced him. "No. I'll try to keep a better eye on where I'm putting my feet."

"This is far enough anyway." He pulled her into the shelter of another tree. "We'll wait for Lizzy to pull up."

The tree line was closer to the road here, and she could see buildings through the trees all around them. A sound barrier picked up where the trees left off some ways ahead of them.

She took a good look at Gabe then, the tension in his jaw. "You *are* mad."

"Not at you."

"What, then?" She tilted her head until it rested against the inside of his shoulder. He'd told her to leave his arms free when they were outside. Even if he had one around her now, she didn't want to hang on to it in case he needed to let go of her in a hurry. So she wrapped her arms around herself to avoid the temptation of holding on to him.

"I should have checked the car more closely before we got into it." He scowled. "I didn't anticipate them finding my car, tampering with it."

His phone rang.

Chapter Fourteen

"Hello." Gabe had an idea of who it might be, but since the caller came up as unknown on his phone, he'd wait to see if life would surprise him.

"Still ever so warm and charming when you answer your calls, I see." Jewel's voice came across the line.

Nope. Not this time.

"Still doing your dirty work from a distance," he shot back. Gabe, one. Recent life surprises, zero.

At his side, Maylin stared at him with narrowed eyes. It wouldn't take her long to figure out who'd called, if she hadn't already.

"Oh, you enjoy my little present? I had one of my colleagues pop it into the tire for you as a teaser and leave the main gift right where you'd see it." She laughed. "How far are you from the car at this point?"

Far enough away to have survived the blast, as she obviously knew. No need to give her any more detail, but he scanned the surrounding area for more gifts.

Seeing the damned second detonator hadn't been a surprise after the initial blowout, but he hadn't been prepared for the shot of fear that cut through him as he'd glanced up to see Maylin watching him from inside the car. Getting her out had overridden any other thought in his head.

"Did you have your new boy toy tamper with the car door and seat belt, too? Or were those personal touches from him?" It'd be good to know. Gabe planned to hunt the bastard down for this, but it never hurt to know exactly which parts had been the other man's idea.

Maylin's lips pressed together in a grim line. She motioned for the phone and mimed her talking into it.

He gave her what he hoped was a quelling look. Her eyes narrowed even further and he wondered just how badly he was going to pay for that later.

"I might have given him some helpful ideas, but the final touches were all his." Jewel had to be aware of Gabe's intentions. Still, she'd thrown the other man under the bus, and she might not even warn the guy unless she liked him. It was one of her habits Gabe didn't miss.

"The detonators are your guilty pleasure." Gabe wondered what she wanted, following up with the call. Maybe her *colleague* hadn't managed to tail them close enough to confirm whether they'd been caught in the explosion or not. She did like to confirm just how much damage she'd done with her handiwork. "Never saw a vehicle you didn't want to explode."

"This is true. I do like to make things go boom." He could picture the slow smile spreading across her lips. A long time ago he might've grinned at the thought, but now only a slow burn of anger built. He and she had been in solid sync once upon a time. Not anymore. "But I don't want your little galley cook dead yet. I just want to put a touch of proper fear into her. She was much too confident when I had the pleasure of meeting her."

He wrapped his arm around Maylin tighter. If Jewel was set on killing her, he'd go under and take Maylin with him. Once they were away, no one would find them.

"Really, Gabe. You are so very serious. It's why I sent you those presents. Without me around, who would keep you guessing?"

Maylin muttered against his shoulder and lifted her fist to give him a solid thump on the chest.

There were going to be dire consequences for keeping her out of this conversation, and he must be going insane, because he was pretty sure he was looking forward to them. He grinned. "Is that what you're doing?"

"Hmm."

"What do you want, Jewel?" Not likely to tell him, but the cat and mouse game had gone on long enough. He was done.

"This was a reminder for you, too, in case your short time out made you forget." Jewel's voice had become hard, the words concise. "I can take out the older sister at any time. Keep her under control. Have her quit looking for her sister and there won't be any more problems."

The last finished on a sweet note. He did not miss these dramatic outbursts from her. A person could deliver a message without the melodrama.

"I think we're getting too close to knowing more than we should." He let his own arrogance shine through. She did bring out the asshole in him. "This isn't about one woman looking for her runaway sister anymore. That's not news. We're about to expose something sensitive to your employers. What will you do?"

Silence.

"While I'm glad I'm not blown to pieces, most of my readily available wardrobe is. The duffel had most of my clothes in it. I'm going to need to go back to my apartment again to get more."

Maylin ignored Gabe's scowl in response to her statement and crossed her arms, leaning back against the kitchen counter. The guest cabin at Centurion Corporation was familiar compared to the hotel the previous night, and felt a little like coming home.

She was being perfectly reasonable, but having gotten her safely back to Centurion Corporation grounds, Gabe seemed less than thrilled with the idea of taking her someplace unsecured again anytime soon. Especially a place the enemy already knew about, like her apartment.

He might have a point. Another one of Jewel's little presents was likely waiting for her. A shudder ran through her. Gabe lived with these kinds of possibilities every day. Would she ever go back to her own way of walking through life, not worrying about intruders and bombs?

Not for a long time.

Still, she wouldn't live in fear of the possibilities. Practicality had to have a place in there, too. "I need clothes and I can't afford to buy new ones. Plus, there's really no time to go through all that."

"You need rest. Real sleep." He might've tried to keep the growl out of his voice. Maybe.

Probably not.

She kept her mouth shut. Obviously he was set to be as stubborn as she was. His dark glower was incredibly sexy, if she wanted to admit it.

"Clothes are a necessity, whatever steps we're taking next." Keep the words measured. Go for patience. Bumping heads was one thing, but she didn't want to pick an actual fight.

Instead of getting more obstinate, he grinned. "Well, I can think of a few activities for the immediate future in which clothes are superfluous."

"Using a big word or two there. Maybe you've gotten practice in your recent conversations." She clamped her hands over her mouth as soon as she said it. Gah, it sounded obnoxious. She was angry he hadn't let her have choice words with Jewel. But the level-headed part of her brain acknowledged there would have been little constructive to come out of it.

In a way, Jewel had been baiting her again.

Gabe shrugged, not bothered. "*You* are a good influence on me. To be honest, it's fun talking with you. It stretches my vocabulary some."

"Really?" Not what she'd expected. Every person on his team was intelligent. Their level of skill was obvious and their confidence in each other only reinforced the impression.

"On missions, conversational skills tend to be reduced to the shortest sentences required to get a message across. Sometimes we don't even use words if a motion is enough." Gabe made a few hand signs. "No one in a combat situation has time for in-depth discussion. It washes over into our day-to-day life, and we get to be frugal about our word counts."

"I don't mind." He had been short with her in the beginning. Concise. Some people might've considered him rude. She'd figured it was about expediency. But she liked this, learning more about why he was the way he was. It filled her with warmth.

"Anyway," he continued, watching her. The heat in his gaze made her breath catch. "It's worth remembering words are meant for more than decisive action once in a while, for special people."

She huffed out a laugh. "And what about the majority of the populace?"

He shrugged and stepped towards her, close. "Not worth the syllables."

Another laugh bubbled up and got lost as she locked gazes with him, and her heart started to pound in her chest. Thoughts scampered away and all she had left was…wow. He was intense, and suddenly a very potent sexual being. "I thought you wanted to hold off on…exploring what's between us until we've rescued An-mei."

It'd been a struggle to remember what phrase he'd used. Actually, her own vocabulary was quickly evaporating.

"What's between us is a whole lot more than physical. At least, for me." His voice had gone darker, roughened with honest emotion. "Not to say it isn't a significant part of it. And right now I've got a serious need to make sure every part of you is safe and sound."

His hands came up and gripped her upper arms with a light, firm pressure. She placed her own palms on his waist and leaned her forehead against his chest.

"The car." He paused and wrapped his arms around her, hugging her close. "When we couldn't get you out of it. I just about died inside."

She'd been frightened. Very. But thinking more about what Gabe might've seen in the past, she wondered what nightmare possibilities had gone through his head when her seat belt jammed?

"I'm here. I'm okay." She rubbed her face into his shirt, breathed in the earthy smell of him. He was her safety.

"I just…" His heart rate was picking up, the beat of it a strong rhythm against her ear. "I need to know you're here."

She nodded. Not sure she understood.

His hands started to roam, rubbing and massaging up and down her back and arms. Everywhere he touched came alive under his palms. He was checking for injuries, she realized, but this was so much more intimate. Careful.

In a sudden movement, he had her by the waist and boosted her up to sit on the kitchen counter. It surprised a gasp out of her and he stilled, looked into her face. She bit her lip and gave him a small smile.

This was okay. "Caught me by surprise, that's all. Nothing hurt."

"Good." The tightness around his eyes and mouth relaxed a little.

Returning to his inspection, he started with her thighs and worked his way down each leg. His touch still firm, massaging and waking up her senses until her awareness of him was at an all-time high. She swallowed hard when he got to her right ankle.

"Swollen." He carefully removed her shoe and sock, taking a closer look.

"I twisted it when we walked away from the car. It doesn't hurt." In fact, the swelling had to be minimal. "Honestly, I've walked off worse just turning wrong in the kitchen. It's fine."

He bent and kissed the side of her ankle anyway.

Fire ran up her leg and to her core. Her breath caught. She swallowed hard.

He straightened then and cupped her face in his hand. "That was closer than it should've been. I should've taken better care of you."

She leaned into his palms. "You saved my life. Kept me safe."

The smile he gave her was sad somehow. She wanted

to take it away and replace it with a different kind of emotion.

And right now, she wanted nothing more than for him to touch her more. Her skin was hot all over. She'd never felt so alive than with him in the past couple of days, and need had built up inside her until she was wet. Telling him was an option, but she preferred decisive action.

Gripping either side of his waist, she spread her knees and pulled him in until his hips were snug against her. He let her, his dark gaze burning into her and his hands sliding to her neck in a slow caress. She wasn't alone in her desire—that much was obvious in the hard ridge of his erection inside his jeans.

"Kiss me?" She whispered the request.

Fire sparked in his eyes and he bent, capturing her mouth in a kiss so deep she decided air was a frivolous requirement. He cupped the back of her head with one big hand, encouraging her to tilt for even more access. His other hand swept down her side and back up to cup one of her breasts. She let out a needful groan, squeezing her thighs around his hips and running her hands over the hard planes of his chest.

He shifted his embrace, his arms circling her hips and lifting her. She locked her legs around his waist and grabbed onto his shoulders, still caught up in the hungriest kisses she'd ever experienced. A tiny part of her mind noticed he was carrying her to the bedroom and approved. What they were about to do would've broken health codes in a professional kitchen. The newer, wilder part of her mind pointed out that it wasn't a professional kitchen and wondered if it wouldn't have been great to stay right where they were.

Any thoughts scattered as he let her down on the bed.

He stepped back and peeled off his shirt. Her mouth went dry, then watered as he unbuttoned his pants and set his erection free of both pants and boxer briefs. Oh, she really didn't mind the change in location.

Getting to her hands and knees, she stalked him across the bed. He stilled and watched her approach. Still bold with the wild streak she'd found, she reached out and wrapped her hand around the length of his cock. He groaned, stepped closer for her.

Stroking the soft skin along his shaft, she parted her lips and took him into her mouth. His hand buried into her hair but didn't push her, so she took her time swirling her tongue around his tip. The taste of him, the smoothness of his skin. She opened wider, taking as much of his length as she could, and then withdrew, sucking as she did.

He groaned and his fingers tightened in her hair.

Peeking up at him, the storm in his eyes warned her things were going to escalate very soon. Her nipples tightened and wetness grew between her thighs in response. But first, she was going to suck him again. And she did. She took as much of him into her mouth as she could, until his head bumped the back of her throat, and she sucked gently as she backed away. If it was at all possible he got harder, bigger. She licked the length of his shaft and turned her hand to cup his balls, running her fingertips over the superthin soft skin there.

"Maylin." He was short on breath. "You're going to make me come."

"Mmm." She ran the tip of her tongue along the underside of his shaft. "Is that a bad thing?"

"No." He let go of her hair and started to pull her shirt up. "But I am damn well going to bring you first."

She let him pull off her shirt, arching back as he buried his face in her bra. He cupped her breasts in his hands, nibbling at her nipples through the fabric.

"This needs to go." He reached around and undid the clasp, freeing her of the undergarment.

She gasped as the heat of his mouth closed over one nipple, and clutched his shoulders for balance as he sucked. Distracted, she didn't resist as he pressed her backwards onto the bed. He took a moment to give similar attention to her other nipple until she was squirming underneath him.

"Easy." He murmured the word against her skin, then kissed his way down her navel. As he unbuttoned her pants and hooked his fingers over the waistband of both pants and panties, he looked up the length of her. "Are you wet for me?"

She swallowed, caught up in desire and aching. If he didn't ease the need soon, she'd go insane. "Yes."

He grinned, sliding her pants and underwear off in one smooth motion. "Good."

His big hands parted her legs and gripped the inside of her thighs, holding her open for his pleasure. He never broke their eye contact, even as he leaned down and blew a puff of hot air over her tortured flesh. He hadn't even touched her yet and she quivered for him.

Suddenly, he dragged his tongue through her folds and she cried out, tossing her head back as the sensation shot through her. His hands shifted to cup her bottom, lifting her hips as he feasted on her. All she could do was grab the bedsheets in her fists and writhe as he sucked, licked, even nipped.

"You taste so good." He didn't let up his onslaught, darting his tongue into her opening. "Sweet."

Her body tightened and she moaned. His tongue flicked against her clit and she bucked. Couldn't help it.

He chuckled. "Oh, you're close, aren't you?"

"Yes," she gasped. "Yes."

Letting her hips back down, he continued to lick and kiss and swirl his tongue while his hands ran up and down the backs of her thighs. She reached down and grasped his head, holding on as the sensations built more and more. He penetrated her with a finger. Each stroke drove her closer to the edge.

But she wanted more. Something more than one or the other of them finding release.

"Wait." She pulled on his head, made him look back up at her. "Wait. I want you inside me."

He paused. The storm in his eyes rocked her to the core.

"Please. Come with me." This time it was important to her. She didn't think about why, just that it was.

He rose up and fished in his discarded pants pockets, coming up with a condom. Without taking his gaze off her, he freed it from its wrapping and rolled it over the length of him. When he climbed back onto the bed, he stopped to kiss her breasts before covering her. She parted her legs, shifting her hips to help him until the head of his cock nudged at her entrance.

For a long heartbeat he held himself poised over her. Then his mouth came down on hers hard and demanding as he slid inside her, stretching and filling. She moaned into his mouth, reaching up to grasp his shoulders.

He kept on kissing her as he rocked his hips into her. Every stroke drew a moan or a cry from her and he swallowed all of them as his tongue danced with hers. Wild wasn't the word for it. She was lost in him.

"Maylin." He uttered her name and she tightened hearing it.

He groaned. Then he leaned back just long enough to hook an arm under her right leg, bringing it up high and opening her wider. Every thrust went deeper, stroking different places inside her until she felt herself climbing back to the edge of climax.

All she could do was hold on. "Yes, Gabe, this. Please!"

A guttural sound rolled up out of him, something between a growl and a sound even more primal. He drove into her and they both went over the edge together. Her orgasm gripping her entire body as pleasure rushed over her mind in a tidal wave.

Awareness came back to her slowly. He'd let himself down on top of her and she savored the weight of him, reaching to run her hands over his back and shoulders.

He nuzzled her neck. "I can't resist you when you ask all nice like that."

"Nice?" She squirmed under him until she could angle her head to look into his face. "More like begging."

And wasn't that embarrassing?

He must have seen the flush rise up on her cheeks. Concern in his eyes, he propped himself up on his elbows so they could look at each other without craning necks. "Hey. It *was* nice. And I like when you tell me what you want. Please keep telling me. Okay?"

He was so earnest, so sincere, she couldn't help but absorb his words. Biting her lip, she nodded. The embarrassment receded gradually.

He kissed the bridge of her nose. "Good."

Since he was leaning over her she indulged herself, running her hands over his chest and torso.

"Aw, you are too tempting." He lowered himself down

on her for a long kiss with a fair amount of caressing and hip grinding. She might have been guilty of some groping. Okay, a lot of groping. "Minx."

"What?" She nipped at his earlobe. "I can't help it. You're I don't know how many pounds of delicious muscular übergorgeousness."

Now she was making up words.

He chuffed out a laugh. "And you are definitely starting to fall asleep. You just don't know it yet. Wait right here."

She almost protested when he rolled off her, but he was back in record time with a damp washcloth. Cleaning up a little was a good idea, and then he climbed back into bed and tucked her against his side. "Nap."

"Is that an order?" She said it lightly but she had to admit, it was a good idea. Exhaustion had snuck up on her and sleep was dragging her under faster than she'd anticipated.

He nuzzled her hair. "I'm here. You're safe. Rest. Then we'll take on whatever comes next."

Snuggling in the circle of his arms, she let go and fell into sleep.

Chapter Fifteen

"So. Your car is still on the side of the road." Lizzy was sitting at the breakfast counter when they returned to the main house.

The dark-haired woman lifted her chin at Gabe in welcome and gave Maylin a smile.

Warmed, Maylin returned it with one of her own. "Hungry? I was about to make up dinner for us."

Lizzy peered down into her plastic cup. A metal ball inside clunked against the side. "Normally protein shakes are fine for me around dinner time, but I'm game for real food."

"It'll only take twenty minutes," Maylin promised as she reached the refrigerator.

Someone had stocked it with a few more fresh ingredients. Plus the freezer had a few surprises, too. She wondered if the Centurions might be hopeful she'd do more cooking to calm her mind.

Glad to.

"Need help?" Gabe stood at her shoulder.

She handed him a box of frozen shrimp, easy peel kind. "Could you dump some of these into a bowl of cold water? It has to be cold to defrost properly. Warm will spoil the shrimp. Figure about four or five for each of us. Oh, and could you start the rice cooker with about one measuring cup of uncooked rice? There should be a cup for the rice cooker, not a standard measuring cup."

There was a beat of hesitation and then he took them from her, dropping a kiss on her cheek before turning towards the sinks. "Really glad you'll let me help."

Maylin paused. Blinked. When was the last time she'd let anyone help her cook in a kitchen? She couldn't remember. Usually if they were catering, she'd assign simple dishes to the staff but did special dishes on her own. Declining help.

Trying not to ruin it by thinking too hard, she nabbed the carton of eggs from the refrigerator and bustled over to the counter, peeking into the cupboards to see if someone had stocked them with a few basics.

"Car is still burning itself out?" Gabe asked Lizzy as the sound of running water started.

"For the time being. Authorities will probably wait until danger of fire is gone before letting their investigative teams near it." Lizzy snorted. "I pulled the remnants of both your bags out of the trunk to avoid identification, but none of it was worth saving. Too much damage."

"Interior?"

Lizzy shook her head. "Too hot and too much fire and smoke damage. No way is a forensics team going to lift prints out of the interior."

Maylin looked up from her mixing bowl. "You make it sound all sorts of easy. Like the car couldn't explode more."

Was that even a thing that could happen? It seemed like it could. Lizzy had taken an extreme risk going anywhere near the thing and she made it sound like no big deal.

Fear squeezed her chest at even the thought, so she walked over to the sink to splash water from the tap into her bowl of flour, corn starch and baking soda, then started beating the contents hard. Taking her worry out on the mixture until it became a thin batter seemed like a practical thing to do.

"They're not going to blow up the car after we've left it behind," Gabe stated, his gaze focused on the bowl tucked into the crook of her arm.

She set it down with an audible thump and cracked an egg, carefully separating the egg white into her batter and tossing the yolk and shell into the garbage disposal. "How do you know?"

Picking up the bowl, she resumed her beating. Earlier in the day, being yanked out of the car and running for the woods counted as the strongest fright she'd experienced in her life. Mostly because Gabe had been scared. And she couldn't imagine much he'd be afraid of, but whatever it was would end her without much effort.

Lizzy looked from Gabe to her and back. "It's one thing to blow up the car with you two in it. It's Jewel's special kind of twisted to take out the tire, then set an explosion to incinerate the inside of the vehicle. She obviously wanted to give you a chance to get out. So there's no reason to have set a third charge to wipe the car off the map. Waste of valuable explosives."

Maylin pressed her lips together. Neither of them had said Jewel wouldn't have blown up a car with a person in it. She added a bit of vegetable oil and finished combining her mixture. Hesitated, then added a tiny pinch of salt. Another few seconds of beating gave her a smooth, light batter and a little less anxiety.

Setting it aside, she rummaged for a large pan. Somebody had bought the kind of wok with a flat bottom you could set directly on a burner. Handy. She pulled it out, wiped it down, and poured a large amount of oil into it. As she set it on the stove to heat up for frying, she glanced back at Gabe. "You don't think you're worth it to her to blow up?"

He met her gaze, his expression very serious. "She had the opportunity to kill me from a distance. She didn't. If she does in the future, she'll make it up close and personal."

His statement had the kind of ring of truth to it that sent a cold shiver down her spine. She headed to the sink. The shrimp were mostly defrosted, and she drained the water from the bowl and patted them dry with a paper towel before seasoning them liberally with salt and pepper. Then she went back to the fridge and pulled out green onions and a jalapeno.

"Someone really did some shopping." She needed a change of topic. For just a minute.

Lizzy laughed. "Victoria and Marc figured if you could make breakfast out of nothing but leftovers, getting you a little bit of everything from the grocery store could only mean good things in our future. The internet may have been involved in assembling the shopping list most likely to tempt you into making stuff we all like."

Maylin smiled, some of the tightness leaving her shoulders. It made her happy when people enjoyed her food. Really, it was why she did what she did. "I'll make something nice for tomorrow morning."

"They're doing some recon. Won't be back until late morning."

"Even better." Maylin pondered. "I'll have time to make dim sum."

She cleaned and chopped both the green onions and jalapeno fine, then washed her hands. She'd have to remember not to rub her eyes for a few more hand washes. Once wasn't enough to get the burn of the pepper off her fingertips, and it transferred readily.

Both Gabe and Lizzy were sitting in awkward silence. Gabe was texting on his smartphone but he was keeping an eye on Maylin.

She realized they were being sensitive to her. But she couldn't hide from serious discussion every time she got anxious. It would slow down their main purpose. And honestly, she needed to grow up some, step up to the issue at hand. "Are they doing recon on the biotech company Gabe found out about?"

It was Lizzy who answered first. "Marc and Victoria headed down to California to check out the biotech facilities and get us some basic intel. If your little sister is being held there, though, they are either incredibly smart or insanely arrogant."

Leaving the chopped stuff by the sink, Maylin grabbed the shrimp and dumped them in her batter, giving them a light toss to coat. She nabbed a pair of long chopsticks from her personal kitchen tools. Glad she'd brought the box of cooking tools with her from her place. It had seemed stupid at the time, but she hadn't been willing to leave without them in case she needed to return straight to work. Having them here was a comfort.

"Why arrogant?" An-mei had to be there. Where else could she be?

The oil in the wok sizzled as she started frying the shrimp a few at a time so as not to drop the oil temperature too low.

"You can run an easy internet search and view satellite photos of the whole facility," Lizzy answered.

Gabe grunted.

Maylin kept her eyes on her shrimp, ensuring each one fried to a light golden brown before nipping them out of the oil to drain on a plate layered with paper towels. "What?"

"Generally, biotech or tech companies with things to hide have high enough security to lock down satellite images of their facilities. Not usually available to the public or the casual internet surfer." Gabe pushed away from the counter and took the plate with the fried shrimp from her. As he held it for her, she transferred the last few shrimp to the plate and turned off the heat under the wok.

In a fresh skillet, she poured half a tablespoon of the oil from the wok and tipped the skillet this way and that to coat before setting it on the stove at high heat. "So Marc and Victoria went all the way to California to confirm?"

Lizzy laughed. "It's not a long flight and they were getting a little cabin fever. Some light reconnaissance did them good."

Maylin considered that as she tossed the green onions and jalapeno onto the skillet, stirring them with a wooden spatula as they sautéed and released fragrant scent. Turning to Gabe, she relieved him of the plate of freshly fried shrimp and added them to the skillet, tossing to mix the shrimp with the greens. Then she added another sprinkling of salt and dusted it all with pepper. As she finished, the rice cooker beeped. "Perfect timing."

She flew about the kitchen then, putting out plates and arranging them with a nice scoop of rice topped with the salt and pepper fried shrimp. Gabe had taken a seat at the breakfast bar with Lizzy, but neither of them started on their plates until Maylin sat with them to eat.

"Leave the dishes. I'll do them since you cooked," Lizzy said between mouthfuls. "S'good."

"Do you get any communication from them while they're gone?" Maylin figured Lizzy would have told them if they'd found An-mei, but it seemed odd for them to head out and not send back any information at all.

"Standard procedure is to check in every twelve hours for a short trip like this. We know you're under surveillance, so we're keeping communication to a minimum to reduce the chance of our *friends* tapping into us." Gabe was eating his portion quickly, too. "They'll be sad they missed this. It's delicious."

Pleased, Maylin applied herself to her own plate. "Normally, I'd serve this as part of a meal with several other dishes. But it seemed like it'd be good tonight on its own."

"It is," Lizzy agreed. "Last check-in, they confirmed the location seems to be legit. No signs of underground labs or unusual shipments. Personnel come and go on a normal schedule. They're maintaining observation through the night to see if there's any interesting activity in the dark when the normal employees go home."

"There's probably another facility if this one is filled with normal employees." Gabe stood, taking his plate and Lizzy's to the sink.

Maylin swallowed hard, only halfway through her dinner. They ate fast. No. They inhaled. Minimal chewing.

"We'll find what we're looking for," Lizzy said, standing away from the breakfast bar. "We're systematic to be sure we don't miss anything. And we will find anything they're trying to hide. You'll see."

Maylin turned on the stool to face Lizzy. "Thank you."

The smile Lizzy gave her was gentle, and somewhat awkward. "Good night, you two. Try to get some actual sleep."

Gabe opened the door to the guest cabin, listening hard to ensure the silence. They were safe on Centurion Corporation ground, but he was too keyed up to ignore ingrained habit. Instead, he moved through the rooms and cleared each as Maylin waited for him just inside the door.

She was getting good at following his directions. Her trust evident every time she did it without question. He'd repaid each time with answers once they were safe. Explanations he'd never taken the time to make for anyone else.

And her trust was misplaced.

So far, none of his queries had turned up feasible solutions. He'd called up some old favors and could pull together a small task force, but not one sufficient to go up against Edict and other unknown opponents. He'd been checking messages while Maylin cooked. He'd even talked to Lizzy to double-check his logistics and it didn't look good.

He had feelers out and at the very least, he'd know what freelance contractors were out there. Some of his old contacts were looking for information on Phoenix Biotech to find out who else they might have on their payroll.

Something might come through. Maybe. But realistically, it wouldn't be soon.

He closed the door once his sweep was complete and Maylin headed straight for the little kitchenette area. He smiled. She was more at home in a kitchen than anywhere else in a place. Not because of any stupid saying about women and kitchens, either, but because she created things there. It was her domain, where she could make things happen and do things to help the people she cared about. It didn't matter if she'd just come back from another kitchen.

"I'm putting on a kettle for tea," she called over her shoulder. "Did you want any? Or would coffee be better? Were you planning on doing any research tonight?"

He stepped up behind her, placing his hands on her waist as she straightened. "Coffee would be great."

She set the kettle on the stove over high heat, then turned in his arms. As her arms slipped around his waist, he kissed the top of her head. He should tell her.

"We're close to finding her." Maylin pressed her face into his chest. "I know we are. Even if she's not in California, we're on the brink of something."

And if they were?

"It will be good to find your sister." Lame he couldn't think of anything better. He'd promised her false hope.

"Should we start planning? How will we get her out?"

No more dodging.

"Centurion Corporation isn't going to."

She froze in his arms.

"There's four in my fire team. Chances are whatever facility she's in has more security than just we four can handle." He kept his arms loose, let them fall to the side as she stepped back and away from him. "I won't send my team into a massacre when there isn't a chance of any of us making it out. It's a lose-lose scenario."

"This isn't new. You've known. Since we were in DC." Each sentence came out carefully measured. Precise and cold. With plenty of time for him to refute her.

And he couldn't. "I was looking for solutions. There aren't any."

The kettle behind her began to go off, a low whistle building in pitch and volume. Maylin ignored it. "You're giving up. After all that talk."

He met her gaze, squashed the urge to cringe under the accusation in her clear green eyes. "This 'small' biotech looks to have a lot more resources at its disposal than any legit company its size should. It means that wherever your sister is being held is going to be a fortress. Even if we find it, and we haven't yet, the only result to come out of us rushing in there will be a missing fire team. We'll disappear off the grid with no evidence to follow."

And Centurion Corporation would want to come after them, avenge them. But Harte wouldn't go to war for them when they'd gone ahead of their own accord.

"But you're the best." It was the first time he'd heard Maylin raise her voice. Heat flushed her cheeks and her mouth twisted with pain and anger.

"We're the best because we know how to prepare for the situations we'll encounter and we're good enough to recognize what we can and can't do." God, he hated himself for what he was saying. But it was truth and he always gave her the bitter truth. "We. Can't. Do. This. You need to walk away."

She stared at him. Shock. Pain. Despair flashed in her eyes.

"*Qù nǐ mā de!* Oh, wait, let me translate that one for you. Fuck off!" Maylin balled up her fists. "From the very beginning you've told me 'no.' Won't help me. Can't help me. I am so done with dragging you all along against your pathetic practicality!"

Gabe held his peace. He couldn't be angry in return.

Couldn't find anything to refute her because she was right. It'd been her indomitable will that brought them this far. The rest of them had only been caught up in her wake.

"How good am I when I admit I can't do this without you?" Maylin continued to rage, tears falling down her cheeks. "Does it make me any better to admit what I can't do? Will it bring my sister back safely?"

"No." He had to give her the word again. It was the only answer he had to give and it ripped apart his heart to do it.

Maylin's nostrils flared as she breathed in deep, pulling all of her spectacular temper back into herself. When she spoke again, her voice trembled with contained anger. "What can I do?"

Stay with me.

He wanted to say it, but he'd shoot himself before hurting her even worse with the selfishness of that statement. He was failing her. "I don't know yet. I'm looking for more options for us."

"But your Centurions won't help us?" Still so carefully controlled.

He shook his head. "The kind of resources we'd need to do this infiltration and extraction would put most companies in the red for years. A single person with your income? You could mortgage the rest of your life and your first-born child to us, and it still wouldn't be enough to cover the cost. We wouldn't let you sign a contract for it."

And she would've. No doubt. She'd give her life for her sister.

Wouldn't he give his for Maylin? Yes, but it wouldn't be enough.

She pushed past him, the kettle still screaming on the

stove. He reached out and switched off the burner. When he turned around, she was standing at the front door. "Did you tell me because there was no hiding from it anymore? The way you told me about Jewel? Is this what you do with every important piece of information in your life?"

He opened his mouth and nothing came out. To say he wasn't the type to share was too flippant, but he couldn't think of a way to properly explain. Probably because any explanation was really an excuse.

Her back became poker straight and she brushed her hair off her shoulder so it fell in a cascade down her back. Perfectly composed from this perspective. None of the turmoil he'd seen a second ago visible. He was effectively shut out.

"How is Centurion Corporation supposed to be better than Edict?" Her voice was low and measured, cool and distant. "How could you let me hope?"

She put her hand on the doorknob.

"Don't go, Maylin." He didn't try to stop her physically. All he could do was ask, and he didn't even have the right to that anymore. "Please let me keep you safe. Your sister would want you safe."

It cut her and he hated himself for it. But Maylin could be used as leverage to make An-mei do the research she'd been taken to do. It was another reason Jewel wouldn't have blown up the car. Maylin was valuable.

"I need air." Maylin turned the doorknob. "I'll be outside. When I come back in, I'd rather sleep alone."

Chapter Sixteen

Gabe winced but didn't try to change her mind. As she stepped outside, his phone rang. Hell of a time, but damn, it'd be better to answer it and distract himself than to stand by the window like a creep and watch Maylin put walls up between them. He hit the answer button. "Diaz."

"Is your girl still with you?" asked Harte. The man did not sound chipper.

But Gabe wasn't the type to guess what anyone was about to say. He'd answer and deal with what came next. "Yeah."

"Good. We're going to need to talk to her again. And review the reconnaissance information from your team."

"Something change?" Centurion Corporation policy wasn't about Harte and his decision. He'd stand by it if it was the right thing for the corporation. But if new developments became a concern, Harte would reevaluate as needed. It was what made him a good CO. So whatever was going on had to be a true game changer.

"Some of the feelers you put out turned up interesting information." Harte didn't sound irritated, but Gabe figured they'd have a discussion about how he'd continued to investigate a disapproved contract after all this was over. Harte had a long memory.

"Yeah? It came straight to HQ?" Not what Gabe was expecting, but whatever it was, it'd moved Harte to call him.

"Contracts information comes to me." Harte made it a simple statement of fact. "I'm not familiar with the exact wording of your inquiry, but your source decided it'd be prudent to send it through to me first."

"Okay." Gabe wasn't going to argue.

"Phoenix Biotech has put out a request for proposal on a contract. Security for an extremely sensitive shipment of biohazard material. The RFP is by invitation only, so we wouldn't have known about it without your inquiry as we were not invited to submit a proposal."

Ah. And that probably chapped Harte's ass some. Centurion Corporation prided itself on being in demand.

"This shipment is not headed for any standard disposal location and in fact is to be 'handed off' to another unit for the next leg of transportation." Harte maintained a pleasant tone.

Pleasant wasn't a natural state of being for Harte. Someone, somewhere, was in for a world of hurt.

"Interesting." Generally, any shipment intended for not-so-legit destinations was easier to hide from surveillance when a corporate sponsor hired multiple paramilitary contractors to move the cargo in segments along an unpredictable course. Each contractor team only knew where to pick it up and where to drop it off. No knowledge of where it came from or where it was going next meant chain of custody was fairly easy to document, but it wasn't so easy to be sure the actual contents had remained intact from the true beginning of the journey to the final destination.

"I made some friendly inquiries of my own," Harte

continued. "Your recent playmates are on the roster as one of the already contracted teams, but the others? Not really any players we've worked with in the past."

The paramilitary-contractor industry was fairly large considering the sheer turnover rate of people entering the military in the US alone, and subsequently leaving with specialized skill sets. The number fluctuated from year to year but hovered easily around the six-digit range across the various armed forces. That was a lot of people with the potential to become private contractors. But few had the business acumen to exist as solo contractors, and the actual number of organized corporations was significantly reduced. Players as efficient or successful as Centurion Corporation or Edict were limited to a small circle of elite, and each of them had high standards for working with others.

"Edict isn't likely to play nice with other teams." Gabe doubted Centurion Corporation would work with them at all unless they were new and being given a chance to prove themselves.

"I know at least two of them have a reputation for not playing well at all." Harte barked out a laugh. "It's a train wreck waiting to happen."

Meaning the cargo was intended to go missing.

There were a couple of possibilities for where the shipment was actually meant to end up. The most likely destination was into the hands of a buyer.

"What kind of research was your missing scientist doing again?"

Gabe wasn't liking where this was going. "An-mei Cheng is a geneticist."

"Do we know more?"

"She lives and breathes gene sequences. She's immersed so completely the sisters send each other family notes in DNA-based codes." Which still boggled Gabe's mind a little. He was familiar with codes and had basic experience in reading them, even breaking them. But it'd been an added layer to Maylin's intelligence he hadn't anticipated.

"Your girl owns a catering company, right?" Harte was obviously caught off guard, too.

Gabe grinned. "Apparently Maylin was pre-med. Her best course of study was developmental biology before she decided she wouldn't be happy in a medical career. She followed her heart, built herself the kind of business she wanted."

And he was more and more impressed with every new thing he learned about her.

"Interesting family." Harte grew serious. "I've got a couple of guesses lined up here, but the actual answer depends on exactly what kind of research An-mei Cheng was doing. Quick internet search goes into genetics. But there's one article catching my eye."

Gabe strode over to the small desk in the corner. He'd left most of the research files Lizzy had pulled together in the beginning there. Retrieving the folder, he spread the files and quickly scanned them. "Gene-editing therapy."

"In adult test subjects. Not in petri dishes."

The applications were broad, and in his line of work, they were the stuff of nightmares. Biological warfare went beyond the definition of horrific and straight to unspeakable.

"Phoenix Biotech is not a US government–contracted research company," Harte pointed out. This was mostly good news. They wouldn't be going against the country they loved. "But we can assume they're not going to appreciate us retrieving a wayward geneticist. We'll need to crack them wide open so they're too busy dealing with the US authorities to even try to reacquire the girl."

"We." Gabe zeroed in on the key point. It changed everything.

"It is in Centurion Corporation's best interest to aid in the investigation of potential criminal activity when we have literally been invited into a unique position of observation. The US government is more than willing to have us on point in their already established investigation."

"I thought you said we weren't invited to submit a proposal." And yet, Gabe was really beginning to enjoy where this was going.

"Well, we might have made contact with Phoenix Biotech and presented a strong proposal for high caliber services they did not yet have. Phoenix Biotech was more than happy to open up their RFP and offer a handsome advance for a proof of concept demonstration." Of course they did. Harte was very good at presenting the services Centurion Corporation could offer. Over the course of several years, his shrewd business sense had grown the company into one of the best. "Being the mercenaries we are, we couldn't very well resist. Could we?"

"You're funding our mission with Phoenix Biotech's money." Gabe knew Harte was good, but this was above and beyond.

"Call me Robin Hood." Harte continued, "The US government is also offering a substantial bonus for any information we may acquire regarding the nature of biological weapons being developed."

Gabe peered out the window, straining to catch sight of Maylin. She'd quit pacing on the porch and begun wandering through the trees between the guest cabin and the main house, weaving back and forth instead of heading for one building or the other. In the gray mist of the day, she was going to end up chilled and damp. "How are we going to proceed?"

And then he'd figure out how to make things right with Maylin.

Harte cleared his throat. "You continue your angle. Send me an updated status report and an estimated breakdown of the support you'll need by morning. We'll send you reinforcements by EOB tomorrow. I'll work my end with a separate team. Get the girl out, and any of her research you can retrieve safely while you're at it."

"The girl is the primary objective."

"Confirmed."

Relieved, Gabe grabbed a jacket for Maylin and took a step towards the door. Jesus. If he'd waited minutes longer, they wouldn't have had to have that fight.

No. That was cowardice speaking. He should have had the conversation with her back in DC. And if delaying it had damaged what was between them permanently, then he'd own it. What mattered more was doing what he could for her now, whether she forgave him or not.

"An-mei Cheng may not be the only scientist in their custody." Harte brought him up short. "She is the objective for this mission, and her research is secondary. Any additional intel on the number of other projects in the facility would be extremely helpful for us to move forward."

And they'd need to move fast. If all of the scientists were off the radar the way An-mei was, whoever was making the big decisions at Phoenix Biotech might decide to shut down the facility after Centurion Corporation retrieved her, and the people still in the facility might not get out in time.

* * *

No amount of cooking was going to help her find her
way past this roadblock. Maylin stumbled between the
trees, reaching out to press her palms against the trunks
until the bark bit into her skin. The mist had settled under
the trees and darkness chased the sunset until the only
light came from the external lamps on the main house
and guest cabin. She didn't want to go to either one, and
there was no light leading the way to the answers she
was looking for.

Drops ran down her cheeks, hot tears and cold rain.
This wasn't her. She never admitted there were no other
options. She kept working towards a solution until she
found a path forward. Even her parents had said it was
her strength. When they couldn't see where her life would
lead after she'd quit her pre-medical course of study,
they said they'd learned to give her time to find her way.

But it'd always been for *her*. Her troubles and her solutions.

This time An-mei was lost, and what was needed to
bring her back was beyond any individual's means. Hell,
as good as Gabe and his team were, Maylin had known
she was asking for more than they could do, too. And
she'd let herself hide from the obvious when they'd returned from Centurion Corporation's corporate headquarters on their own. She was angry and embarrassed
because she'd set herself—and them—up for failure. She
was as mad at herself as Gabe.

What good was being independent if the only person
she could keep safe was herself? And even to do that,
she needed to hide amongst others.

"Hating every part of me right now," she muttered
into the rain.

But what decisions could she have made differently? Even...even if she hadn't become intimate with Gabe, things wouldn't have come out another way.

Would she take it back if she could?

"*Coração*. Should I translate it for you?" The weight of a jacket settled around her shoulders. Gabe sneaking up on her should've scared her, at least made her jump. Instead she fought the urge to lean back into the shelter of his arms. "My heart."

Hers skipped a beat.

Warmth spread through her even as she tried to keep it stuffed away. Her anger simmered, but she couldn't bring back the flash of rage she'd had earlier. It was too hard to scream at him for something he couldn't change.

"I don't know where we go from here." Saying it out loud buried her under sadness. What was she going to do?

"I broke something between us, *coração*, and I am sorry." Gabe grasped her shoulders and gently turned her to face him. In the dark, he was backlit by the light from the guest cabin, but she could still see his face in the fainter light from the main house. "Won't ask you to forgive me right away."

"Good." She bit her lip. Why did she have to sound so petty?

"But I have news." His hands squeezed as he spoke, like he wanted to be sure she listened. "I got a call from my CO. We'll have the reinforcements we need. We are going to get your sister back."

"Just like that?" She whispered her question, blinking away the mist and rain.

"Come inside. Let me get you warmed and dry. And I'll tell you about the call."

Her brain stuttered as relief blanked everything. "We still need to find her."

Gabe nodded. "But you were right. We're on the brink of something and I don't think it's finished yet. Last thing we need is for you to come down with pneumonia."

She didn't know what to say.

"Let me take care of you." He murmured the request. "At least this much. Let me take the lead."

Trusting him again. Seemed like she was continually taking a leap of faith for him. But he was An-mei's best chance.

She nodded, afraid to open her mouth and say something she'd regret later. Whether it started another argument or sparked a step back towards intimacy, she wasn't ready for either one. Instead, she let him pull her in to his side and guide her back to the guest house.

One step at a time, she'd decide how much trust she could give him again. They'd start back at the beginning, with finding An-mei.

Chapter Seventeen

It'd been a morning of cleaning.

Gabe had watched Maylin go through the guest cabin like a whirlwind, sweeping every room methodically. She'd start around the outer perimeter and sweep inward towards the center of each room. The resulting pile of dust was gathered in a dustpan and taken out the back door, even if the front door was closer.

He'd asked about it at first but she was nowhere near chatty. And he couldn't blame her. Coaxing her to take a hot shower and tucking her into bed the night before had been the limit of what they could repair between them for the time being. She'd taken the news from Harte with her to bed to think on, and from the dark circles under her eyes, she'd slept about as much as Gabe had.

An inner drive pushed at him to take better care of her, but he couldn't make her sleep. And he wouldn't ever suggest she set aside her worry.

His phone rang, the caller ID popping up Lizzy's avatar. "Diaz."

"Marc and Victoria will land in two hours." Lizzy probably knew Maylin had been out in the night, but she didn't ask. "I'll pick them up from the airport and check on what's left of your car on the way back. If the police have cleared out, we'll sweep the area for any leftover fragments they might've missed."

"Be careful." He was fairly certain Jewel had been messing with him. But the hard part about dealing with other good mercenaries was the way they all took pains to be unpredictable.

"Always." Lizzy paused. "Our ETA brings us back here about lunchtime. Should we pick anything up on the way?"

Gabe leaned back from the desk to get a line of sight on Maylin cleaning the bedroom. "She set a bunch of rice to soak overnight. I'm thinking she's planning on cooking something."

Lizzy chuckled. "No arguments here. Way better than protein shakes and takeout."

True enough. And as stress behaviors went, Maylin had way more constructive quirks than most people did. Gabe couldn't count the number of clients they'd had who'd done nothing but pace. He had no patience at all for the ones who went hysterical or screamed at everyone.

"Any chance she'd consider staying after this?" Lizzy sounded as wistful as Lizzy ever got. "The real meals go a long way towards making a body sound. And you two seem to be getting along."

Not since he'd screwed up royally. "She's got a catering business to run when all this is done. Pretty high profile."

"Ah." She didn't push. "Well, can't say I'm surprised. She's a stand-up woman. I knew I liked her for a reason."

The more he learned about Maylin, the more he respected her and the more he ached for what he'd crushed with his mistakes.

Once Lizzy terminated the call, he stood. Stretched. Admitted he was procrastinating and took the few steps to catch up with Maylin in the bedroom. Coming to a halt at the door, he rapped his knuckles on the door frame.

"Yes?" She straightened from smoothing out the bedspread.

Gabe lost his words for minute, struck by a simple thing. God, she was beautiful. No makeup, no sharp dress suit or nicely coordinated blouse and slacks. Her hair hung over one shoulder in a simple ponytail. And he couldn't take his eyes off her. Not even for a second.

"The team will be back in time for lunch." He offered the latest news because there wasn't anything else he thought she'd care to hear.

A small smile touched her face and he missed the brighter smiles she'd give him before. "The lunch I had planned takes some time to prep. Mind if I head up to the main house?"

Gabe stepped out of the doorway so she could pass. "Sure. You can go up there anytime."

"As long as someone knows where I am?" There was a hint of something there. Not bitterness. Something.

"We want to keep you safe." *He* wanted to most of all. "But we want you to be as comfortable as possible, too."

He didn't try to suggest she needn't cook. It'd be an insult. As if he hadn't learned anything about her at all. And he was afraid to ask her if he could help.

Instead, he followed her up to the main house with his laptop and parked himself at the breakfast bar to do more research and planning while she cooked.

"Still making dim sum?" He'd had some once, in Seattle's Chinatown-International District. The ingredients she was setting out were varied but didn't seem as wide an array as he'd guessed would be needed for all those little dishes and dumplings.

She shook her head. "Didn't have the ingredients to do it really well."

"I would've gone out on a supply run for you."

She hesitated and he heard her unspoken thoughts loud and clear. He wasn't allowed to help anymore.

"I figured with the rainy weather, comfort food would go better."

"The team will like whatever you make." He tried to infuse his words with sincerity, since she'd probably bristle at reassurance. Walking on eggshells was not his strong suit. "It's all been incredible so far."

She gave him another small smile, and he let go his breath, happy she believed him.

They both fell silent then. He continued his research online, catching up on response emails to his queries and running a few specific searches. At the edge of his peripheral, Maylin went about dropping her uncooked rice in a blender complete with the water she'd used to soak it overnight. While it was blending, she took out a deep Dutch oven from the back of the cabinet and put a bunch of large spoons in the bottom. Gabe couldn't figure out how the hell she'd be cooking with that setup. Next she took out a cake pan and greased it lightly with vegetable oil. Then he was really confused.

She set the Dutch oven on the stove over fire set to the highest setting and poured some water in it. As she turned away, he craned his neck to see inside. The water didn't quite cover the rounded backs of the spoons on the bottom.

What the hell?

Next, the cake pan was set on top of the spoons with

what looked like a thin layer of the rice batter she'd made. Then she covered the whole thing.

No idea what was going on there. But Maylin turned to other ingredients, browning ground pork and fresh minced garlic in a medium pot and filling the kitchen with savory scents to make his mouth water.

Gabe jerked when she turned to look at him with a raised eyebrow, and gave her a guilty grin. Caught staring. But hell, the magic she worked in a kitchen was beyond him.

"Do you mostly cook Asian foods?" Was that a safe question? Might not be.

But Maylin didn't seem to mind. "I cook dishes from a lot of different cultures. I love Italian and Greek. But when I'm worried or anxious, I tend to fall back on the dishes I learned to make growing up. Less likely to mess those up when my mind is working through other things."

Made sense. "Like any Brazilian dishes? Or Portuguese?"

"Love eating the food, not so good at cooking it… yet." Maylin continued to work as she spoke, pouring water into the pot of browned meat and garlic. "I'd love to learn."

"I've got a couple of dishes I remember." Maybe. Sort of. "Really simple dishes."

Maylin laughed. It was short and quiet, but it was still a laugh and he'd take it. "Simple is usually the best place to start with any new cuisine. I like to learn the basic foundation dishes and then build from there."

Smart. Practical. Methodical in the way she approached things. And so very talented. He could see why her parents had thought she'd do well as a doctor. And he was very glad she'd followed her heart instead. People tended to lose some of their spark when they were forced into a profession they didn't have a passion for, and he wanted to see Maylin happy.

"I take it you didn't do much cooking as a kid." Her statement was a hesitant invitation, and he was not going to pass it up. Not this time.

He owed her a few more pieces of himself.

"No. Not much. My dad worked and my mom was home until I hit high school. She wanted us to be the perfect white-bread family from the television show reruns she watched every day. Mostly she made sure we sat down to meals on a regular basis, even if we didn't talk to each other any other time of the day." His dad hadn't been the "toss the ball around in the yard" type. He worked too hard.

"Did you ever help her in the kitchen?" Maylin lifted the cover on the Dutch oven, releasing a big cloud of steam. Reaching in with mitt-covered hands, she pulled out the cake pan and immediately flipped it onto a clean cutting board. A smooth, white circle fell flat on the board. She re-oiled the cake pan, poured more rice batter into it, and back it went into the Dutch oven. Then she returned to the stuff on the cutting board and rolled it with nimble fingers. Using a sharp knife, she cut it into half-inch-wide segments and dropped them into a bowl of water next to the sink.

He still had no idea what they were. "No. I was kind of a prick as a kid. Never occurred to me to do anything but my chores. And then only because I had to." He'd been ungrateful.

"You were young." The kindness she gave him was more than he deserved.

"I've had plenty of time to wish I'd been a better kid."

A pause. "They're gone now?"

"Yeah. Car accident when I was a freshman in high school." And hitting the foster care system at that age had been a bitch.

"I'm sorry." How was she still so sincere? So empathetic without smothering him with pity.

God, he didn't want her pity.

"It is what it is. I was lucky to get foster care. Not gonna lie, though, it's hard enough for young kids. No one wants you when you're almost old enough to care for yourself. Especially when you're angry at the world and not worth the trouble."

"But someone did, I hope?"

He considered, sifting through old and bitter memories. The whole sharing thing was coming easier than he'd thought it would with her, but it still wasn't what he'd call easy. "Somebody kept me because it was the right thing to do. And they gave me some good perspective on life. But I wouldn't say there was more than that."

His foster family hadn't kept in touch once he'd turned eighteen. Not even letters during basic training.

"So this team is your family now. You watch out for them, make sure they all get out of danger before you do." Maylin was still busy working with her batter, steaming those…things. Her other pot simmered and filled the kitchen with an incredibly delicious smell, some sort of soup. He wanted her to be a part of his life more than he'd ever wanted anything else. His team was family. She'd become more.

"Don't tell them." None of them were the sort to say that kind of thing. Part of the reason each of them functioned in the team was because, while they'd lay their lives down for each other, they also understood not to waste those lives. To go on if they had to. "But yeah, I guess so. We're there for each other. Most people with actual families don't fall into this kind of work."

"Families by blood. You all are an actual family, too, by choice."

He didn't argue with her because it resonated with him. Truth. Even if there were some complications in there.

"You're all good people." Maylin was setting out bowls and filling them with those white segments unraveled.

Well, shit, she'd made noodles from scratch.

"Whatever is going on in the kitchen, it smells like heaven!" Marc called from the front door.

Maylin met Gabe's brooding gaze and smiled, hoping to lighten up the dark place he'd gone to. "Perfect timing."

His answering lopsided grin tugged at her. "Yeah."

She busied herself ladling clear broth from her pot into each bowl of noodles, making sure each of them had a good helping of the ground pork and vegetables she'd included. Ho fun soup was one of her favorite comforts, and considering the confused state she'd been in when she'd woken, comfort was definitely on the menu.

One phone call last night and their fortune had changed. All they needed to do was actually find An-mei and they could get her back. Nothing should've dampened that hope.

But she teetered back and forth between wanting to hug Gabe and to put as much distance between them as humanly possible.

When he'd brought her inside and told her about Harte's call, he hadn't expected everything to have been repaired between them. If he had, they would've been finished. But it was because he'd understood it didn't erase her feelings, the break of trust, that she was struggling to decide what they were now.

He'd made his intent clear: he wanted to repair what was between them and explore even further once this nightmare was over.

And most of her wanted it, too. There was a tiny part of her warning of betrayal and whispering about keeping secrets. She didn't want to turn to someone she was supposed to be able to trust and have them turn away from her. Wasn't sure she could survive Gabe turning away from her.

Coward.

Yup. She was.

"We have news and we are starving." Marc came into the kitchen full of barely contained energy, giving Maylin a rakish grin. Victoria and Lizzy were barely a step behind.

Gabe had already closed his laptop and moved it out of the way, so Maylin started putting their bowls up on the breakfast counter for them.

"One of these days, perhaps we should use an actual table." Victoria perched on a stool despite her words and leaned forward to take in the scent of the steam rising from her bowl.

"Do you ever have time?" Maylin placed spoons and forks across each bowl. "Normally we'd go with chopsticks, but there aren't any here besides the ones I use for cooking."

"With food this good, we should start making time." Victoria sipped delicately and closed her eyes, uttering a hum of appreciation. After a moment she looked around again and nudged Marc. "We could stock chopsticks, couldn't we?"

"There were way more kinds of chopsticks than I thought possible when I looked." Marc set his fork and spoon aside in favor of picking up his bowl and sipping straight from the rim. Totally okay in Maylin's opinion. She did the same when she was alone in her apartment. "Plastic ones, metal ones, wood ones. Some of them were pointed at the end. No clue which kind worked best and I wasn't about to get the disposable ones we get from Chinese takeout places."

Maylin warmed at the thought he'd put behind it. "I'm all about whatever works."

Besides, she wasn't sure how much longer she'd be here. Or if she'd be a regular visitor…after.

There would be time to think on it later, closer to when they'd gotten through it all. But now there were much more important things.

"What did you find out?" Maylin couldn't touch her bowl, even though she'd mostly decided to make this dish for herself.

Marc glanced at Gabe before answering her. "Your sister isn't in the California facility. We suspected as much the last time we checked in and this trip confirmed it."

"But Phoenix Biotech had quite a few interdepartmental communications going by actual physical mail to locations throughout the US." Victoria tossed the information out there between noodles. "It's very likely she's being kept at one of three of those, judging by the lengths taken to secure the envelopes and then make them look like normal mail."

"Only three to search through? And we know the addresses of each of them?" Maylin almost bounced in excitement. Then she caught sight of Marc wielding his spoon. "Ah! Don't cut the noodles!"

Gabe paused midbite and slurped up the rest of his noodle instead, almost choking.

Marc slowly put down his spoon. "Okay. Why?"

Embarrassment burned Maylin's cheeks but, well, they needed all the luck they could get. "To cut the noodles is to cut short longevity."

Silence.

Marc's eyebrows were raised, but after a minute he shrugged. "Okay. Good a reason as any. They're pretty slippery anyway, so cutting 'em would be more trouble than it's worth. It's fine to slurp them, though, right?"

In answer, Maylin handed him an extra paper towel.

Lizzy chuckled next to him.

Maylin's loaner phone screen flashed, catching her attention from where it sat on the counter. It was a game notification. Hope flared and Maylin headed for her phone.

Victoria managed to gather her noodles in her spoon and eat it all at once. After a moment to chew and swallow, she continued. "Montana, Oregon, North Dakota. All northern tier. We'll analyze the three locations tonight to see which is most likely. It's going to be time consuming if we need to do reconnaissance on each one."

"I'll see if we can leverage trainees to do some of the analysis in parallel. Can you work some satellite magic?" Gabe had directed his question towards Marc, who was working on slurping.

Maylin shoved her phone in the midst of them. "There's a new message in my inbox. It's from a new account. But it's got to be An-mei. *Got to be.*"

"Are you sure?" Victoria sounded suspicious.

Excitement buoyed Maylin and she nodded vigorously. "My account is set to private. Only users who know my exact user ID can send me messages, and who is going to know an eleven-digit user ID off the top of their head?"

Gabe stared straight at her. "You have your sister's memorized."

"And she has mine," Maylin finished with a grin. "Besides, look at the message!"

There it was on the phone screen:

aTaaaaGc aTTaaaaG aTTaGccG aaTaaacc aTaaGccc
aTTTcGcG

Marc hastily grabbed a napkin and scribbled out the code. "Short and sweet." He started the conversion on the napkin, writing the binary under the letters.

"So you say," Victoria muttered.

Marc continued to scribble without acknowledging his partner. "So the DNA translates to binary code. And the binary code translates to letters. I got that far. But this is what it says—"

aTaaaaGc aTTaaaaG aTTaGccG aaTaaacc aTaaGccc
aTTTcGcG
01000010 01100001 01101001 00100000 01001000
01110101
Bai Hu

"Why? That's how I translated it, too, but I thought there had to be some change to the code." There was something tickling the edge of Maylin's mind. "Bai Hu isn't even a monster or character in the game."

"What is it?" Lizzy asked.

"It's a white tiger." Maylin stared into her ho fun. Thinking. An-mei sent her the answer. "It's one of four celestial gods. Creatures. It depends on how you translate it. They're also a part of the Chinese constellations."

Gabe had his laptop out again and Marc was scribbling notes as she spoke.

"Keep talking. Something will catch," Marc encouraged her.

"None of the locations had a white tiger or even a stylized animal as a logo." Victoria tapped her spoon against the side of her bowl.

"There's Xuan Wu, the black turtle in the north." Maylin scraped at her memory for the mythology. It'd been a favorite back when they were children. There'd even been a Japanese anime based on the mythology, which An-mei had watched over and over. "Then there's Qing Long in the east. He's the azure dragon. Zhu Que is the vermillion bird in the south and Bai Hu is the white tiger in the west."

"Vermillion, red?" Victoria asked. "Like a phoenix?"

"Yes, Zhu Que represents the fire element."

"And it's in the south."

"Basically."

Marc jumped up off his stool and leaned over Gabe's shoulder. "Bring up a map of the United States."

While Gabe complied, Maylin rushed around the counter to look, too. She had to crane her neck and get up on her tip toes to see over Gabe's shoulder.

"If Phoenix Biotech in California is the south—" Marc pointed "—we assign the other celestial god animal things to the other states: Oregon, Montana, North Dakota. Your turtle could be either Montana or North Dakota depending on whether north refers to the state or the actual facility location. But what we care about is your tiger in the west. Seems pretty simple to me."

Victoria piped up. "Each of these facilities are left-overs from the cold war, believe it or not. A satellite check showed the Oregon site is underground. Couldn't get close because there's high-level security restricting access to detailed imagery."

"More and more likely," Gabe commented.

"Oregon." Maylin whispered, because stating the obvious seemed unnecessary, but she needed to say it for herself. "All this time and An-mei might be so close."

"Might be. We need to get a closer look at the facility and get more intel on it." Lizzy reached around Marc to pat Maylin on the shoulder.

"I'm betting it is." Marc slapped his notepad on the counter. "If we're right, it'll save us days of recon. It'll make a huge difference now that Edict knows we're looking."

Maylin froze. "Are we running out of time?"

Gabe turned on his stool as she settled back hard on her heels. He took her hands in his. "You've just won us back more time than anyone is expecting. Even if they try to move her, we'll be watching in the right place now. We'll see."

"What do we do next?" Maylin meant the question for all of them, but she was looking at Gabe.

"We confirm with preliminary reconnaissance that the location is active, receiving the sorts of supplies to indicate the research we're looking for, and bulked up enough on security to indicate our target is there. Then we start planning. This is going to move fast and we might have random questions for you." Gabe gave her hands a squeeze. "It's a lot of hurry up and wait."

"Anything I can do."

Chapter Eighteen

"Oh, Maylin."

She paused at the front door as Marc popped his head out of the surveillance room.

"Thought you might want your smartphone back." Marc strode towards her, hand outstretched. "I only used it once or twice while you were gone to make it look like you were checking your email. Didn't check it at all once you two ran into Jewel in DC. Not much point since she and her team knew you weren't here."

Jewel wasn't someone she wanted to think about right about now. But Maylin took the phone with a smile anyway. "Thanks."

"It doesn't hurt if you use it while you're here. It's pretty obvious you're under our protection." Marc flashed Gabe one of those male looks that wasn't as indecipherable as they thought it was. "There's probably a charger that fits it in the guest cabin."

"I'll show her." Gabe sounded grumbly. He probably wouldn't appreciate the description but to her, it was perfect.

The walk to the cabin was silent and awkward. When they reached the porch, Gabe came to a halt. "It's going to be a busy afternoon for us, and probably a late night, too."

She nodded, clutching her phone to her chest to keep herself from fidgeting. "There's plenty of noodles and soup left if you all get hungry later in the afternoon. And I can come up and make dinner."

"Only if you want to." Gabe shoved his hands deep into the front pockets of his jeans. "You should take the time to rest if you can."

"I'm not going to get much sleep while we're this close."

"I know, but this kind of operation is something we need to prepare for in every way before we go in. Too many things can go wrong if we're not ready, and these people—Edict at least and probably their sponsor, too—they aren't the type to have regrets if they end up killing people."

Fear cut her breath short. For An-mei, for Gabe, for the people who'd so quickly become friends. "If there's any way to do this without people getting hurt…"

"Being prepared will minimize the damage." Gabe looked up, catching her in a fierce gaze. "We do what we do to ensure the best outcome. Believe that."

Maylin swallowed hard. "I do."

His expression softened. "Not like you've had much reason to believe me recently, but it's true. We're going to do everything we can to get your sister back safely for you. Let us do what we're good at."

She ached to hear his words. He was right, and she wasn't going to lie to him or herself and say her faith in him had been completely restored. But it was rebuilding, and maybe he didn't realize how much it had to do with him taking accountability for what he'd done, acknowledging how she'd felt and committing himself to rebuilding faith with her. Those things all mattered.

And most of all, she didn't want things between them to be broken.

"Will you be coming back here at all?" The last few words came out in a whisper. She didn't want him to feel obligated but she'd miss him.

His expression softened and yet his gaze intensified, heated. "There's a lot of work to do. To be honest, if I come back here I'm going to be tempted to do all sorts of things to bring us closer together that have nothing to do with the mission or the team."

She blinked, surprised by the answering heat coursing through her. Damn it, her nipples tightened.

"Shouldn't play with temptation." And she was going to have a nasty discussion with herself about priorities. Her body was distracting in the worst possible way and she wasn't ready yet to give in that way again. Was she? She needed to edge them back towards steady ground. "Why don't I come back up in a few hours and cook the kind of dinner you can grab and get back to whatever it was you were doing? The kind we can leave out on the counter for you all to snack on through the night."

"Wouldn't say no." Gabe grinned at her and her breath caught to see it. "Entire team appreciates how you've been feeding us. We're going to have to up our PT, though."

"PT?" Nope. Her brain wasn't capable of recovering fast enough to remember simple acronyms yet. Full-blown fantasies of kissing him were taking up the majority of her mental capacity at the moment.

If anything, his grin widened. As if he could know. Well, maybe he could. "Physical training."

And how did one volunteer for it?

She dragged in a full breath of chill air. Cold shower might be better. "Good food is worth it."

He winked. "Agreed."

If he didn't turn down the charm, her heart was going to crash right through her chest. Or stop for good.

"I'll see you later, *coração*." When he leaned in, she didn't duck. His kiss seared her lips and when his fingers touched her jawline she opened her mouth so he could deepen the kiss. In moments, she was lost.

Then the kiss ended and he took a step back. Off balance, she almost stumbled forward and he reached out to steady her, letting her go as soon as she had regained her equilibrium. Physically, at least.

She thought he might say something. He opened his mouth, closed it. Then he turned and headed back.

What had she been hoping for? Had to be something, because the pang of disappointment hurt and she didn't think it was Gabe's fault. There was no doubt of the attraction between them, and he was walking away to do exactly what she'd wanted him to do from the first time she'd met him. Every minute she spent with him, her reasons for holding distance between them crumbled. And he had to know.

And he was giving her time. She should be thankful for it. But she wasn't sure whether she wanted to help him close the distance or run.

She turned and walked inside the cabin, heading for the kitchen out of habit. But standing there, she couldn't lock on to anything. Cleaning had been a great way to burn off the combination of confusion and frustration she'd felt this morning, but she wasn't about to do it all again. There was keeping busy and then there was being crazy.

Pacing helped for about a minute or two.

Heading into the bedroom, she flopped onto the bed and stared at the ceiling.

It'd be silly to go back over there right away, even with the excuse of starting to cook something complicated. Gabe had just walked her over here, possibly to keep her out of their hair.

Besides, seeing Gabe and having him ignore her in favor of something else? It'd be hard. And not fair to want him to devote all his attention to what mattered, then be around distracting them both with the obvious lust issues they had.

No. That was unkind and unfair to the both of them. Whatever this was, it wasn't just lust. It was more, for her at least, and Gabe wouldn't be trying so hard if it was passing desire for him.

At lunch, she'd had a harder time than she liked to admit resisting the urge to tap at his shoulder and ask him to help her while she'd been cooking. He hadn't been ignoring her at the time, but she'd wanted his full attention. And she didn't like the way she wanted it because it hadn't come from affection. It'd come from insecurity.

Where did they stand with each other?

The ball was mostly in her court. He'd made it obvious. So the indecision was all hers, too. Great. She had no patience for indecision, especially her own.

She needed to trust him again. On a whole lot of levels.

Sitting up, she pulled out her smartphone and turned it on. It had about a twenty percent charge. Not bad but she hated having her electronics anything less than fully charged if there was an outlet nearby.

She started poking around in drawers and cabinets for a stash of chargers. There were a couple of interesting things, like a first aid kit and a mystery duffel bag in the little alcove under a shelf in the closet, but no chargers.

Out in the living area, where Gabe had been sitting with his laptop earlier in the day, there was a power strip and—found it, a charger that fit her phone. Hah.

She hadn't checked email or messages in days. It'd been one thing to install the game app on the temp phone but Gabe had warned her not to check the things most likely to be under surveillance.

There were messages in her digital voice mail so she decided to clear through those first. A few client messages in response to her out of office notification asking her to respond as soon as she returned. Nothing urgent. She saved each of them to address later, when she was officially back from her "vacation."

"Maylin. I need you to listen."

She froze. Charlie's voice was so strained, she barely recognized it.

"*Please*. There's people. They won't let me go. They're giving me forty-eight hours and then they're going to kill me. *Kill me!* They said all you have to do is let them come get you and they'll take you to your sister. It's what you wanted, right?"

Oh, no. Charlie. *No, no, no.*

His voice dropped to a pleading whisper. "Everyone gets what they want, right? Please tell me this is the right thing to do. Please. I don't want to die."

A sinking feeling in her stomach turned and twisted into a tight knot of fear. How long had it been? Fumbling, she saved the message and cursed as she got the voice mail service to replay and announce the time stamp. It'd been a day and a half ago. A day and a half.

She should run to the main house. Right away. Ask Gabe...

Shuddering, Maylin went to the bathroom and threw up.

As she ran cold water from the tap and splashed her face, she pulled herself together piece by piece. She needed more information for Gabe and the team. This would split their attention, take precious time away from finding An-mei. But she wasn't about to leave Charlie with whoever had him.

Still not sure she was doing exactly the right thing, she opened an app on her phone and set it to record, then she dialed Charlie's number. She'd done it in the past to be sure she recalled details when planning an event, but this time, it mattered a lot more.

Before she bothered Gabe, she'd find out more about who had Charlie and what they wanted.

"Maylin, it took you this long to answer your friend's call for help?"

Jewel's voice came across the line, crystal clear.

Maylin fought to modulate her voice to calm and cool. "What do you want?"

"He told you." Jewel chuckled. "Just allow us to come get you. We'll let him go back to his life and we'll take you to your sister. And everyone goes on into happy-ever-after."

"If you know where I am, you know I can't just walk out to the sidewalk and hop in a car. And I don't know why I'd be of use to you anyway." An-mei was the scientist, the brilliant resource. The closest Maylin could come to creating a biological warfare weapon was cooking up a devastatingly spicy batch of curry. Why, why, why were they after her?

Maylin started to wander back through the cabin, taking stock of what was actually tucked away. People like Gabe and his team had useful things at hand squirreled away in every nook and cranny. Even in their own base of operations, they didn't seem like the types to keep everything in the obvious locations. Not that she'd know where they kept their weapons or anything anyway. But they all walked around with something on them. Harness, knife, sometimes even their guns. They were always ready for something to happen.

How likely was it there would be something in every building? She was betting they had small caches stashed everywhere in preparation for the worst-case scenario, including the guest cabin. And well, the mystery duffel bag she'd seen earlier wasn't likely to be extra toilet paper.

"I'm sure Gabe's told you by now. We have history." Jewel said it in a way that left a million things implied. But Gabe had already told Maylin, so it irritated her but it didn't catch her flat-footed. "I used to be a Centurion and I know the area and their security precautions quite well."

"As if they wouldn't change things." Maylin didn't know for sure but it sounded good.

The duffel bag was heavier than she anticipated as she hauled it out of the closet. With no idea what was in it, she handled it carefully and placed it gently on the bed.

Jewel sighed. "Change, yes, but they're so predictable."

Unzipping the bag, Maylin pushed it wide open so she could survey the contents and try to figure out what might help her. If—and this was a very tiny *if*—she ended up going with Jewel and the Edict team, she wanted something with her.

There were several guns and boxes of ammunition, but

she'd never fired one and didn't even know what ammunition went with what gun. Besides, she'd read articles about how women carrying guns usually had the very weapons they carried for self-defense used against them. Probably not her best option.

Some of the weapons were unidentifiable to her eyes. The letters and numbers printed on the sides didn't help, either.

Then there were the canisters. "Flash Bang" was printed on the side of each one, along with a delay time. Simple pictures for directions. It didn't take much to get the idea. Recognition and relief. Those could buy her time.

"We'll manufacture a distraction. All you have to do is come along quietly and your friend lives." There was ambient noise on the call, but Jewel was raising her voice to cover it. "Are we agreed?"

Maylin's mind raced. "You haven't asked me not to tell Gabe."

"Oh, honey." Jewel laughed. "I wouldn't give you time to do that."

In the background, someone said, "Location confirmed."

Panic gripped Maylin. She was out of time. She didn't know how, but it was a fact.

The explosion sent Gabe and his entire team crouching for cover and moving. Gabe headed for the front door, staying low, with Victoria right behind him. Both of them had handguns drawn and ready. Marc was two steps ahead, breaking off into the surveillance room. Lizzy had headed in the opposite direction, towards her room.

Gabe called out, "Anyone get a visual?"

Lizzy answered first, leaning out the doorway of her room as she slung her sniper rifle over her shoulder. "Came from the training side."

"Contacting Training now to see if it was a misfire," Marc called out from the surveillance room.

"Not likely! That was an ASM." Victoria spat out a curse. "Heard too many overseas. Unless they added the missiles to the training program here, that wasn't a misfire."

No. Training hadn't added to their program or they'd have notified the fire teams on site for rest and rehabilitation.

Marc appeared in the doorway of the surveillance room, tossing Gabe and Victoria portable communications units.

Gabe slapped on the throat mic and threaded the earpiece over his ear, shoving the rest of the receiver into his shoulder harness and giving it a tug to be sure it was clipped securely.

"Need to get eyes on the asset, stat." Lizzy's statement was actually a question for Gabe. Who did he want going to secure the asset?

Maylin.

Gabe continued towards the front door. "Victoria is with me. Marc, get reinforcements from Training. Suspected incursion on the guest cabin. Lizzy, go high. We need a bird's eye view. Everybody count in on the comm in ten."

"Apaches, incoming." Victoria's voice came in clear on his comm—her sharp hearing had given her a split-second advantage on the rest of them. The low, distinctive sound of the attack helicopter blades beating the air reached them all.

"Go." Gabe was out the door and proceeding through the trees at top speed, eyes open and scanning the area as he took a curved path towards the guest cabin. The front door faced outward to the creek running past the Centurion property. Intruders were going to come from the perimeter right to the front door.

He was headed for the back of the cabin, and hoped Maylin had remained in the bedroom at the rear. His heart kicked into overdrive, pounding hard in his chest. He sucked in air, held it for a beat, and blew it out to get his shit under control. She needed him. If she was in the kitchen...

Chapter Nineteen

The explosion had sent Maylin to her knees, instinctively ducking and throwing up her hands. The ground had shaken, and it felt like the cabin had shifted a little on its foundation, even. Or maybe she was just scared out of her mind.

Yeah, she was definitely afraid.

"We'll see you shortly, Maylin Cheng," Jewel sang out from the phone still clutched in Maylin's hand.

Tā mā de.

Adrenaline coursed through her as she looked around wildly for something she could do, some way she could go. The windows were still intact somehow. But Jewel and her people were coming. Did she have time to run to Gabe and the others in the main cabin? What if Jewel had a surprise waiting for her outside?

The loud strike on the front door sent a fresh spike of fear stabbing into her chest, and another hit to the door followed.

No. She didn't have time. Not unless she bought herself some. Otherwise, they'd just grab her while she was trying to wrestle the damn window open.

She swallowed hard. Go with them? Charlie knew too much about An-mei's kidnapping if they'd told him they knew where her sister was. That they were taking her to An-mei. No. If they had Maylin, they'd probably kill Charlie to erase proof of An-mei's abduction. He didn't deserve to be caught up in all this.

Worse, if they had her, they had the leverage to make An-mei do what they wanted. Based on what Gabe had told her—and she believed what he'd said about biological warfare—a lot more people could be hurt than Charlie if An-mei did the research.

She was going to hell, but she wasn't going to go with them. Maybe she could sell her soul to get Gabe and his team to rescue Charlie, too.

Please forgive me.

Another bang at the front door, followed by gunfire. Maylin ducked back behind the doorjamb in the bedroom, breathed for a two count, then made herself peek. Hiding wouldn't help her. She needed to know what was coming towards her.

There was a man. He'd shot out the lock of the door. Someone was cursing behind him. "What if you shot the girl? Keep it under control, idiot."

"If I'd shot her, she'd have screamed. Asshole," another man answered. "She'll be fine. Let's grab her and get out."

They sounded nothing like Gabe and his team. She'd listened as they'd murmured communications to each other that first night, forever ago. Even in banter, they'd been professional. Concise. These people weren't Centurions.

How long before they managed to shoot her, on purpose or by accident?

Someday she was going to learn to come up with answers instead of so many questions.

Her heart pounded. She tightened her grip on the cold cylinder she'd grabbed from the duffel, hoping her hands wouldn't sweat and make her slip. One chance. And she had to hope she understood how to use the thing. It was heavy in her hand, weighing a lot more than she'd expected. No wonder the bag had been so hard to get out of the closet.

The man came through the door, his gun held out in front of him as his gaze swept the room. She waited—and she might be stupid for losing the precious moments— until his attention was on the far end of the room. Pulling the pin, she tossed the flash bang grenade hard.

His partner shouted a warning.

It landed short, its arc only taking it part of the way to the man, but it rolled the remaining few feet towards him. She turned away just as it exploded. The sharp bang was deafening and she clutched her head. There were shouts, but they came to her as if her ears were stuffed with cotton. She didn't wait for her hearing to come the rest of the way back. She ran for the window, lobbing one of the metal batons she'd found in the bag through the glass. No time to climb through. Instead she threw herself through the window headfirst and tried to tell herself to roll.

She hit the ground hard, rolling onto her back, the wind knocked out of her.

"Stay down!" Gabe's voice, still muffled as if she had earplugs in her ears. One side was worse than the other.

But okay. She could do that. Happiness and relief cut through her fear. He was here. Relief might have been a wonderful thing if her hands and shoulders weren't stinging. The pain was actually increasing steadily. Oh, she had to have landed on something bad. Like glass.

"Victoria." Gabe was crouching over her and she could

see the muscles in his neck strain like he was shouting. Maybe he was. The whole world was a muted cacophony for her. His hands patted her down in a gentle but thorough progression over her entire body. This checking for injuries was becoming a thing between them. Maybe it wasn't a good thing.

Maybe she was going to be hysterical.

Victoria was at their side, firing her weapon. "Covering. Go."

Gabe's mouth was set in a grim line as he grabbed Maylin by the wrist and pulled her to a sitting position, urging her to her feet. "We're going to need medical. Have them meet me at the main cabin, stat."

She tried. Honestly, she dug into her reserves and pulled up every contrary, stubborn moment in her life to drive herself to her feet. But nothing was working right. Everything throbbed, punctuated by piercing pain in random places. And a hot wetness was running from her ears down her jawline.

Gabe had her up, though, and he hoisted her over his shoulder. The jostling hurt more, blood rushing to her head as her view consisted of the ground and his feet running. She might throw up.

The world went black instead.

"You're safe." Gabe's voice came clearer this time, but not by much. There was still cotton, or maybe dirt, clogging her ears.

Around her, people were rushing back and forth. There was an IV in her left arm and a man in fatigues was injecting something into the line leading to her. Beyond him, another man in fatigues was being led by. The skin up and down his arm and the side of his face darkened, burned.

"Here. Focus right here." Gabe stepped into her line of sight. He caressed her cheek and she turned in to the caress, letting her eyes flutter closed as his thumb gently brushed across her skin.

"We're giving her Toradol for the pain..." The stranger's voice faded away.

It was a lot quieter when she woke up.

"Welcome back." The voice was familiar but it wasn't Gabe or Lizzy, not Victoria or Marc either.

Maylin inhaled and exhaled nice and slow, each breath clearing away more of the grogginess. She opened her eyes and blinked a few times before focusing on the slender man seated next to her.

"Caleb."

He grinned. "Glad you recognize me."

"I don't know where I am, though." The room looked something like the nurse's office from high school. Not really, but it was the closest comparison she could think of with the curtain partitions around her stretcher partially open to reveal several similar beds. There were doors at either end of the long room but no one seemed to be walking by. A couple of curtains were drawn around stretchers at the other end of the row.

"You're still on Centurion Corporation grounds." Caleb stood and poured water into a tiny cup. He handed it to her carefully, making sure she had a good hold on it before he settled back into his chair. "Sip slow. If it stays down, we'll see about getting you whatever chow the medics say you can try first."

"Where's Gabe?" She followed directions, the water

cool against her lips and her dry throat. Since the initial sip seemed to go down fine, she took another then returned her attention to Caleb.

"Well, Diaz and the team are fine. Not a scratch on them." Caleb waved a hand in the direction of the hallway. "You, on the other hand, look a lot worse than you are."

"Thanks?" Most likely she'd regret asking for a mirror.

"You fell on broken glass." Caleb eyed her, maybe to gauge how well she was reacting to the news.

"I remember. I jumped through a window."

"Not recommended. We all try to avoid it if possible."

"I can understand why." But she wasn't in pain, per se. Stiff, yes. And maybe there was a dull throb over most of her body.

"Most of the cuts were superficial. A couple are held closed with butterfly stitches, so don't mess with those. One or two spots, we had to stitch closed after the glass was removed. When those itch, don't mess with them either." Caleb stood and refilled her little cup with more water. "How's it staying down?"

"No nausea." She pondered. "So if I start itching, you're going to put a cone of shame on me?"

Caleb grinned. "Nah. But they make these mitts we can put over your hands to keep you from scratching."

"I'll pass, thank you." And the conversation was starting to wear on her. It wasn't that he wasn't nice, and the banter was pretty light, but there was a nagging…something at the back of her mind.

"Everything sounds weird. Kind of hollow." The words popped out.

"Yeah." Caleb set the pitcher down. "About that. Nice

distraction with the flash bang, but you were too close. You blew out your eardrums."

"Ah." Well, considering the alternative, it might be the better of the options. "Is it permanent?"

"Medic says the ruptures on your tympanic membrane are fortunately minor. Obviously you can hear some, and what trouble you're having isn't likely to be permanent." Caleb tapped a finger to the side of his own ear. "I can tell you from personal experience it'll probably be fine. Could even get back to close to one hundred percent in a few days to a week. But if you don't have your full hearing back in about three months, what's gone is probably gone for good."

Sobering thought.

"Considering most of your injuries were minor, we decided to keep you here at our medical facilities, but we can provide you with protection at a civilian hospital if you really want to move."

Some of the tension left her shoulders. There was a world of difference when someone gave her a choice. "This is okay. Especially if I can get up and leave soon."

"So long as you promise to rest, you can be moved to the rest and rehab cabin, but the guest cabin is a mess. We'd rather you stay in a more secure building for the time being."

Memory came crashing back. "Charlie!"

"Whoa, whoa." Caleb jumped up as she started to swing her legs down off the stretcher. "You've still got an IV in, don't rip it out by accident. Your friend is going to be fine. Our men retrieved him from one of the Apaches when we responded to the offensive action."

She blinked back tears. How could she have forgotten? "Really?"

"To be honest, Edict shoved him out of the helicopter." Caleb held her shoulders. "But he didn't fall far. He's got a few bumps and bruises, but you look a lot worse than he does. Plus, with the damage to your ears, let's take it slow with the standing up or one of the medics is going to come in here and yell at us both. Your balance might be off."

"They just…let him go?" Maylin had been so sure they'd kill Charlie, and maybe her, too, once she wasn't of use as leverage. Maybe she'd been watching too many television shows.

Caleb grimaced. "Well, there's no being sure. But Lizzy took a distance shot at the person holding him in the copter. So whatever they were going to do, their mind was changed. Lizzy is a pretty incredible sniper, in case you didn't know."

"I didn't." Really, she didn't know much about any of them. Except Gabe. "Where are they all now?"

Caleb paused. "I promised Diaz I wouldn't lie to you. He said he owed it to you."

Maylin's breath caught in her throat.

"You have been out for a good twenty-four hours. They've been cleaning up and analyzing the attack, including a captured recording of your call with Jewel. Nice presence of mind, setting it to record the call, by the way, and keeping your wits about you with her. That woman is too clever for her own good." Caleb sat and crossed one leg over the other, tapping his knee with his fingers in a rapid staccato beat. "Harte and I arrived with several other fire teams, enough to make a couple of squadrons. That's two dozen more people to support Diaz's team, by the way."

"Okay." It was a lot of people. All to the good, she

hoped. Elation bloomed in her chest and spread through her body, clearing away the last of the fog of her injuries. They had enough people and firepower. They were going to get her.

Her heart contracted and expended in her chest almost painfully. After being told so many times to give up, by everyone, this was finally happening. And she couldn't help holding her breath against the fear that all of this could still end badly.

A few tears welled up and she blinked them back. Happiness and apprehension warred with each other inside her head until she clenched her hands in her lap to stop them from trembling.

Caleb didn't say anything as she worked through her tumble of emotions. He seemed so nonchalant about it or, she was realizing, his expressions weren't reflective of what he was actually thinking.

She'd blinked away the tears and sat staring at him for a few moments before he continued as if he'd never stopped. "Diaz and his team were ready with a plan, and it was determined they should execute, with certain tweaks, before Edict or their sponsor decided to move your sister since the acquisition of you failed."

In his own way, Caleb was really hard to read. She couldn't help but watch him close. He seemed so genial and pleasant, she almost missed the tightness around his eyes and at the corners of his mouth. His tone had barely changed. But he was angry. Maybe.

"Caleb, I…"

He waved her apology away before she could finish. "It's not your fault. Not any of this. And Edict is ballsy as fuck for taking action here. There has been tension between the two organizations ever since they cherry-picked a couple of our resources, but this took it to a whole new level. Trust me. If it hadn't been you, it would have been a different contract and a different altercation."

"How are you and Harte different, Caleb?" She'd wondered before, and maybe it was a stupid question now. But she wanted to know. Isabelle and Victoria had nicknames, but most of the men had been addressed by last name.

Caleb blinked. "Different?"

"Everyone calls you and Harte by your first names."

"Oh." He might have been blushing. Maybe. Hard to tell, but he did look sheepish. "I was an officer when I was active with the US military. So was Harte. I'm in training now, but I have special subject matter expertise in intelligence and other things. So I guess since we don't use rank in the Centurion Corporation, being private sector and all, the first name usage is our version of addressing someone who is the equivalent of an officer. Sort of a gentleman's agreement. It's not quite that simple, but that's the high-level version of it."

"So you have authority." She kept her gaze steady on his. No dodging on this one.

"Yes." He said it slowly, like he was realizing she'd maneuvered him and was deciding whether he should slip out of whatever she had in mind.

"So you can take me to Gabe and the others."

"Not exactly." Caleb studied her. "They're not on premises and there's no way I'd take you to where they are. Besides, we'd only be in the way. The operation is planned and in progress. If we want them to succeed then we trust them to do what they need to do."

"There's got to be a way to know what they're doing, though. You don't just wait in the dark for them to come home." Even as she said it, she watched his expression go pleasantly blank. Wow.

"This time. No. We aren't waiting in the dark." Caleb met her gaze with his own and it was inscrutable. "If you and Diaz are a thing, it's important you accept who he is and what he does. Most of the time, not sometimes, you will have to wait with no word until he comes back. Decide if you can handle that."

Not a light matter.

"I won't answer that right away, because what you've said deserves time to really absorb." Maybe other people said something different. But she wanted to give it serious consideration, because it was another truth, a reality of who Gabe was. "But this time, you said you weren't waiting in the dark, and you didn't say I had to."

Caleb chuckled, the seriousness evaporating. "Promise you'll eat something first. The operation won't start for a while yet, not until 0200 hours. When it does, I also need your word that you'll stay in the back of the room with me. You have questions, you ask me. Don't interrupt anyone else no matter what you hear."

She pressed her lips together. Despite his levity, she got the impression he'd take her right back out of whatever room this was going to be if she couldn't follow his instructions. If he was taking the time to make this clear to her in advance, it was almost certain there'd be *something* going on she'd want to question. Could she watch and not ask questions? Not attempt to interfere? A hundred possibilities ran through her head. It was that or sit here waiting.

She wanted to know what was happening. "I promise."

Caleb dragged his hand through his short cropped hair,

rubbing his scalp with his palm. Abruptly, she wondered if he'd stayed the entire time watching over her.

He chuckled. "I'd have never done this before, but I figure you should be there as our good luck charm. You're the bird dog that flushed up all of this trouble in the first place."

Chapter Twenty

"One Alpha, in position." Gabe kept an eye on the corridor, scanning left, then right, and back again as his team crouched around the access to the old air ducts. Literally one eye open since his team had invested in the better-quality night vision gear that covered only one side, allowing the mcn to retain depth perception and leaving them free to open the other eye in case of a quick change in lighting. It took some getting used to, but allowed for faster reaction time.

It was the edge needed for survival and success, in that order.

"Roger that, One Alpha." Harte's voice came low through the comm in Gabe's ear. "Squad Two in place, maintaining surveillance. You are clear to proceed. Unless you need a minute to recover from the run. It was a long way through those tunnels."

Gabe grinned in the dark. Sometimes he wondered if he missed the more strict communications practices of active military duty, especially during operations like this one. But then, their frequency was secure and Harte had a good sense of when there was time for banter versus times every word mattered. "A mile or two underground? Didn't break a sweat."

"Roger." Harte might be chuckling, but his words came through clear. "Proceed."

"Proceeding, sir." He clamped down on the anticipation driving him to rush forward. There'd been a lot of hurry up and wait to reach this point. His Delta fire team had to break the seal of an airlock fused shut decades prior by the Army Corps of Engineers decommissioning team while Alpha, Bravo and Charlie fire teams stood by on watch. Once breached, Alpha led the way into the tunnel with Bravo and Charlie following, leaving Delta to stand watch at the entrance.

At the entrance to the air ducts, Marc and Victoria had scouted the next stage of entry into the underground complex while he and Lizzy had held their position. Meanwhile, Squadron Two's fire teams had taken up positions above ground to keep an eye on the site's activity.

It'd been a lot of waiting. Now that he and his team were inside and on point with a primary plan and a backup, everything they did would be action and reaction. Which was good, because An-mei Cheng had waited long enough.

Using hand signals, he motioned for Marc and Vicky to lead them forward. They crawled through a short stretch of air duct before sliding into the space between a wall and a massive pipe. There was a long-forgotten built-in access for a repair crew on the side of the pipe, allowing them to enter and climb down under the main part of the facility, still underground but a level or two above the matrix of tunnels branching out from the old site. The drain in the utility closet was industrial sized, large enough for them each to emerge and take position before heading out into the more dangerous hallway.

"For a decommissioned ICBM, the facilities are in

surprisingly good repair." Harte's comment was nonchalant, confirming for Gabe that the camera feeds each of his men wore were in working order despite the underground distance.

"Well-lit, clean," Gabe responded. There were a lot of these decommissioned sites dotting the United States, leftover from the Cold War when intercontinental ballistic missiles were scattered among "dummy" sites. Over time, they'd fallen into disrepair, and most were condemned. "Funny how this one didn't show up as having a long-term lease."

Sites like these could be contracted to local governments and corporations, even private military contractors in decades-long leases for preservation or training purposes. Cheaper for the federal government than maintaining the site, perfect for organizations like theirs to establish a training facility. In fact, Centurion Corporation had similar contracts for other types of sites.

Once his team cleared the glorified broom closet, they set up on the door and communicated through silent touches their readiness to breach it. Marc opened it quickly and the other three poured into the hall, Gabe at the lead, all weapons at high ready.

Never breaking step, the fire team embodied the mantra "smooth is fast, fast is smooth" as they flowed past other doors and danger points in a modified T.

"Not a spider or rat in sight."

"You'd think someone wanted to maintain good laboratory practices for some reason." Yeah. They'd confirmed this was their target when surveillance had caught some very interesting supplies arriving. Coated slides for protein and DNA microarrays, multi-well microarray substrates and a long list of other things, harder to pronounce and definitely for genetic research, all received in fairly regular shipments from various sources.

Whoever was maintaining the site had done a good job of hiding the supply draw from the eyes of anyone watching for a virtual paper trail, but for someone with eyes on the site? It was painfully obvious. Right up there with the number of fairly new surveillance cameras installed on the premises.

His team reached a juncture in the hallways and, having established a beachhead, crouched at the corners to wait for Bravo and Charlie teams.

The Bravo team would emerge with a mirrored formation to his own fire team a minute or two behind them to ensure they had heavy support on both sides. Charlie team would follow after, with Delta team holding position at the access point, ready to run in with medical support if the worst happened.

Once the teams had all emerged from the drain and were able to move quickly, he took them forward.

Based on the surveillance and intel they'd been able to gather, there were likely minimal patrols at this time of night. 0200 hours fell well into the graveyard watch, when those assigned to the shift became complacent with the night's silence and, hopefully, bored enough to doze off. Any other personnel in the facility, maybe more kidnapped scientists like An-mei, should be asleep, and all were likely kept in separate quarters to prevent them from communicating more than was necessary.

Hang on. You have a big sister looking for you.

Gabe hoped they were in time. Edict shouldn't have had time yet to move An-mei. They'd have needed a green light from a decision-maker in their backer's organization, Phoenix Biotech, on any semi-permanent location to take her to in any case. And the Centurions were betting on An-mei's value as a scientist to keep her alive. Anticipated retaliation after the attack on Centurion Corporation ground would push Edict and, by extension, Phoenix Biotech, into taking defensive action. Hopefully it wouldn't pressure them into making An-mei disappear permanently.

Harte's voice murmured into his ear-comm, "Squadron Two Bravo reports normal movement above ground. Guards on watch show no change."

Which was an indicator that all was well below ground, if luck was on their side.

Gabe proceeded forward, working his way through the network of hallways and stopping to check the labels for each of the rooms as they passed, trying to find the labs or the sleeping quarters. The search would be painfully slow unless they found someone to help them. Gabe wasn't above asking for directions.

Politely, of course.

They moved forward two more hallway junctions before he heard exactly what he was hoping for: footsteps. They echoed around the corner as his teams halted. The person was alone and unhurried. Perfect.

"What are they doing?" Maylin squinted, trying to make sense of the images on the various monitors. Apparently Gabe and each of his teams were wearing cameras, but the images had been too dark until Gabe's team emerged in the lighted hallways of the facility. Even so, the video feed wasn't crisp and the color was a little closer to gray scale. Focus was sharper in the center of the screen but stretched along the periphery. It made it more like a scary movie for her, surreal and tense. As if anything could come at them from any side. They'd all become people who mattered to her. And Gabe? Much more. Indescribably so.

"They're about to ask for directions, most likely." Harte stood in front of the monitors, arms crossed. His head turned slightly as he scanned each of the monitors in turn. "It's what I'd do."

"We had a good idea of what the layout was inside the underground lab based on the way the military tended to build those old silos. They're cookie-cutter in some ways. Not the same, but following the same architectural logic." Caleb tapped a monitor showing an outside view of the area. "But these people could've repurposed the interior in any number of ways. It'll take too long to do a room-to-room search. Our teams need to get intel directly from someone familiar with the operation."

Possibilities crowded into Maylin's mind and none of them were the stuff of sweet dreams. She had to remind herself, chant silently. *We're saving An-mei.*

The people who had her sister would've done worse to her, would've killed Charlie. An innocent man dragged into chaos and it was all Maylin's fault. Maybe when it was all over she could figure out a way to make up for it, but she wasn't in a place to think about it. Yet.

For now. There was only the screen and the sudden blur of movement as Gabe rushed forward and grabbed a person mouth first. There was a struggle as they grappled. Gabe had the other man subdued in less than a second. Frightening how quiet, how fast it had been.

"The scientists. Where are they kept?" Gabe's voice was barely recognizable, the low growl distorted. Maybe he did it on purpose or maybe it was a measure of how different he was with her.

The captured man started to curse through the thing shoved in his mouth, but his words were cut off by a rapid clicking sound and he convulsed. Maylin jumped. Couldn't help it.

"Taser." Caleb's comment was neutral. Harte said nothing, his face a hard mask.

Gabe waved a tiny cylinder under the unconscious man's nose. As the man came to, Gabe fired off the question again. "Where are they? Where are the scientists?"

The man spit out another muffled insult. Defiance was in the set of his jaw and his stubborn glare.

Gabe tased him again.

"Maybe you should wait outside." Caleb made the suggestion gently. "I'll come get you when they move to the next phase."

Maylin shook her head and hugged herself. Made sure to watch every moment. Gabe was doing this for her. He might have committed other things in the past and this probably wasn't the worst he'd ever done, but this was for her. If there was nothing else she could do, she could bear witness.

Caleb didn't argue, only returned his attention to the screen.

The man finally broke, stuttering out a set of directions.

"One Charlie, secure him." Having given the order, Gabe and his team moved forward.

They moved quickly through the halls, and the cameras blurred a little more on the edges. They encountered one more guard, overwhelmed him with a speedy efficiency that made it look simple. It couldn't be, but Maylin had no doubts they were very good at what they did.

"Note—no unit insignias on the uniforms. Their badges are worn. They've been here awhile."

Harte responded, "Understood, One Alpha."

Finally, Gabe's camera trained on a door. He touched a badge he'd stripped off the first guard to a sensor on the left and it flashed green as the lock disengaged with an audible click. Inside, a tiny form lay curled up on a bare bunk. Gabe moved forward and pinned the girl down as she woke, covering her mouth to silence her scream. Gaunt, exhausted, but a beautiful sight.

"An-mei." Maylin whispered her sister's name.

Harte didn't even glance back at her. "Identity confirmed. Acquire the package and get the hell out of Dodge."

Still gruff, the version of Gabe's voice she knew returned. "An-mei. Maylin sent us. Can you walk?"

Panic receded from An-mei's eyes when Gabe made no move. After a long moment, she nodded. He released her and helped her up. Her sister took a moment to gain her balance but then seemed steady on her bare feet.

"She looks okay." Dizzy with relief, Maylin leaned back against the wall.

Clothes, boots. They could get An-mei those. What mattered was she seemed whole and mostly well.

"They'd want her in good enough shape to conduct their research." Caleb sounded so incredibly reasonable. "Scientists need steady hands. If she didn't eat, they'd have force-fed her to make sure she was getting nutrition."

Hopefully, it hadn't happened.

They were on the move again and Maylin had to look at Marc's camera to see An-mei. Gabe had taken the lead again and they were back in formation.

Caleb moved to lean against the wall next to her. "They might have done other things to try to get her to cooperate. Isolation, sensory deprivation. Your sister will probably need counseling. I'd recommend you both stay here for some time until we can find new options for you."

"They aren't safe yet. Can we talk about it after? We need them safe first." It was unlucky to talk about the future before the immediate danger had been overcome. It was tempting fate.

Gunfire burst out in a staccato beat across the speakers. Marc's camera ran into An-mei's back; from one of the Bravo team's monitors, Maylin could see Marc pressing An-mei into the floor as he loomed protectively over her to shield her. Gabe had gone down into a crouch as he returned fire.

"One Alpha, Code 13. We're under fire. Request immediate assistance."

Maylin's heart stopped.

Harte barked orders. "Two Alpha, proceed inside. Two Bravo and Charlie, retrograde to vehicles and prepare for secondary exit scenario. One Delta, stand by."

"What...?"

Caleb placed a steadying hand on her shoulder. She was glad he kept his distance, though. She might have shoved him off in her anxiety. Instead, his touch grounded her. He stepped into her line of sight. "We're switching to Plan B. The other squadron was waiting above ground just for this. One of the fire teams is heading in to help and then lead them out to the ground level where the other two teams are clearing a path out. Squadron One Bravo is moving inside now while One Delta will stay below ground in the tunnels to guard that escape route in case they have to go to Plan C. The teams have this under control and are still moving."

And they were. Marc had hoisted An-mei over his shoulder and was walking fast. The cameras of the Bravo team bounced as the teams moved forward at speed, not quite running but definitely heading somewhere in a rush. Here and there, gunfire burst and Gabe's teams responded. Victoria wielded an impossibly large gun, lighting up the hallway as she fired. Maylin wasn't sure if it would be a memorial or a nightmare, but the sounds of shouts and pained cries burned into her brain. So far, though, every one of the Centurion cameras continued to move.

The teams seemed to converge and all head through a wider open area.

"They've reached the front door." Caleb said it like such a place had one, complete with reception area.

All Maylin could see was open space and a pair of doors ahead.

Suddenly, all of the cameras flashed with light. Terse words jumbled together as the teams reported in, and she couldn't sort them. How any of them did, she didn't know. Couldn't imagine getting used to it.

Anxiety wound up inside her so tight she had to force herself to let go of the air she was holding in her lungs. Her jaw hurt from clenching and her heart pounded. Please, please let them come through okay.

"Flash bangs." Gabe's voice came across. "One Charlie has one man blind. Injuries minimal."

The cameras resolved to images again just in time to go black as they passed through the front doors into night.

She could barely make out shadows as they moved to vehicles. The engines and shouting were enough to tell her they were moving. More gunfire. And the cameras flared again as another explosion went off ahead and to the left of one of the vehicles. The jeep Gabe was in.

It was Lizzy's voice over the speakers. "Fucking Jewel and her IEDs."

Chapter Twenty-One

Gabe concentrated on breathing. Not easy with acrid fumes clogging his lungs. He blinked rapidly to clear his vision. The world was upside down. Actually, they were. Could've been worse.

"All posts, status. One Alpha, go."

Lizzy reported in first, broadcasting across their radio channel even though she was right next to him in the passenger seat. "Scott. Green. Moving into position to provide cover but we need to get mobile again. Stat."

As soon as she'd checked in, she released her seat belt and scrambled out of the overturned vehicle. Gabe would do the same, but he had a suspicion his mobility was going to be more of a problem. Pain fired off at intervals down his lower back and through his legs. He'd have to go slower.

Victoria checked in next, already halfway out of the vehicle. "Ash. Green."

"Lykke. Green. The package is unconscious. No visible injuries. Ash is assisting with extraction from vehicle."

Good. An-mei was their highest priority. If he had to, he'd send his team back to Maylin without him.

The other fire teams continued their check-ins. No

other cars had been caught in the small blast. It'd been the kind of present designed to flip a single car and cause confusion in the caravan while enemy forces focused fire on the vehicles caught behind. Only Squadron Two had already subdued what enemy units there were on site. They had a small window of time to recover and get out.

Gabe reassessed his own situation. The immediate pain had subsided. He braced himself as best he could and released his seat belt. Nothing happened.

"Fuck." He reached for his utility knife and yanked the hooked end across the seat belt, the cutter parting the reinforced fabric with ease.

Did Maylin have one of these in her car? Not likely. He should get her one and teach her to use it.

Harte's voice came across the comm, cool and calm. Meaning he was worried. "One Alpha Diaz, status?"

"Green." Gabe kept his growl to a minimum. "Minor seat belt issue. Not a problem. Enemy units have not been reinforced yet. We are clear to move for now."

Twisting and crawling out the window wasn't an easy feat, but he made it. Muscles protested in his lower back, but he didn't suffer any further sharp pains. Peering out into the darkness around them, he watched the deep shadows for any sign of movement.

Nothing. Yet.

Good thing his legs were working. He counted it a small win as he joined his fire team on his own. Running would be a problem if it came to it, but for the time being they doubled up in one of the other vehicles.

"Proceed slow. Use extreme caution." Speed was not their friend at the moment, even if there was a need for it. Enemy reinforcements might be on their way, but they hadn't shown up yet and it could be because they didn't want to be caught in their own blast zones. There were other improvised explosive devices. Had to be. His team couldn't afford to rush out of here and potentially trigger another mine.

The vehicles moved forward at an agonizing crawl. It would've been a good time for a military explosives detection unit, but they hadn't brought any of the dogs with them. All they could do was hope there weren't any more in the path out.

The sound of gunfire surrounded them as multiple hits sounded against the side of their vehicle with a distinct *thwang, thwang, thwang, thwang*.

There was a metallic click from inside their vehicle as Lizzy flipped up the rear iron sight on her assault rifle. The rest of his team reacted a split second later. Marc opened the west-facing window and Victoria moved to cover An-mei's unconscious form while Lizzy shifted into position to return fire from her seat.

Gabe made the report. "One Alpha. Shots fired from the west. Scott, you got this?"

Two shots rang out. Then Lizzy reported in. "Two down. Two to go."

Even with a regular assault rifle and iron sights instead of her sniper rifle and scope, Lizzy was one of the best he'd ever encountered. She took another shot. "One to go."

"Roger that."

Harte's voice murmured over the comms in their ears, "Two Bravo and Two Charlie, move to intercept additional enemy units to the west."

Gabe cursed. They were sitting ducks all lined up. The only comfort was that any shooter would have to stay far enough back to be clear of the potential blast zone. Too far to take aim for anything but an area target shot, so the best their attackers could hope for was a lucky hit on one of the tires. Unless there was a sniper set up out there to take a point target, his team had a chance of getting out. Problem was, their luck was running out and they couldn't pick up speed without risking running over another mine. "Convoy, continue at current speed. Stay sharp for any additional IEDs."

Thwang.

The point of impact was higher, the bullet ricocheting dangerously close to the window. They all ducked down a little lower in the vehicle, covering as best they could. Marc had joined Victoria in physically providing cover to An-mei.

Lizzy took one more shot. "All targets eliminated."

His team rode in grim silence as they crept along. All of them would end up under medical surveillance once they got home. The blast had been enough to shake every one of their brains inside their skulls, and even if they thought they had green status to get up on their own power and get the hell out, they'd need to spend the next several days letting their minds physically recover from the blast trauma.

They'd been damned lucky.

But the sticking point was one he needed to figure out: with Jewel, a person didn't get lucky more than once. Even the chances of surviving her toys once were minuscule. He'd survived, what? Three times. Something was off.

As they hit a main road, they picked up speed finally. Gabe had started to report in when the ground under the vehicles shook enough to make them slow again.

"Holy shit." Marc let out the curse as he braced An-mei's still-inert body against him.

Dust clouds rose up over the trees in the direction

they'd come. The base was going down in a series of explosions.

"Keep driving." Gabe gave the order. "Let's get clear in case there's more to come."

"Damage is limited to the core facility," Harte's voice reported over the comm. "Perimeter damage limited. You should be clear. Status?"

Gabe cleared his throat. "Clear and headed to next checkpoint. One Delta, withdraw and meet us there."

"Roger that, Diaz. Satellites show enemy pursuit has veered off and your path is clear. Travel safe." Harte's acknowledgment was damned cheerful. "Your girl is awake and looking forward to seeing you."

Was she there? Listening? He couldn't think of something clever to say. The words he had for her were for her alone, not two crazy squadrons of mercenaries and a boss who'd never stop ragging him for it.

But if she was listening…

To hell with it. If he'd learned anything from her, it was to speak his mind. And his heart. Or he'd keep on regretting his entire life. "We're coming home, *coração*."

"Right here, waiting." Maylin's sweet voice came across the comm, low and trembling. "Thank you, all of you. Travel safe."

Every one of the men and women in his vehicle had shit-eating grins plastered across their faces.

He studied An-mei, propped up now between Victoria and Marc but kept low enough to protect her from possible injury if they came under fire again. A possibility if they had any other delay to their exit. They were likely in the clear, but it was better to be sure. None of them would relax until they were safely back on Centurion Corporation land.

"How is she?" No more broadcasting until the next check point. This was just with his team. He hoped the girl was okay.

"Still out cold." Marc shrugged and An-mei's head tipped against his shoulder. "Pretty sure she passed out before we even flipped."

Actually the best they could hope for. Unconscious and limp, her unresisting body was least likely to have taken damage.

"No visible signs of injury." Victoria had a hold of the girl's wrist. "Vital signs are all there. Didn't find any broken bones once we got her clear back there. No bleeding. I honestly think it's simple exhaustion, but we'll know more once we make the next checkpoint and Delta team has a chance to take a more thorough look."

"They've got field diagnostic gear on the copter." More than An-mei would need the Delta team's medical expertise. Once they arrived at the checkpoint, Gabe would make the tough decisions to prioritize the injuries. If An-mei was just unconscious, he had other team members in greater need of attention. Broken or bleeding trumped even damsels in distress.

Looking at her, she appeared to be sleeping. Hopefully a good sign.

The family resemblance was clear. An-mei shared Maylin's delicate bone structure and incredibly fine hair. He'd gotten a good look at the same brilliant green eyes when they'd first found her, too. But An-mei was shorter and lighter, somehow more fragile with a paler complexion. He didn't think it was only from her time in captivity. The younger sister had a sort of waif quality to her. Breakable.

The last person he'd been sent to save had been a

physically fit man. Worn down from days of captivity, but so much more able-bodied. Or so Gabe had thought. His mistake. Sound of body didn't help much if a person wasn't sound of mind, and the man had been a babbling, panic-ridden mess.

It'd been a struggle for Gabe and his team, getting the guy out of his cell. Ultimately, the man had died and his mission had been a failure. They'd barely gotten out and Gabe hadn't come through it on his own two feet.

He needed to get An-mei back in one piece for Maylin, and for himself, too. Acknowledging it freed up something deep inside him he hadn't admitted all this time.

Every mission mattered. He cared. Couldn't not. And it made him human even if he pretended he wasn't.

Half an hour after Gabe had told her they were coming home, she was back in the kitchen again.

Maylin ran her fingertips along the cool marble counter. Funny how it had become home to her, more so than her apartment back downtown or the kitchens she used for her work. Before all of this, when her life had been An-mei and the catering company—well, to be honest, mostly her catering company—no kitchen had been home for her because she was always stepping into the commercial-grade places meant to feed hundreds in a single night. None of those places was the central gathering place of a family.

Gabe's team was a family, though they might not think of it that way. Non-traditional, unconventional, but in so many ways closer in understanding and purpose than a normal family might be.

In the space of a few days, Maylin trusted them more than most of her own family ties.

She reached under the stove for a big stock pot. It was funny how they'd bought an entire cook set without knowing how to use any of the cookware. When she'd commented on it, Lizzy had shrugged and said somebody should figure out how. Or somebody who could cook would eventually find themselves there for recuperation, too.

Nabbing several bones from the refrigerator, she tossed them in the stock pot with a drizzle of olive oil. Bones always made the best soup stock. Gave it a heartier quality than just bouillon. Over a medium-high flame, she'd brown them and start adding other ingredients for a nice clear soup. It'd be ready for the team when they got back.

No matter when they returned.

And that was something she had to think hard about. Reaching into the refrigerator, she pulled out carrots and celery, plus a big onion. As she washed them and cut the ends, placing the prepped vegetables on a cutting board, she let her mind run free. What was between Gabe and her was real. Undefined, but tangible. She didn't want to give it up.

But Harte and Caleb had let her peek into the work Gabe did. She hadn't been sure her heart could take the fear she'd had for every one of his team, and most especially for Gabe.

When the bomb had flipped his vehicle, she thought everything she loved had died.

Gabe. An-mei. His team…they'd all been in there. And with the exception of her sister, they all did this on a regular basis. They only came to Washington State to recuperate when their jobs hit them so hard they had no choice but to come here to heal. And that was only if they'd been lucky. The alternative was…unthinkable. And permanent.

Methodically, she began dicing the onion. Small, uniform pieces so they would cook at the same rate. Measurable. Everything was predictable in cooking. There was room for creativity and personal taste, but mostly cooking was a logical set of outcomes. Add something and get a quantifiable and predictable result.

Culinary chemistry, really.

In a kitchen, she had control over everything and the freedom to tweak things back and forth to reflect her mood and intentions. It was always constructive. And in her business, her rewards were in direct proportion to the level of effort she'd put into it. Fair.

What Gabe and his team did usually had a cause, as far as she understood it. There was usually a clear understanding that they were doing the right thing. But they went in with a plan and a backup plan, plus several alternatives in case everything went to hell. All they could control was their reaction to the insanity they'd gone into. And most of the time, things didn't make sense.

She'd have no way of helping them in the future. No control over when they came back or whether they returned unharmed. She'd only be able to wait like this and maybe have something warm on the stove for them. Something that would keep because there was no knowing exactly when they'd get back.

She added the onions to the stock pot and gave the contents a stir to coat the onions in the olive oil and the drippings from the pork bones. Then she returned to the cutting board to dice the carrots and celery.

Same uniform size. Same comforting measurements. She was a creature of habit. Nothing about the last few days had been anything resembling routine except this. Cooking. And it'd made her happy to cook for Gabe and his team. She'd even gotten a feel for how to cook for each of them individually. Thoughts of dishes they specifically might like. She'd planned to make a special meal for each of them someday soon.

And then the bomb had gone off under her car and she'd understood how someday could be never.

She shook her head. Lifting the cutting board, she brought it to the stock pot and slid the entire load of diced carrots and celery into the pot with the back of her knife. Setting both board and knife aside, she liberally sprinkled salt on the veggies and then gave it all a good stir. It smelled lovely.

After another minute, she used another pot she'd filled at the sink to pour water into her stock. Covering the meat bones and vegetables and filling the stock pot to three quarters of the way full, she figured it'd take only a short while for it all to come up to a boil. Then she'd season and add a few more ingredients to finish the soup.

She'd need something else to keep her hands busy. Bread was out of the question because no one had known to buy yeast and she'd not even thought to get a sourdough starter going. That would have taken a week or so.

Tears welled up and she picked up a ladle to stir the soup even though it didn't need it. Stupid. Her place was back in Seattle, so why be upset about not having the ingredients she needed to make Gabe nice things? And why think about long-term supplies or things like sourdough starter when she didn't know what her future with him was going to be? Especially if he got his stupid self killed before they ever figured it out?

She couldn't make a home here because the entire place was transitory, temporary by nature.

But she wasn't sure she could go back to the home she had, either.

"You'll be coming with me now."

Chapter Twenty-Two

Maylin's heart stopped. No way. Couldn't be.

"Surprised?" Jewel laughed. The sound was low and almost a cackle. Theatrical.

The thought brought some courage back to Maylin, and she forced herself to continue to stir her soup pot, slow and unhurried. "Why are you still here?"

And how? If Jewel got hold of her for Edict, would they use her to bring An-mei back under their control? Maybe. Or revenge. Either way, it'd hurt An-mei...and Gabe.

"Final bit of insurance. Once I saw the squadrons deploy, I figured security on you would be lighter. My gamble paid off. And since I hear our Gabe was successful, you become even more valuable." Jewel was continuing her villain act. "I know this base as well as any of the idiots here. I was a Centurion."

And verb tense meant everything in that statement. Maylin glared at Jewel. "But you're not anymore."

Jewel shook her head and made a clicking sound with her tongue. "Doesn't make me any less good at what I do, darlin'."

"I think it does." Maylin stuck her chin up. Refused

to let Jewel frighten her out of thinking. She needed to get away, call for help.

"What do you know?" Jewel sneered. "You've met a handful of them over the course of a week. I've blown up three times as many in half the time."

True. And what was she? A cook. If it'd been her stepmother speaking, she would have squared her shoulders and listed her accomplishments. She was an entrepreneur. She'd never had to ask her parents for money, and she was independent. But against a woman like Jewel, a woman capable of going head-to-head with Gabe, what was Maylin?

Stubborn. Headstrong. Too determined for your own good. Her stepmother's words came to her at the worst of times. This was not the time to let the woman's words get her down.

Besides, they were discussing the Centurions. And she could multi-task.

"They do the right thing even when the money isn't there." Deliberately not looking at something had never been so hard. "Greed isn't a handicap for them."

"How philosophical," Jewel crooned. "Even a little Zen-sounding. Or some shit like that. You learn that growing up? Or do you have a crazy family uncle who vomits up pieces of wisdom? Maybe one with blond hair and green eyes. Did you ever wonder where you and your sister got them from? She is a geneticist, isn't she?"

Maylin didn't rise to the bait. She gave Jewel a serene smile instead. "My father came from northwestern China. There's a possibility we're throwbacks to a lost Roman legion. Or, we could be the result of a random combination of genetic factors plus environmental influences. Eye color is a complicated thing."

Jewel's eyes narrowed. "In any case, the Centurions as a whole are fools, Gabe and his team even worse than the rest, and their chivalrous code doesn't make them heroes. What it does is make them suckers and makes you a fool for believing in them. They're mercenaries, like me, and people like us have done awful things for no good reason."

Jewel stepped forward, the grin on her face broadening when Maylin didn't bolt. "You're going to come with me as bait for your wayward sister. Let's get going before the idiots on watch actually manage to pull together a timely response team. If they realize you're in danger at all. You see, they're used to bigger threats. A single woman talking to another woman? It'll take them time to recognize the back of my head as not belonging to any of the Centurions on site. If they recognize me at all."

Maylin hadn't even known where the cameras were, only had faith they had to be somewhere. As much as Jewel knew, there wasn't any hope of a miracle rescue in time to stop her.

Jewel raised her right hand, training a small gun at Maylin.

Don't look away. Keep your eyes wide open and look for your own solutions. Maylin didn't think her father had meant his advice for life-threatening situations, but hell if it didn't apply.

She kept her eyes on the gun, with Jewel behind it, and yanked the ladle out of the now-boiling soup pot, knocking it over. Jewel screamed as scalding liquid splashed across her hand and the gun she was holding, and Maylin scrambled around the kitchen island as the stock pot clattered to the floor between them.

Jewel was cursing behind her, and Maylin sobbed as

she bolted for the hallway towards the front door. Maybe she'd knocked the gun from Jewel's hand. Maybe…

Her feet were yanked out from under her and her head hit the ground as she fell. Stars shot through her skull like a billion piercing needles, and she fought to keep conscious. She was roughly flipped onto her back and a frightening click sounded off right next to her head.

Jewel was kneeling over her, gun held in her left hand as she cradled her right close to her chest. "Little bitch."

Dead was better than taken. Maylin swallowed hard. It'd be better if the mercenary killed her than use her against people she loved. Like An-mei, or Gabe.

And he didn't even know she loved him.

But Jewel only held the gun steady and cocked her head sideways. "Gutsy. I'll give you that. I've blown you up, driven you through glass, and now I'm holding a gun to your head. Did it even occur to you to leave Gabe? It's not a major concern to me, mind you, more a point of curiosity."

Leave?

Jewel regarded her with a small, patient smile.

"He…he's not staying." Maylin blurted it out. No idea where Jewel was going with this. The woman was crazy.

"With you?" Jewel cocked an eyebrow.

"Here." Maylin blinked over and over again, trying to clear her vision past the pounding of her head. "This place is only temporary."

Jewel had to know that. It was for rest and recovery only.

"Yeah, yeah. I do know." Jewel sounded exasperated. Maybe Maylin had been babbling out loud. "And what about the two of you? Did either of you talk about anything besides what was directly in front of you?"

Maylin's throat tightened. "I don't know. We haven't figured it out yet."

"Did it occur to you to take your sister and leave once they all bring her back?"

"Without saying good-bye?" Leave things unfinished? "No. There's too much. Too many questions."

"So you were going to just play house here until they came back?" Jewel laughed, a genuine sound of mirth bubbling up from deep inside. The amusement chased away the hard lines and made her look years younger. For a moment, you'd think she was a normal woman. Not capable of shooting people in the back. Not holding a gun on Maylin.

Embarrassment burned Maylin's cheeks. "It's what I can do for them. Have something comforting when they get back. I couldn't go with them, be real help to them. I don't have the medical training to treat their injuries. This is what I could do."

And it was something. It was needed.

"You know, I mistook your quiet little demeanor for submissive." Jewel nudged Maylin's hip with a booted foot. "You've obviously got no combat skills. You played the respect game very well inside the embassy back in DC. Most American Chinese would've gone in there and tried to roll over everyone and gotten nothing but passive-aggressive bullshit in return. But you, you walked the fine line and got results. Give a little ground, gain a lot more than they realized, until they were tripping over themselves to help you. More effective than I figured you could be. Takes a lot of patience to be that kind of person."

Maylin tried to squirm away, but Jewel nudged her harder.

"Ah. Don't move. I've got a point here and I'm going to take my sweet time getting to it. You don't give up and I like that, too, but now's not the time to get all uppity." Jewel spit to one side.

Better than on her. Maylin was grateful for small blessings.

"You know the problem with the kind of life we lead?" Jewel continued. "We're not patient. And if we happen to fall in love, the people we fall in love with aren't either. It's not a common enough virtue. There's too many other priorities out there. And we find ourselves having to choose. But you. You kept your focus through this and you're loyal to a fault. You belong with them, with him."

How...? Maylin opened her mouth to ask but Jewel hushed her.

"Nope. Don't want to hear you talk. You might be headstrong enough to be good for him. Maybe. If you don't get yourself killed first." Jewel's gun hand steadied and the musing expression wiped away from her face until there was nothing at all. "Me and him, we butt heads, but in a bad way. You, you're better for him, and I'd have to scratch out my eyes not to see it. The problem with the both of you is tunnel vision. You only see what's in front of you. It's too simple. You want to do real good? Learn to notice the other things."

Fear pinned Maylin down as she stared back up at death. Not too melodramatic, not when Jewel looked as cold-blooded as she did. The word was meant for Jewel when she looked like this. Then Maylin couldn't look at her face anymore, not when she could only stare at the woman's finger as it tightened on the trigger.

Another loud click.

"Good. Don't ever close your eyes when there's a

chance to get away. I like that about you." Jewel stepped away from her. "You keep that stubborn streak and stay with him. Give him what he deserves." She turned then and disappeared down the corridor, past the kitchen and right into Gabe's room.

Maylin wanted to have the courage to go after her, see where she was going. But her practical mind told her it'd be stupid. And the part of her that was truthful admitted she was too frightened to do it. Her body trembled uncontrollably. Because twice there, she'd thought she was about to die.

People came in the front door then and crowded around her. Caleb was there, and others, moving to secure the building and asking her if she was hurt. She was in shock, they were telling her. And yes, she was. But she was busy remembering what Jewel had said. Because it was important.

Chapter Twenty-Three

"She's waking up."

"Come see me when you're done here."

"Roger that."

The voices echoed inside her head, low rumbles at different pitches. She struggled to wake faster, working to draw in more air and shrug off the heavy sleep. She wanted to hear one of those voices more. Wanted to talk. There was something important she had to tell it. Him.

Gabe.

"Easy there." His voice flowed over her, his tone gentle and tinged with worry.

He shouldn't worry.

"Ah, but I do." His lips brushed hers. Perhaps she'd spoken aloud. Or he'd gotten to the point where he could read her mind.

"I'd rather keep speaking out loud. Where's An-mei?" Her throat constricted at the end and she coughed once, twice. A previously faint ache in her skull quickly escalated into a painful throb.

"Nearby, but let's get some water in you first." Gabe sounded amenable.

Suspicious, she cracked open her eyes. There he was,

leaning over her, hale and whole and not a dream. And he was holding a glass of water.

She let her heavy eyelids fall, and she sighed as relief flowed through her. This had turned out much better than she'd been thinking it might not too long ago, however long that was. In any number of scenarios she'd thought it'd be her standing at the bedside with a glass of water and Gabe in the hospital bed.

"Want help sitting up?" The note of worry in his words had gotten stronger.

Careful of the throbbing headache, she nodded slightly.

There was the sound of a click and the bed started to adjust, the top half elevating gradually until she was in a sitting position.

She opened her eyes again and he stood there grinning, all sorts of proud of himself for having pushed a button. Smiling, she reached out and ran her fingertips over the button controls so she could do it herself later. If it was that easy, there was no reason she couldn't do it on her own.

He handed her the water, holding the glass until she had her hands wrapped around it. She took a sip, then another, and her throat eased from its dried-up and scratchy state.

"I've only been gone forty-eight hours, but you managed to get yourself knocked in the head again since I left." He reached out and touched her forehead. There was a tender spot, probably a decent-sized lump. "Did Jewel hit you?"

"No." Maylin leaned her head into his touch and he curved his hand over her cheek. "My head hit the floor when she tripped me is all. Actually, she could have done a lot worse to me."

His brows drew together in a scowl. "Could have. This was bad enough."

"I really need to learn to defend myself more effectively." Guilt warred with a pang of sadness. "Here you are freshly back from a dangerous mission and I—"

"Need to rest and heal." Gabe interrupted her, pressing his thumb over her lips.

Irritated, she caught the tip of his thumb between her teeth.

Heat kindled in his eyes and she blushed in response, releasing his thumb.

Gabe chuckled. "Don't tempt me. That wouldn't be rest. What I could do, if you're feeling up to it now, is take you to see your sister."

She startled to scramble out from under the light covers.

"Easy, easy." Gabe's arms wrapped around her. "You're going to tip right off this bed."

The warmth of his embrace seeped through the thin fabric of the hospital gown and through her skin. He held her for a long moment, whispering endearments into her hair, then he adjusted his hold to scoop her up in his arms.

"I can walk!" She didn't wiggle, though. He had to have been hurt back there on the mission. She'd seen the vehicle flip over. "You should not be carrying me."

He grunted. "I can handle getting you into a wheelchair. Safer than letting you hop out of that hospital bed and try to run around with a mild concussion."

Well, even without a mild concussion she was clumsy enough that she probably would have tripped herself up somehow and fallen out of the bed.

There was indeed a wheelchair nearby, and he placed her gently into the seat. He also got a light robe from a nearby hook on the wall and helped her slip it on.

She tipped her head to look up at him. "How do I look?"

He raised an eyebrow. "Beautiful."

She batted at his hand on the arm of her wheelchair. "Presentable? I need to know if I look presentable. I don't want An-mei worried about me after everything she's been through."

"Can barely see the lump with your hair down." He leaned in and kissed her for good measure. "And you make the robes here look surprisingly presentable. Ready?"

"Ready."

He wheeled her out of the curtained area and out of the larger infirmary into the hallway. It wasn't far, and he turned her wheelchair in to a much smaller room with only two beds, separated by curtains. As he brought them to a stop at the far set of curtains, Maylin reached out and twitched the edge of one aside. *"Mèi mèi?"*

A form stirred under the blankets on the bed. *"Jiĕ jiĕ?"*

Tears welled up and burned her dry eyes at the sound of her little sister's voice. Groggy, hesitant, but it was An-mei. Swallowing to ease the constriction in her throat, Maylin tugged at the curtain to open it more.

Her little sister was sitting up in bed, green eyes blinking away tears.

Without being asked, Gabe pushed her wheelchair forward until she was within reach and leaned forward to lock the wheels. Maylin surged out of the chair and stumbled forward, wrapping her little sister in a careful hug.

An-mei's arms tightened around her in return. "You found me. You found me. You found me."

"We did." Maylin kissed her sister's hair and rubbed

her back, surprised at how thin she had become. She didn't want to ask what had happened to her in captivity. Not yet. "Do you think you could eat something?"

An-mei made a choking sound, somewhere between crying and laughing. "It is so good to hear you ask."

Maylin released her from the hug and drew back to look her over. "We should both have something to eat, and I'm guessing there are medications they'd like us to take, too."

Shadows darkened An-mei's gaze and her slender shoulders stiffened under Maylin's hands.

"You're safe here." Maylin wasn't sure how to give her sister the reassurance she'd need. "These are the people who helped me find you, got you out."

Giving her sister time, Maylin shifted to sit on the edge of the bed and turned to hold out a hand for Gabe.

Gabe took a step forward and placed his hand in hers. His grip was firm, steadying, and he rubbed his thumb over her fingers comfortingly.

"This is Gabriel Diaz of the Centurion Corporation." Maylin figured now was as good a time as any for formal introductions. "He led the fire team that went in to save you."

Recognition replaced the shadows in An-mei's eyes. "You were there. You came and got me out."

Gabe nodded. "This is real. This isn't a new way of trying to trick you into doing their work for them. This is really your sister and you are really out of that place."

An-mei balled her hands into fists, the sheets caught up in her grip. "They drugged me, had an actress come in trying to pretend to be my sister. But I knew it wasn't her. Knew it."

Maylin reached out hesitantly, unsure if her touch was

welcome despite the initial hug. "How did you know? How do I help you now?"

A tired smile appeared on her tear-streaked face. "Their imposter always asked me to take medicine and never, ever mentioned I should have something to eat, until I stopped eating because I realized they were drugging my food."

Maylin bit her lip. This was probably the least of the things they'd done to her.

"There could be addiction to deal with," Gabe said quietly. "Can we take some blood samples? Our medical team has the resources to do a full workup and find out what's currently in your system."

An-mei considered for a long moment, then nodded.

Gabe gave Maylin's hand a squeeze then released it. He took out a smartphone and showed it to both of them before he slipped it into Maylin's robe pocket. "I'll go let our medics know and leave you two alone to talk for a while. I'm just a phone call away."

An-mei had been keeping her attention on Gabe from the moment she recognized him. When he left, she watched him go. Then she finally looked at Maylin.

Maylin had no idea how to prove to her sister she was who she was. All she could think of to do was wait, patiently, and meet An-mei's searching gaze with as open a return gaze as possible.

"I'm so afraid this is another one of their tricks. Their mind games to get me to do the research they wanted," An-mei whispered.

Maylin ached for her. "No one here is going to ask you to do anything. You're safe."

An-mei licked her lips and swallowed. "Can we go outside?"

"I think so." Maylin blinked and glanced back at the wheelchair. "I'm pretty sure I can walk, whether he thinks I should or not. Do you think you can? If you do, let's find a robe for you and make a break for it. It's all green and wooded outside. Nice for a walk. I know where there's a decent kitchen and I can make you some congee. Easy on your stomach."

The tension melted out of An-mei and she lay back against the raised back of her hospital bed. "It *is* you. Food is the way you heal everything."

Relief filtered through Maylin with her little sister's acceptance. "The right food can make anything better."

An-mei sighed. "Next time, you go to China and I'll stay home. They had I don't know how many kinds of dumplings you'd want to try."

"Okay." Maylin huffed out a laugh. "I think we've both had a lot of adventure lately, though. Maybe hold off on any more continent-hopping until we've had a chance to catch our breath."

"You're going to be right here with me, for the next few days?" An-mei's voice got small and timid again. "The medics said I should stay at least that long and that there'd be people to talk to about what happened to me. What happens next."

"I'll be here as long as you need me." Maylin gave her a smile. "I promise."

"What about your catering company?" Her sister bit her lip.

Maylin took a deep breath. Of course her sister would think about it. It was the reason Maylin hadn't been with her in China in the first place. "Well, I've taken a leave of absence and they can do without me awhile longer. So you have my undivided attention."

Her sister didn't answer, but the next question hung in the air between them. This one, too, was a familiar one. *But for how long?*

"And we're less than an hour out of Seattle, so if there's any dire emergency, we could both drive in for the day, if you feel up to it—probably with an escort. But overall, I've realized I need to restructure the way I've been managing the company anyway. I'll adjust my work schedule accordingly so we can stay here as long as you need."

Maylin paused. Considering. "An-mei. You mean everything to me. Whatever the next steps are, I'll adjust to what you need. Don't worry about the catering company."

An-mei reached out to her then, her fingertips touching the back of Maylin's hand in a brief moment of contact. "I don't want you to give up the catering company."

"I would, if you needed me." Maylin was absolutely sincere on this point.

"And that's all I needed to hear. It means a lot." An-mei smiled. "But I don't want you to actually do it. There's a lot of next steps after this and it'd be more than enough if you were there with me."

Maylin smiled in return. "I will be. *Huān yíng huí jiā.* Welcome home, *mèi mèi.*"

An-mei laughed, finally sounding more like the little sister Maylin knew. "So I think there's a robe on the wall over there. If you can grab it, we can make a break for it, and you can tell me how you met that incredibly hot man and what's going on between the two of you while we find ourselves some food."

Chapter Twenty-Four

"How's the family reunion going?" Harte leaned against the far wall of the hallway, out of range but near enough by for his presence to be a sort of brotherly comfort to Gabe. Hard to explain, but there it was.

Gabe had retreated to the hallway to give the sisters space. Left alone, Gabe had to admit he'd probably be slamming his fists into the wall until something broke. Didn't matter if it was the wall or his knuckles.

Truth be told, the walls had survived a lot of Centurions so it'd probably be his knuckles.

"Fine. More than fine." Seeing the damage in An-mei's eyes, knowing from experience what that meant and how much therapy the girl would probably need before she could sleep through a night or take a bite of food without wondering if it was drugged, had been the final straw to ignite his temper in a slow-burning rage. It'd already been prepped and ready when he'd gotten a good look at the lump on Maylin's head after her encounter with Jewel.

"Those two have each other back. It's just going to take a metric shit-ton of time for them to recover. No thanks to Jewel and Edict and fucking Phoenix Biotech." Gabe finished on a growl and clamped his mouth shut, grinding his teeth.

"From what Maylin told us and what she will undoubtedly repeat to you, Jewel could have done a lot worse. I'm thinking there's more going on there."

Gabe spit out a low curse, careful to keep his voice down. Just in case Maylin woke up. Or her sister, who was in the hospital bed next to her. "I've got no fucks to give about Jewel's reasons for stabbing us in the back."

"Or shooting you in the back, as the case may be."

Gabe waved a hand, dismissing the interjection. "She made her choice and joined Edict. Not a whole lot in the world to excuse it."

Harte stepped away from the wall. "See. She knows that. I'm thinking she might've even been okay with never telling us her reasons, either. But things are changing pretty rapidly and what we saw at that location was a lot more than one little biotech company could've funded on its own."

Now might not be the best time to be thinking of a bigger picture. But it was Harte's job and Gabe might be damned for slowing down, but part of what he did best was finding the puzzle pieces for Harte to put together. So he let himself pace, but his mind tracked back to the things he'd seen. Things the cameras might not've caught.

"Their training was standard, not the higher level we're used to seeing from Edict or similar teams. The contingent guarding that facility was complacent and used to being there."

Harte nodded. "They had an evacuation plan, but they moved a lot of equipment before they decommissioned the facility."

"If you want to call blowing the place up decommissioning." Gabe snorted. "It might've been Jewel's work, though. The explosions were controlled, kept perimeter damage to a minimum."

"Based on satellite surveillance, it looked like they got all of the personnel out along with the equipment." Harte began his own pacing, on a path perpendicular to Gabe's. "But we were more concerned with keeping eyes on your escape route to be sure you didn't have any un-welcome pursuit, so we lost them when their paths split up and scattered. Even if they're still in the state currently, they won't be for too long."

Course not. If it'd been Gabe, he'd have scattered his resources and sent them out by various modes of transportation, too. Whoever had governance over that site had plans in place and those people were following them.

"So there's a sponsor behind this Phoenix Biotech." Gabe didn't like it, and the words tasted bitter in his mouth. "Somebody into projects like the genetics they were trying to make An-mei research."

"And with the means to pay several mercenary organizations, not just Edict," Harte added to the list with even less pleasure in his voice. If it were possible.

"Whoever it is won't be happy to have lost a valuable asset." Gabe would be damned if they'd send Maylin and An-mei back to their lives only to see them snapped up again.

"No." Harte settled again, a shit-eating grin on his face. "About that. I reached out to a few contacts."

"Yeah?" Gabe halted and leaned back against the opposite wall. He'd wait to find out what Harte had in mind. If he didn't like it, *then* he'd get up in his CO's face.

"There's a few government sponsors concerned about the potential for biological warfare and the best way to develop countermeasures." Harte lifted his chin to indicate the women in the room behind Gabe. "If An-mei is amenable—and I'm thinking developing countermeasures is better than developing the weapons themselves—they'll provide a new identity and protection for her. Sort of like witness protection but specialized."

"And what about Maylin?" It'd be awful to separate the sisters after how hard Maylin had worked to get An-mei back."

"Option to disappear with her sister." Harte's gaze settled on Gabe.

Gabe held steady. "Maylin deserves to be with the only family she has left."

"Maybe." Harte let the word out slow. "She does have an entire catering company she's built from nothing."

"She could build another one or do something different." Gabe had no doubt Maylin could do anything, start from scratch over and over. She had the tenacity to make anything happen.

Harte nodded. "She could. She's made some changes here, even. I'm realizing the recuperation portion of these facilities could do with a stabilizing influence for the teams stationed here. From what I hear about her cooking, she had a lot more of an impact on your team's recovery than maybe anyone realizes."

Gabe hadn't thought about it. Maylin's impact on him, on his life, was so big he couldn't wrap his head around it. She'd changed his life, and he didn't even know what he was going to do when he went back to who he used to be.

"'Let food be thy medicine and medicine be thy food.' Hippocrates." Harte was looking at him expectantly after the quote, and Gabe wasn't sure he was following his CO's logic this time.

Harte sighed. "I considered hiring a bartender because

most of you really don't like talking to a shrink, and outside the military, I don't have a way of making any of you see one no matter how much good it'd probably do you. But a bartender means booze and some of you would best be as far away from alcohol as possible."

Yeah. Alcoholism. Drugs. Some of them turned to just about anything that could change a mental state when things got bad. Being a working mercenary, having to stay sharp, probably saved all of their lives every bit as much as the continued danger presented by their jobs threatened to end them.

"I'm thinking your Maylin found something a lot better for all of you. And I heard from a lot of the personnel on the training side, too. They were jealous. Not just about the good food, and I hear she is a very good cook, but about the way you all could gather in the kitchen. Talk. Really talk."

"We talked about the mission." Gabe didn't mean to argue. But it was what they'd been doing.

"You relaxed. I've checked with Lizzy, with Marc and Vic. It was more about working together and less about the dark side of what we do. Family-like, complete with picnics in the car."

"If you're going to offer her a job, offer it to her." Gabe wasn't about to try to influence her decision. He couldn't make her promises, and it'd be damned unfair if the only time he came back to her here was in pieces.

"I plan to." Harte said. "But I'm thinking this mission showed us some realities about you, too."

"And what are those?" Gabe couldn't keep the growl out of his voice. He didn't like where this was going.

"Your back injury never healed one hundred percent. Not letting the medics see to it isn't going to hide the issue. You're also stupid as shit trying to walk it off right now."

Fuck.

Okay, so spasms had been running through his back the entire ride home. "My legs are working."

"For now." The words came out short and sharp. Harte wasn't fucking around anymore. "I'm requiring you to pass a PT test before you're cleared for active assignment again. You were damned slow leaving that overturned vehicle, and things could've happened before you got clear."

Cars actually didn't explode the way they did in Maylin's television shows. But sometimes they had help. Especially when your ex had a thing for planted explosives. So yeah, things could have turned out a lot worse. And in a way, he should thank his freaking stars Jewel had been up here in Washington State and not out there with an eye on them.

"Jewel is not the only explosives specialist out there."

Course, Harte could also be a mind reader.

"Didn't happen this time." Gabe gritted his teeth. His back muscles spasmed as he spoke, and having his temper up wasn't going to help him relax.

"Let's not have it happen at all." Harte sighed. "There are other options here."

"Retirement isn't my thing." Gabe would go insane in retirement. Especially if Maylin disappeared with An-mei under government protection. He wasn't sure he wouldn't go after her and if he did, he could end up leading danger right back to them. It'd be stupid. But if he didn't have a job to do, stupid was the least of his worries.

"What about a change of career path?" Harte asked. "Obviously security on this site needs to get to a higher level of performance. Edict shouldn't have ever gotten close. I need someone here to overhaul on-site defenses and adjust the program before we take on more personal-security contracts. Trainees need to be ready for the real thing when they're here, or they won't be when we send them overseas."

Those who can't, teach. Gabe hated the saying because it was incredibly shitty.

And what was it Maylin had taught him?

I take the sayings I like to heart.

And the ones you don't like?

I prove them wrong.

Gabe chuckled. Couldn't help it. She'd changed him and she hadn't meant to. It was probably why she'd been so successful at it.

Harte cleared his throat. "Wasn't the reaction I was expecting."

"Yeah, well. I guess I'm learning new tricks." Gabe sighed. "Talk to me about what you have in mind."

Chapter Twenty-Five

At the first crack of his bedroom door, Gabe came fully awake. He kept his eyes closed, though, and his body relaxed, his breath the long, slow rhythm of sleep.

Soft footsteps told him his visitor was small and female, and his girl. The urge to smile almost broke his facade.

Maylin walked like a cat, especially in just her socks on the hardwood floor. But she wasn't the furtive kind of silent a trained Centurion would be. She was quiet in a non-threatening, make soft imprints in his heart sort of way.

"Don't even try to convince me I can sneak up on you, Gabriel Diaz."

Ooh. She was feeling feisty. It made him even happier, and he didn't fight the grin spreading across his face even though he kept his eyes shut. Apparently a minor concussion didn't keep her in the infirmary for long. And he wasn't even going to hide from how happy it made him. Course, another part of him was up and ready to welcome her, too.

"I've got a tray here for you." Her voice turned to warm honey. "You want it on the desk, your bed, or flipped over on your lap?"

Oops. No more faking sleep. He opened his eyes and couldn't help grinning even broader. Didn't matter to him if he looked like a complete idiot. His girl was there, in his room, standing on her own power.

"Wanted to enjoy being with you again, *coração*, one sense at a time. Hearing you. Seeing you." He tapped the desk next to the bed and waited for her to safely place the tray, then caught her hand in his. He ran his thumb along the inside of her wrist, over her pulse point. "Touching you. I missed you."

He didn't dare more. Not yet. Twice now, he'd kissed her while she lay on a stretcher, and this time the next steps had to be her choice.

The spark of temper faded from her eyes. She drew in a long breath. "I missed you, too. We didn't have a lot of time to talk earlier."

Sounded like a good thing. He hoped it was. "You needed to see your sister."

Her gaze was warm. "I did, and I want to thank you for bringing An-mei home safe."

Aw, hell, he couldn't think of anything to say that wouldn't sound stupid or end up with his foot in his mouth.

"But getting back to what I was talking about before you took me to see my sister." Her eyes narrowed as she continued, "I probably should take some self-defense classes. I bet there's some in the city, but those are usually big group seminars."

"I can teach you." He wasn't going to leave it to some civilian instructor.

She nodded. "I'd like that. Maybe Lizzy or Victoria could help? They're closer to my size and they have to adjust for…a few things."

He dropped his gaze to the tempting curves of her chest. "I'm very fond of the things that make you different from me."

She cleared her throat. But when he looked up, there was heat in her gaze, not embarrassment. Good. "So, self-defense classes. Hopefully you all can teach me the basics before you have to leave again."

She stepped back and away from him, turning to retrieve the tray. He swung his legs over the side of his bed, but before he could stand she set the tray in his lap and sat next to him.

There were two bowls of clear soup with vegetables in it. Next to the soup was a platter of crackers, thin slices of salami and pepperoni plus a selection of cheeses.

Maylin reached across him to layer a cracker with a couple of slices of meat and cheese. "I sort of dumped the first pot of soup I made on Jewel and the kitchen floor. Caleb let me loose in the pantry over at the main facility, so I brought back a few supplies to make sure you all had a warm meal when you woke up."

The kitchen had been a mess when they'd gotten back. Security detail had still been taking pictures before they cleaned up, and verifying how Jewel had gotten in and out. Still, Caleb and Harte had made sure everything was taken care of so Gabe and his team could hit their bunks.

"Not that I don't appreciate this." He paused as she held the cracker and meat, and took a bite. It took another minute to chew and swallow. Awkward, because he'd never had someone feed him before, and hot, because she took the rest of the loaded cracker and ate it herself. Food was good. "But I didn't want you to think you still had to take care of us when you could be with your sister."

She took one of the bowls and a spoon, nodding. "Who

do you think raided the kitchen with me? But she ran out of steam quickly. Your medics say she's going to be very tired for a few days yet. Dehydrated. They've put her on an IV and they say rest is the best thing for her. When she fell asleep, I needed to make myself useful."

"You mean you stress-cooked." He lifted his bowl and took a sip directly from it. Spoons were for chasing peas and fancy dinners.

She sipped at her soup and huffed out a laugh. "Exactly."

"Thank you." And he put every bit of sincerity he had into it. "This is delicious."

He had no idea how she managed to put together these meals over and over again. From bare minimum supplies, no less. Hell, Harte had asked if they could challenge her to make MREs edible. She probably could, but it'd take some serious effort, even for her.

"I'm the one who can't thank you enough." Her words came out in a whisper and he saw a tear fall into the bowl in her lap.

"Hey." He got the tray back on the desk and took her bowl from her, kneeling down in front of her so he could look up into her face. "No tears. She's back safe and sound."

"I'm not sad. I'm so incredibly happy. You found her and you brought her back," Maylin whispered. "How can I ever repay you and the others?"

He cupped her face in both hands and used his thumbs to wipe away her tears. "Don't cry. It kills me to see you cry. Every one of us glad to do this for you."

"You were hurt. You all could have been killed."

It was the truth, and he didn't insult her by making less of it. "This is what we do."

She nodded into his hands. "I get it."

Most people didn't want a relationship after they realized what they'd be getting into. The waiting sucked. The time apart made people bitter. And it was too easy to pretend the awful things weren't happening.

"I don't want to hide this from you." He tried to choose his words carefully. "Because I want us to have a future, and this is a big part of it. Truth."

"Managing expectations?" Her question didn't sound bitter. It was actually very neutral.

He turned his head to the side, searching for how to say things. "Expectations, I try not to have. More like informed decisions for both of us."

"But you want there to be an 'us' going forward?" That sounded definitively hopeful.

"That's an affirmative."

She turned her head and kissed his palm. "I do, too."

Back to grinning like an idiot. "Yeah?"

"Yes." She slid her hands up to his and pulled them away from her face, holding them instead in her lap. "So what are our choices?"

He liked the sound of that. "For starters, I'm going to be here a while longer, healing. Not going to hide it from you, but I messed up my back more this last mission." He squeezed her hands in his before she could apologize. "If it didn't happen this time, it would've happened farther away from home. So don't you think it's your fault."

She was overthinking and about to argue again, so he stopped her the best way he knew how.

He kissed her.

Just one kiss, and he was on fire. It started simple, but then she yielded her mouth to him and he was caught up in the feel of her lips against his and her sweetness against his tongue.

When they both pulled back, it took a couple of seconds to remember where he'd been going with his line of thought.

"I know you've got a couple of choices."

She nodded. "There's a government representative here already. Harte introduced him to An-mei and me while she was awake enough to talk. He's offered to extend protection to me if I go with her, or to assign a protection detail here with me until they're reasonably sure I'm not a risk."

For her own safety or to be used as leverage against An-mei.

"It's a big decision." He ached to know what she wanted, before he gave her his news. But he'd learned by now she liked to have the full picture before she made her choices. "I've got a few things for you to consider, too."

She watched and waited then, her clear green eyes unreadable.

Okay. Lay it all out there, Diaz. She's worth it.

"I wanted you to know I'll be right here." He held her gaze steady with his. It meant everything for her to understand. "I'll be training new recruits at this site, and wherever you go—if you call me—I will come to you. Doesn't matter when or how often. I'll make it work."

He'd make *them* work, if she wanted it. Or he'd leave her to her life if she asked, no matter how badly it'd rip him to pieces.

Her eyes widened as his words sank in. "You're not going overseas anymore?"

His mouth twisted a little, but he wasn't going to hide from her. "Looks that way. This is where I can do the most good, training the rookies to be good enough to be

Centurions and developing a new domestic personal-security branch of the Centurion Corporation. Harte wants to call it Safeguard. So this is where I stay."

He gave her hands another squeeze. "You don't have to decide right now, but I'm hella curious about what you're thinking."

She huffed out a laugh. "I was really confused before I got here."

"Did I help or did I make it worse?"

Her smile did crazy things to him. "You made everything simple."

He raised his eyebrows. "Nothing about us is simple."

"No." She bit her lip and freed one of her hands to trace a fingertip along his jawline. "This is. I want to be with you, Gabriel Diaz. And I was going to try to come to you wherever you were whenever you were back on domestic soil, or even where you might be able to meet me abroad. Come hell or high water. And here you are, meeting me halfway."

He turned his head and kissed her finger, then rose up to gather her into his arms as he settled them both on his bed. "I'm liking this meeting in the middle thing."

"Me, too." She cuddled into his arms. God, she fit so well against him. "I want to keep running my catering business. Charlie might quit and I don't blame him, but he might stay on. He's got a few things to think about, he said."

Gabe gritted his teeth hearing her talk about another guy. She was in *his* arms, after all.

"But the company is a part of me and I want to keep it going. The government officials gave me some resistance about being able to visit An-mei wherever they take her, but Harte said there might be some provisions made in conjunction with Centurion Corporation, plus he had a talk with me about the kitchen here."

"You provide a calming influence for us." He kissed her forehead. "Stabilizing. And you feed us good."

She pressed kisses along his jaw, just about driving him crazy. "Basically what he said. So long as I can commute from here to the city when I have catering engagements, I like the idea of living here. He said we could have the guest cabin, or another residence could be built. I'm kind of blown away by the idea."

"We." He couldn't hold back anymore. Rational conversation was going to have to hold for a while. "You said 'we.'"

She kissed him then, hot and inviting, until they were both breathless. "I love you, Gabe. So yes, 'we.' *Zhí zǐ zhī shǒu, yǔ zǐ xié lǎo.* For life or for death, holding your hand, and aging with you."

He'd tried so hard to go it alone for so long. He'd fucked up a lot of things in his life. But somewhere, sometime in his truly crazed life he must've done something good, because here she was, and she was his.

And he was hers.

"I love you, Maylin." And he was going to show her. Over and over.

* * * * *

*Read on for a preview of DEADLY TESTIMONY,
the next book in the* SAFEGUARD *series
from Piper J. Drake.*

Chapter One

The people standing between Isabelle Scott and a hot bath needed to move. Immediately. Or violence would occur.

However, the event she'd been covering as private security had just ended and she wasn't technically on the clock at the moment so she wouldn't be paid for the violence. Nor would she have a convenient justification should legal repercussions ensue.

So she'd try to be patient with the four men managing to block the way to both elevators of the hotel. As she approached, she assessed the situation automatically out of habit. The four of them weren't friends, per se. Actually, three of them looked to be surrounding the fourth and the poor bastard was backing right into the wall between the two elevators. He was obstructing her access to the button she needed to call her ride up to the ninth floor and she'd be damned if she was going to take the stairs if she didn't have to.

Not that she had a problem with stairs in moments of necessity. Stairs were a lot safer than elevators in certain situations and there were times when making the choice to step into the elevator was basically the equivalent of entering a kill box.

She drew her brows together in a scowl. Not the line

of thought she wanted to end the night with and, allowed to go further, those kinds of memories would result in nightmares. No thanks.

"Look, fellas." She tried to pitch her voice for politeness. Pleasantry? One of her former teammates, Victoria, was better at it than she was. But she wasn't the ruffian Victoria liked to say she was, in teasing. Well, not completely. "Could you please step aside?"

There. Victoria would've been proud.

One of the three threw a hostile glance over his shoulder without taking time to get a real look at her. "Walk away, bitch. Go get a drink at the bar or something. This'll take a few minutes."

Lizzy clenched her jaw.

The bar was crowded and she wasn't in the mood for a drink. After heading up security for a private party for eight hours and watching important people schmooze with others of equal or greater "status" in a wine-infused corporate boondoggle, all she wanted was to soak out the tension of the day and get some sleep. Maybe order room service. Their client had reserved a block of rooms for the security detail as part of this particular engagement and she'd been looking forward to putting the hotel's hot water heaters to the test.

Her plans aside, the three men closing in on the fourth had the kind of build and stance that stood out in a hotel full of less rough-and-ready corporate types. These were men of physical action. From the less than perfect fit of their suits and the way the fabric of said suits draped oddly over their forms in a few strategic places, she was guessing they were hired help and armed. Very out of place and definitely moving on the fourth with a predatory intent.

The remaining man was about six foot, give or take an inch with his dress shoes. His suit was properly fitted across broad shoulders and an athletic build. He had a well-defined jaw and high cheekbones. Sharp intelligence was evident in his dark eyes as he took in everything around him, darting around to each of his aggressors and beyond them looking for exit routes.

His pale complexion was not unusual for Seattle in early spring. But in combination with his facial features and thick, stylishly crazy hair, his skin tone was a characteristic of East Asians as opposed to Southeast Asians, who were a few shades darker in skin tone throughout the year.

She'd guess he was Korean as opposed to Chinese. Taller than most Asians and in better shape than most people in general. But it wasn't going to do him much good against three opponents of equal or larger size unless he had the kind of training to handle multiple aggressors. The kind of training she had.

And if he did, he'd have stepped out of the situation by now.

Isabelle sighed. No wingman or cavalry coming to his aid. He needed help but it wasn't forthcoming. This was not going to resolve in the next thirty seconds and that was all she was willing to wait. Besides, she couldn't leave a person alone to face odds like these. She'd been on her own in these situations plenty of times and it'd never been fun.

"Gentlemen, get out of my way."

Humor and interest sparked in the Asian man's eyes. He understood English, apparently. Seattle being a major city for travelers, it was always good to note rather than assume a listener could understand the conversation. Especially if she might have to advise him to take action.

The hulking goon who'd originally spoken to her turned then. "What did you say?"

Maybe the English language, or conversation in general, wasn't goon number one's strong point.

"Get. Out. Of. My. Way." She put some steel into her voice this time. No need to increase volume when intensity works better.

Beady eyes narrowed at her as goon number one flexed his thick fingers into a meaty fist and released them. Threat clear.

Ah, well. Intonation could work on people with more neurons firing inside their heads. She might not have a whole lot of stature going on at five foot four, but her new friend should've at least spared a moment to ponder that maybe a woman in a black suit with white dress shirt and an earbud hanging over her collar from a wire might mean something.

He was a thug dressed in a monkey suit.

She was a much higher pay grade.

He advanced on her and made a grab for her arm. She saw it coming with plenty of time to react, rising up on the balls of her feet and keeping her limbs loose in anticipation, her joints relaxed to maximize her range of motion. As his left hand reached her upper arm, she stepped forward slightly with her left foot to meet him and seized his wrist from the inside, her thumb pointing downward. Swinging her hips and right leg around so her butt lined up with her attacker's forward leg, she bent her knees briefly and hip bumped him to rock his weight upward. She completed her move with a full upward body twisting motion, throwing him completely over her and onto his back.

She wasn't entirely heartless, though. She kept a hold on his arm to prevent it from breaking or dislocating as he fell. It'd been known to happen when a person was caught by surprise. And judging by his yelp midair, he was definitely surprised.

The man didn't get thrown by a person almost half his size all that frequently, maybe. He should experience it more often, though. It'd make him a better fighter.

He crashed down on the very hard, cold marble floor of the elevator lobby and she turned to address his companions. They were just beginning to respond, their postures open with their surprise as they started to reach for their weapons.

Not the wisest decision for either of them. Her position was easily within most people's reactionary gaps—the distance needed between a person and an attacker to have the time to react to an aggressive attack. She'd allowed the first man to make a move against her because she needed a reason to cite self-defense but she preferred to take her fight to her opponents.

He'd started it. She'd finish it.

She covered the ground between her and the nearest man standing with a slide step, landing in a Bai Jong or ready stance and immediately lashed out with her rear leg in a powerful front kick directly to the man's chest, then instantly drew her leg back to return to her stance. The air left his chest in a whoosh and he stumbled backwards into the wall behind him.

Pivoting to face the third man, she struck with a hooking kick as she came around, catching his gun hand and sending his weapon clattering to the floor. He didn't have time to react as her other leg swept up in a high round-house and caught him on the side of the head. The man remained standing for a second, clutching the side of his head, then toppled over.

Three opponents, all downed and barely groaning.

The entire altercation took less than ten seconds. She leveled a stare at the only man left standing. He prudently kicked the fallen handgun to one side, well out of reach of the downed men, and pressed the elevator call button for her.

"Thank you." The elevator opened immediately and she stepped inside without turning her back to him.

There was a faint smile playing on his lips and one eyebrow was raised as if he had found something incredibly interesting. She scowled at him. His smile widened.

"Believe me." His voice had a rich, sensual quality to it. It hinted at intimacy he had no right to and a lot of naughty things. "The pleasure was mine."

As the elevator doors began to close, police jogged up to him, huffing with effort. "Mr. Yeun. We can't guarantee your safety if you don't cooperate with us and stay where we can protect you."

Isabelle was curious. Especially as she caught snippets of them arresting the downed men just as the very slow doors finally closed all the way shut. But the call of a hot bath was stronger than curiosity.

She was done for the night.

Her phone rang and she reached out with unerring accuracy, snagging it from the nightstand. "Scott."

Damned thing was sturdy enough not to break under a pounding or from being thrown so she'd learned to grab it as quickly as possible to shut it the hell up. Even if she wasn't quite awake yet.

"Morning, Lizzy. You were involved in an incident with the police." Gabe's voice came through, crisp and businesslike, maybe mildly amused.

She breathed in through her nose and out in a sigh.

Gabriel Diaz was her superior in the Safeguard Division, newly formed within the Centurion Corporation. He—and two other people who had made up their fire team—was one of the few people she allowed to use her childhood nickname. They'd spent time in the field, survived enough combat situations to not bother counting anymore and, in general, trusted each other with their lives.

Currently, she wanted to end his.

"What time is it?" She refused to look at a clock. The hotel's heavy curtains were doing a fantastic job of blocking out daylight and she had planned to sleep in this morning.

"Oh-eight-hundred." There was definitely amusement in Gabe's voice. The bastard. "Are you with company?"

The face of the very attractive stranger by the elevator last night flashed into her mind.

She grunted and sat up. "Negative."

There'd been police, as Gabe so cheerfully reminded her. The hot guy would've had complications in joining her for the evening. And while she had no issues with law enforcement in general, she did not want them parked outside her hotel room door advertising to the world she had company. Multiple deployments in the military gave her a preference for discretion. She'd rather forego fun times than have her choices in off-duty entertainment subject to misogynistic judgment.

"Then you can tell me about it." He obviously didn't have a snooze button.

As commanding officers went, Gabe was a good one. But aside from admitting whether their conversation could be overheard or not, she wasn't prone to give him insight into her love life either.

Fortunately, he wasn't asking about it. Police. He was asking about police.

"Technically, I was involved in an incident and finished before police arrived on the scene." She could've stuck around to answer police questions but she really hadn't overheard anything before she'd decided to clear her path to the elevator. "Looked like a shakedown or similar disagreement. One of the men attacked me and I defended myself. When he was neutralized, the other two engaged. I eliminated the threats with nonlethal force. Then I entered the elevator and came up to my room."

Gabe was taking notes on her story as she related it. He'd craft it into an even more diplomatic statement if needed. "No worries, Lizzy, the police aren't interested in questioning you or involving you in the charges for those men. They had some interesting history, more than enough to keep the police busy without needing to talk to you. Especially when it was determined you were a Safeguard resource on-site for an unrelated contract."

"Then why did you wake me up?" she growled. If Gabe was using her nickname, they weren't being formal so she didn't have to be polite.

"Because seeing you in action can be inspiring." Gabe remained unfazed. If anything, he sounded downright cheerful. "And in this case, it lined up another contract for you."

She growled again without even trying to verbalize anything intelligible.

"Now, Lizzy, when you're good and people are impressed, there isn't any sense in being irritated about the cause and effect." This time he actually chuckled. "If you give people a demonstration of what you can do, can you blame them for wanting your services?"

She clamped her mouth shut, refusing to rise to the bait. More often than not in the past year she'd had to deal with chronic instances of underestimation. Clients looked at her and didn't believe she could be effective as personal security.

When she'd been active duty, she'd spent a decent amount of time proving herself. In the service, soldiers did as ordered and they worked as a team if the mission was to succeed—and in more cases than she wanted to remember, if they were going to survive—so people learned to trust her. She'd carried her own weight. The men and women who'd served with her had come to respect her for it.

Civilian clients didn't tend to react the same way. The past year with the Safeguard Division had been smattered with a fair share of clients looking for big, burly bodyguards and not willing to believe little Isabelle Scott was capable of defending them. Or, and this bothered her somewhat less, she wasn't the image they were going for when they'd decided adding a bodyguard to their entourage was the most trendy accessory.

Still, she had her pride to consider and she preferred to be on assignment as opposed to working the administrative side of things or training recruits over at the Centurion Corporation facilities just outside Seattle. She was too on edge to train, and she needed the active assignments to help burn off the deep anger still inside her.

Maybe she'd been looking for the scuffle last night. Just a little.

She sighed. "What do you want, Gabe?"

"You've been requested for an assignment. Specifically. And both the US Marshals and police are more than happy to coordinate with you." Gabe snorted. "I need you to get to the office in the next hour to meet the client and coordinate with his assigned protection."

"If he has a marshal and police…" She didn't want to finish the question she had at the tip of her tongue. Full respect to the city's finest but there were instances where augmenting a police detail with private military contractors were advantageous. It was unusual, but not unheard of. Well, this would be a first for her working with a US marshal but she could imagine instances where it'd happen.

"This is by request of the client and he's paying for this with his personal funds. You won't be on the government's or city's payroll."

Wasn't that interesting?

She'd had a good long bath last night and a decent night's sleep. Curiosity was winning this morning. "I'll be there at the top of the hour."

Don't miss DEADLY TESTIMONY
by Piper J. Drake, available in ebook now,
and coming next month in print.

Acknowledgments

Thank you to Courtney Miller-Callihan, for believing in me and for endless patience with my random insanity.

Thank you to Katee Robert and Christi Barth for your encouragement and concise advice. Without you, I don't know how long it would've taken me to gather the courage to make the leap.

Thank you to Angela James and Stephanie Doig for your help in bringing this story from rough to polished.

About the Author

Piper J. Drake is an author of bestselling romantic suspense and edgy contemporary romance, a frequent flyer and day job road warrior. She is often distracted by dogs, cupcakes and random shenanigans.

Play Find the Piper online:

PiperJDrake.com

Facebook.com/AuthorPiperJDrake

Twitter @PiperJDrake

Instagram.com/PiperJDrake

Get 2 Free Books,

HARLEQUIN®
ROMANTIC suspense

Plus 2 Free Gifts—
just for trying the
Reader Service!

Get 2 Free Books,
Plus 2 Free Gifts—
just for trying the Reader Service!

Get 2 Free Books,
Plus 2 Free Gifts—
just for trying the Reader Service!

HARLEQUIN
INTRIGUE

YES! Please send me 2 FREE Harlequin® Intrigue novels and my 2 FREE gifts (gifts are worth about $10 retail). After receiving them, if I don't wish to receive any more books, I can return the shipping statement marked "cancel." If I don't cancel, I will receive 6 brand-new novels every month and be billed just $4.99 each for the regular-print edition or $5.74 each for the larger-print edition in the U.S., or $5.74 each for the regular-print edition or $6.49 each for the larger-print edition in Canada. That's a savings of at least 12% off the cover price! It's quite a bargain! Shipping and handling is just 50¢ per book in the U.S. and 75¢ per book in Canada*. I understand that accepting the 2 free books and gifts places me under no obligation to buy anything. I can always return a shipment and cancel at any time. The free books and gifts are mine to keep no matter what I decide.

Please check one: ☐ Harlequin® Intrigue Regular-Print   ☐ Harlequin® Intrigue Larger-Print
(182/382 HDN GMWJ)   (199/399 HDN GMWJ)

Name _____ (PLEASE PRINT) _____

Address _____ Apt. # _____

City _____ State/Prov. _____ Zip/Postal Code _____

Signature (if under 18, a parent or guardian must sign)

Mail to the Reader Service:
IN U.S.A.: P.O. Box 1341, Buffalo, NY 14240-8531
IN CANADA: P.O. Box 603, Fort Erie, Ontario L2A 5X3

Want to try two free books from another line?
Call 1-800-873-8635 or visit www.ReaderService.com.

*Terms and prices subject to change without notice. Prices do not include applicable taxes. Sales tax applicable in N.Y. Canadian residents will be charged applicable taxes. Offer not valid in Quebec. This offer is limited to one order per household. Books received may not be as shown. Not valid for current subscribers to Harlequin Intrigue books. All orders subject to approval. Credit or debit balances in a customer's account(s) may be offset by any other outstanding balance owed by or to the customer. Please allow 4 to 6 weeks for delivery. Offer available while quantities last.

Your Privacy—The Reader Service is committed to protecting your privacy. Our Privacy Policy is available online at www.ReaderService.com or upon request from the Reader Service.

We make a portion of our mailing list available to reputable third parties that offer products we believe may interest you. If you prefer that we not exchange your name with third parties, or if you wish to clarify or modify your communication preferences, please visit us at www.ReaderService.com/consumerschoice or write to us at Reader Service Preference Service, P.O. Box 9062, Buffalo, NY 14240-9062. Include your complete name and address.

HI17R2

READERSERVICE.COM

Manage your account online!

- Review your order history
- Manage your payments
- Update your address

> *We've designed the*
> *Reader Service website*
> *just for you.*

Enjoy all the features!

- Discover new series available to you, and read excerpts from any series.
- Respond to mailings and special monthly offers.
- Browse the Bonus Bucks catalog and online-only exculsives.
- Share your feedback.

Visit us at:

ReaderService.com